Acclaim for the
The Devil Doesn't Want Me

"*The Devil Doesn't Want Me* is a runaway train of violence and mayhem, packed full with a collection of one-of-a-kind characters all speeding toward an explosive and inevitable end. Beetner is a maestro with his action scenes, filling the novel with cinematic set pieces, but the real heart of his story is Lars, an aging hit man forced to confront his own morality as the world goes to hell around him. A great read."

—Owen Laukkanen, author of *The Forgotten Girls*

"Eric Beetner is quickly becoming one of my favorite new crime writers. If you're a fan of fast paced, well-written hardboiled crime fiction, you're going to love this book."

—John Rector, author of *The Ridge*

"Told with heart, humor, and sizzling cinematic prose, Eric Beetner's *The Devil Doesn't Want Me* is crime fiction at its most entertaining."

—Peter Farris, author of *Last Call for the Living*

"I found the story awesome, with characters you will love to hate and hate to love."

—Bookloons reviews

"In the wrong hands this story could have been a cliché-ridden minefield. Author Eric Beetner, however, is incredibly adept at crafting characters who defy their expected roles."

—Book Reviews by Elizabeth A. White

"A tightly woven web that shocks with static electricity at touch. I'm ready to read more from Eric Beetner and you should too after you have bought this book."

—Lurid Lit reviews

THE DEVIL DOESN'T WANT ME

ALSO BY ERIC BEETNER

McGraw Crime Series
Rumrunners
Leadfoot

Lars and Shane Series
The Devil Doesn't Want Me
The Devil Comes to Call
The Devil at Your Door

Stand Alones
The Year I Died Seven Times
Criminal Economics
Nine Toes in the Grave
Dig Two Graves
White Hot Pistol
Stripper Pole at the End of the World
A Bouquet of Bullets (stories)

The Fightcard Series
Fightcard: Split Decision
Fightcard: A Mouth Full of Blood

The List Series (with Frank Zafiro)
The Backlist
The Short List
The Getaway List (*)

With JB Kohl
Over Their Heads
Borrowed Trouble
One Too Many Blows to the Head

The Lawyer Western Series
Six Guns at Sundown
Blood Moon
The Last Trail

(*) – coming soon from Down & Out Books

ERIC BEETNER

THE DEVIL DOESN'T WANT ME

A LARS AND SHAINE CRIME NOVEL

DOWN&OUT
BOOKS

Down & Out Books
3959 Van Dyke Rd, Ste. 265
Lutz, FL 33558
www.DownAndOutBooks.com

The characters and events in this book are fictitious. Any similarity to real
persons, living or dead, is coincidental and not intended by the author.

Cover design by Eric Beetner

ISBN: 1-946502-41-3
ISBN-13: 978-1-946502-41-4

To Maybel.
I don't know how I'll write another word
without you snoring by my feet.

"One of the great dogs of our time."

1

Seventeen years is a long damn time. A long damn time. That's how long Lars had been on the hunt for Mitchell Kenney.

Mitch the Snitch. Mitch the Bitch. The former accountant gathered up quite a few nicknames since turning state's evidence. Seventeen years ago.

Lars spent his fair share of time in cemeteries over the years, and he knew headstones didn't lie. *Tempus fugit*, motherfuckers. Those old Latin bastards were smart.

Now I'm being replaced, he thought as he stared down into his beer glass. *I guess my time has flown.*

The air in the bar tasted stale. Equal parts nicotine and sweat. If bad breath had an address, directions would lead you here. Lars sat alone at the bar, allowing himself his weekly drink. On the job, Lars had rules. Sticking to them was how he kept getting more jobs. Doing those jobs well was how he got this one. Nikki Senior himself picked Lars. Said he needed a man he could trust. A special job, requiring a special man.

Going after Mitch the Snitch wasn't going to be easy, and Lars told the boss so. Said it might take a long time. When the FBI hides a guy, they intend for him to stay hid. Nikki Senior said, "Take as much as you need." Twenty-six times before, Lars had fulfilled contracts for the boss. Twenty-six men dead. Nikki Senior could trust Lars with a gun or a secret or the combination lock to his daughter's underpants. For Lars, letting down Nikki Senior would be worse than letting down his own father. Then again, letting down his dad had been the central preoccupation of his adolescence.

The rules: One drink a week. No smoking. No personal relationships. Sure, he saw a professional girl once in a while, but a lot less now than when he started. Forty-seven years old. *How the hell did that happen?* Lars scoffed, drained the beer.

And now the inevitable—replaced by a young gun. Had to be Nikki Junior who called for it. Little shit was still finding his own dick when Lars got the job in the desert. Lars made a booming business killing people for money before Junior's dad even squirted him out. Now Lars is too old to finish the job. Says him, the little prick.

Not that Lars didn't want a break. God*damn* he wanted a break. All those years. The heat. Hunting, tracking, false leads, dead ends, mistaken identities. Christ, it'd been tedious as hell. If it wasn't for the side jobs every now and then, he'd have gone bonkers a long while back.

Lars waved to the bartender, who looked through him like a ghost.

This bar is a joke, he thought. Supposed to be a biker bar. You could still see the pit where the mechanical bull used to be. A sign over the pool table advised not to scratch the felt. Half the draft beers came from some California microbrew bullshit. And the shit on the jukebox...Lars smiled to himself. *Well, listen to me. The proverbial cranky old man.*

Maybe it would be the best thing, being replaced. He only wished he'd been the one to decide. Or at least that Nikki Senior himself had called him personally on it. But fuck, the old man was too busy being muscled out, same as him.

Lars pushed away from the bar to make his way past weekend Harley douchebags to the jukebox. Time for some real music. Not much to choose from, but he spotted Black Sabbath's "Paranoid" and—did his eyes deceive him?—Judas Priest. Remnants from the real biker bar days. Punch the numbers, shred those guitars.

He found his seat at the bar and waved again for a beer. Nothing.

Halford wasn't even to the first chorus when a young guy, young to Lars anyway, tapped him on the shoulder. He wore the outfit of a biker in a movie—one of the background extras, not even the leader of the gang—but his haircut and trimmed nails gave away his day job.

"Hey pops, is that your nickel?"

Nickel? Fuck, that cost me a dollar for three plays. "Yeah. You don't like Priest?"

"This ain't the eighties, man. That operatic shit gives me a headache. Why don't you let people pick who don't still own eight-tracks."

Lars's first thought: *I should kill this guy. I should kill him just for the practice. It's been a while.*

The last job didn't go so well. That had been six months ago. Yeah, maybe it's time to retire. At least he could get out of this heat.

"I'm gonna talk to the manager. He's a buddy of mine. Get that shit taken off. Fucking hair metal bullshit."

Lars pitied the man. He obviously knew nothing about Priest.

The skinny bartender set down another beer in front of Lars. Halford sang out the ode to breaking the law. Lars said nothing to the faux biker, only picked up the longneck and sipped the foam off the top. The douchebag walked away, feeling victorious.

Yeah, I should kill him.

But he didn't.

2

Lars couldn't stop thinking about the guy in the bar the night before. Criticizing his taste in music. Who the hell did he think he was? He was glad it didn't escalate. Lars built a career out of keeping his cool. His job depended on it.

More than twenty years ago he took up yoga. He'd always done deep breathing exercises, the same kind that snipers in the military use to steady the hand before a shot. Yoga was the next step. It kept him centered all day. He sometimes went weeks without speaking to anyone else, and his slightly monastic life lent itself to ancient Indian rituals. Lars was limber, reed thin and toned from the daily exercise. His brown hair had lightened over the years of Southwestern sun and a creeping invasion of gray above his ears.

Growing up in Queens, he never dreamed of living in the desert. They can pump all the Colorado River water they want over the sand and dirt, but no matter how many golf courses spread fake islands of green, New Mexico is still the damn desert. Lars needed to look no farther than the impossibly bright midmorning sun already softening the asphalt.

He sat in his car watching Trent. He was the new model come to supplant Lars's aging chassis. The kid stepped off the curb at Albuquerque International Sunport airport. Lars already didn't like him.

Trent slung a backpack over one shoulder and hefted a beat-up black suitcase covered with stickers of bands and left-wing political messages in his right hand. An unlit cigarette bounced in his lips as he lifted a finger to block one nostril

4

and fire a snot rocket out the other. A nostril that sported a small silver ring through it. Tiny wires led from headphones tucked deep into his ears to an iPhone clipped onto the studded belt he wore. The stupid belt did nothing to keep his jeans around his waist.

Lars knew this was not what he looked like when he started on the job. The stubble that grew on Trent's chin had been manicured to look unkempt. Lars had a three-day growth that showed he was his own boss.

Trent broadcast industrial metal. Lars, old school rock and roll. In his youth, Lars played bass in a garage band that literally never played any place but a garage. He snuck into a bar at sixteen to see George Thorogood, had his first shot of Jack and got into his first fistfight all in the same night. He knew the value of shutting up at the right time. He knew his limits with alcohol, treated women with respect, and when he was working, Lars was the most dedicated professional you could ever want.

When he got the assignment to go west and find then kill Mitch the Snitch, Lars was already thirty years old, a senior citizen in the murder game. Since then, every month ten thousand dollars had been wired into one of several accounts across the country. Living expenses and fees.

Still, Lars lived frugally. The '66 Mustang he sat in had been his only indulgence. When he first saw it, metallic blue with two thick white stripes across the hood and over the roof, he half expected Steve McQueen to step out from behind the wheel. Luckily for him, it had been owned by a motorhead who took meticulous care of the dazzling machine but let other expenses pile up in the meantime and needed to get rid of it ASAP. Lars took it off his hands for six thousand cash.

He got out of the car and let the New Mexico sun take its daily shot at boring a hole in his skull. Most of the past seventeen years had been spent in sun-baked scrub brush like this. First outside Waco, Texas, then Sedona, Arizona, and now

Albuquerque. Lars's face had the tan-hide look of an old wallet. Sunscreen? What's sunscreen? Forty-seven was starting to look seventy-four on him. Most guys think about retiring to some sun-drenched beach, but Lars thought of places like Alaska. Six months of cold darkness would feel damn good.

Trent waited for the crossing signal and took the opportunity to light his smoke.

When he started walking again, Lars could hear the rattle of his chain wallet, the three bracelets he wore on one arm and the buckles on his boots all over the near-distant scream of airplane engines. Amateur.

Lars nodded. Trent smiled at him from behind his mirrored shades, which reflected back sharp flashes of sunlight. If the noise didn't alert anyone to his coming, the twin spotlights on his face surely would. Doesn't anybody train these kids anymore? Or do they just show up with a record and an untraceable gun and get hired on the spot?

"You Lars?" the kid asked.

"Put that out before you get in."

Lars didn't care much about first impressions. This was a handoff, and then Mitch the Snitch would be Trent's problem. He could tell already the kid stood no chance at all of finding him, let alone lasting seventeen years on the hunt.

Trent sucked hard on the white tube of his smoke then crooked his middle finger under it and shot it skyward over his shoulder, leaving the finger extended for a little extra. He tossed the backpack through the open window into the backseat, which bought him a few more seconds of holding the smoke in his lungs before he had to exhale.

Lars swung his door open and sat back down. The kid got in also, pushing his suitcase into the backseat.

"This thing got AC?"

"Not enough to do battle with this heat. Windows down is the best way to go."

"Fuck me."

"You get used to it."

Lars was ready to be done with New Mexico. It'd been four years here. At least the six years in Arizona before this were in an area known for spas and medicinal hot springs.

In Sedona he almost had Mitch. Somebody caught wind or somebody snitched, because a few days before Lars was set to bring the hammer down, Mitch up and disappeared. Nine months later the tip came that he was in New Mexico. Lars was hoping for Hawaii. At least L.A. There has to be some punishment to witness protection, though. They weren't sending him to the penitentiary, but it wasn't a golden ticket to a new life. Lars wasn't so sure he wouldn't pick prison over Albuquerque.

The Mustang cut a wake into the wavy heat lines coming off the highway.

Trent still had his earbuds in. "So they filled me in on most of it. Anything else I need to know?"

"You tell me what you do know and I'll tell you the rest."

The highway speed of the car did little to cool down the breeze that blew through the open windows. Dragon's breath, the locals called it.

"Well, the way I heard it," Trent spit a fat gob out the window, "was that this Mitch turned rat on the big boys a long time ago. Let them peek at the books, dropped a few names and addresses. He gets a new life and five top guys go to summer camp for twenty-five to life. They put you on it. Quite the hot-shit hotshot in your day is what I hear."

Trent turned his mirrored lenses to Lars, who showed nothing. He was without ego when it came to work. "Then you've been out here for sixteen years looking for the dude."

"Seventeen last month."

"Yeah, well, Mitch is bound to die of old age if you keep up this pace."

"My job is to kill him. No one said how. If waiting him out is the way, then I still did my duty." Lars was calm, centered. No way would he let the young punk rile him.

"Fuck, man. Don't you lose your shit being out here for so long?"

"I get side work every now and then. That breaks it up."

"Yeah, like that last one."

So word had gotten around. The changing of the guard. Nikki Senior was a lame duck, Nikki Junior angling to get the big chair before his old man even kicked it. Across the board the old was being replaced by the new, especially when the old screwed up a job like Lars did.

He knew he wasn't what he used to be. In his prime Lars was a killing machine. Feared and fearless. Now the years carved lines on his face that the Southwestern sun made deeper and permanent. The baseball caps he wore to keep the glare off his forehead had eroded his hairline. The way kids like Trent dressed these days Lars thought of as ridiculous. Lars was a jeans and T-shirt kind of guy. His denim jacket had seen more years on earth than Trent. He used a red bandana to mop sweat off his forehead, and his cowboy boots fit right in here in the Old West. He looked stuck in time, off the grid. Two years ago he bought a pair of reading glasses at a drugstore and knew time had caught up with him. Six months ago he missed his first shot and he knew his days on the job were numbered.

"So what do you do all day out here?" Trent asked.

"Enough. If someone has a tip, I follow it. If nothing comes in, I make my way around town looking into anyone who might be him."

"And how do you know?"

"I don't. I got pictures, but he may have had plastic surgery. I have a list of his aliases, but they're all old."

"So you sit around and get a paycheck for doing nothing."

"Not exactly."

The Mustang bumped into the parking lot of a two-story apartment building. Lars had switched to a two-bedroom unit when he found out about getting replaced. He planned for a week overlap while he showed the new kid the details. When they'd said *kid,* he didn't know they meant it so literally.

Trent lifted his suitcase out of the back and lit another cigarette. Lars hadn't even seen him take it out. Must have been dying of a nicotine fit the whole ride.

"So how many guys you kill?" Trent pumped smoke into the air. Lars almost felt sorry for how much hotter Trent would get with a lungful of smoke. Sweat rings already spread from the kid's armpits.

"Enough. You want to see the notches in my bedpost?"

"I get it. Trade secrets, right? Y'know," he chugged out another blast of smoke. "My old man was a football player. High school. He played quarterback the year they won state. Mr. Scramble they called him. Got away from three tackles and ran eighty-five yards for the winning score. Talked about it to his dying day. His glorious past. Know how he died?"

Lars stayed silent.

"Hit by a pickup truck crossing the street. Those golden feet didn't do shit for him. Know why? Because the past is the past. What you did doesn't mean shit. It's what you *do.*"

Trent let the fable hang in the air between them like another lungful of smoke. Lars didn't bite.

"I was with him. I dodged. Jumped out of the way at the last second. Never played a game of football in my life."

"I'll show you your room."

3

The apartment frowned, depressed and on the verge of suicide. That's how Trent saw it, anyway. Sad, monotone, no signs of life. The walls contractor white, the carpet tan, the sofa off-white, the curtains beige. It seemed like the desert came in through an open window and coated the entire two-bedroom unit. *As bland and nondescript as this entire state*, thought Trent.

"Welcome to your new home. No smoking," said Lars.

"Which one's mine?" said Trent gesturing to the off-white doors down the stubby hallway.

"That one. No smoking in there either. I left a deposit." Lars smiled a sarcastic grin.

"Yeah, a deposit on...your..." Trent couldn't think of an insult, so he let it die. He went to his room, leaving Lars chuckling to himself.

Trent shut the door behind him and tapped the screen on his iPhone, switching off the music and dialing. Waiting for the signal to reach out across the desert, Trent lifted the lid on a shoebox he found on the bed. Inside were a 9mm pistol and two clips. A welcome gift. Trent scoffed and replaced the lid.

"This dude is a relic," he said when Nikki Junior answered.

"That's why you're there."

"You didn't tell me he'd been pickled in a jar."

"You mean he's drunk? Is he drunk on the job?"

"No, I mean he's a little...weathered is a good word." He shed layers of clothes down to his naked chest trying to beat the heat. It wasn't working.

"Yeah well, don't be too quick to write him off, Trent. The guy could still teach you some things. He was the man back in the day. Dad sure liked him."

Trent pocketed his iPhone. He left his earpieces in as he stepped up to the toilet to let go the six-hour flight's worth of three-dollar Sprite and five-dollar beer.

"Yeah, the day. I think this guy has moved on to night-time. I'll get the lay of the land, but with what I got from my guy at the Bureau I plan to have this wrapped up and get out of this fucking oven by midweek." Nikki Junior could hear the sound of him pissing.

"Sooner the better. You get Mitch and you can kill Lars on your way out of town."

"Dude's already got vultures circling." Trent swiveled his hips making loops of piss in the bowl.

Lars stewed, alone in his room. *Like I needed a fucking reminder my best days are behind me. Punk fucking kid.*

The temptation, when someone questioned his record, was always to tell the old stories. Take him out to the gun range and school him with fifteen dead-on head shots in a row. Tell the kid not to judge a book by its cover. But then that would make Lars a hypocrite.

Several deep breaths, in through the nose out through the mouth. Calm. Centered. In control, as always.

Out in the desert, on call twenty-four-seven, a man can't survive without discipline.

He'd be lying if he said he didn't miss the daily action. Lars hit the gun range, tried to stay fit, alert. But atrophy sets in. Shooting at a target only gets you so far. He preferred to head out to the desert with the rifle to peg jackrabbits. Taking a long-range sniper rifle into a gun range of one hundred feet seemed a bit overkill. Plus, there in the Wild West, no one bats an eyelash at hearing gunshots out in the nowhere.

Lars could still hit one of those long-eared bastards at five hundred yards. He loved the way the bullet split the heat waves. Watching through the scope, it looked like firing into water.

Jackrabbits don't shoot back though. Not exactly real-world experience.

The side jobs came along about once every six months. Lately, once a year. Any place that's close by, or at least within a few hours' drive, and he got the call. The jobs always acted as a little boost, a reminder his reputation still counted for something back east.

Christ, I screwed the pooch on that last one.

It was Las Vegas. A long drive but he'd welcomed it. Tearing ass across the flat fuck-all of New Mexico and Arizona in that Mustang felt damn good.

He never liked to get a contract for a woman, was forever suspicious of any man who wasn't bothered by a T&A job. He'd only done it once before in all his years.

The Vegas contract was bad. Young, blond. Could have been his daughter, if he had one. Wife of one of the big guys back east. Came out to Vegas to fuck a pro-poker player she met when he passed through on tour in Atlantic City. The forty-year age difference with the husband back home must have gotten a little tiresome. Lars kind of saw her point. Doesn't justify cheating though.

Contract specified to take her out, leave him upright. He takes the fall, or even if he doesn't, he sees his girlfriend blown away in front of him and he gets the message. One thing Lars always respected about Nikki Senior was his ability to see the value in killing and the value in not killing. Sometimes it's more painful to leave someone alive.

He got to Vegas, found his hotel. Right on the strip. Volcano out front. Should have been an easy in and out. Security in Vegas is tight, but he didn't need to be surgical, just fast.

He jacked the lock—no sense in kicking it in and attracting a lot of attention. The silencer screwed onto his favorite piece—the Beretta.

Inside, he heard sounds in the bedroom. Best case scenario. Caught in the act. They'll love this at the office.

The bedroom door was cracked so he kicked it the rest of the way open to make a statement. Lars remained professional but wasn't above theatrics.

He hesitated.

He'd never done that before.

The thing that made him pause? There were two blondes in bed. Naked flesh side by side like two filet mignon, pink and raw and ready for the grill. The problem? Lars didn't know which one was the target, his field of vision all boobs and asses and lower back tattoos. They both wore obscene diamond rings. They looked like a lab experiment in cloning, each bearing all the landmarks that made her the target in duplicate.

Mr. Poker scrambled backwards, pulling a sheet up over his dick which still aimed at the ceiling. The two girls stayed in bed, confused, thinking Lars was part of the act. Like, great, another dick to suck. The more the merrier. Probably expected a slightly younger model.

They stayed frozen, nipples touching and backs arched. Shaved clean, both of them. Lars held his gun on one then the other. His brain frozen solid. The room glowed orange as the volcano below erupted.

Mr. Poker made it to the bedside table and Lars did nothing to stop him. Another mistake.

Mistake. Lars hated that word. Never had call to use it before, at least when describing his own work.

Mr. Poker pulled a Glock. He started ripping off shots before he took any decent aim, so Lars wasn't in real jeopardy, yet. Two bullets shattered the window and even from twenty-two floors up, the heat of the volcano wafted in.

Lars had no choice. Take them all down.

He shot lover boy first, a wounding blow to make him drop the gun. Lars could see the moment the girls realized what the game really was.

Two naked, shrieking flashes leapt from the bed in opposite directions. Lars swiveled and popped the one heading for the bathroom first. A bloom of red opened on her left shoulder as the bullet entered on its way through her heart and out the other side, only after passing through a thick bag of silicone. She pitched face-first onto the marble in front of the Jacuzzi tub.

He spun and shot the other naked girl, but she moved fast. Olympic sprinter fast. He nicked her barely in the neck, and she hopped twice trying to keep her balance before tipping out of the shattered glass window.

She caught herself. Athletic, that one. She hung there, hands digging into glass shards, naked ass twenty stories above the Strip being warmed by a man-made volcano.

He lunged out and grabbed her hand, the one with the ring on it. He didn't want her falling. Too public, too sensational. Vegas is expert at sweeping a killing under the rug if it happens behind closed doors. If it happens on the Strip while ten families from Omaha are watching, it's harder to hide it away.

"Are you Vinnie Schrum's wife?" Lars asked.

"Why is he doing this?"

"Why do you think?"

He stuck the gun in his pocket and took her in both hands. Used his leverage, not any upper body strength, to haul her in. She was light, thank God. Rails of coke and teenage bulimia saved her ass from falling into the mouth of an overgrown barbeque grill.

They didn't save her ass for long.

Her naked back scraped along the window frame, sliced by the shards of glass still attached. She hit the floor as the cuts all swelled with red.

"Mrs. Schrum?" Lars tried to catch his breath, panting like

a Saint Bernard. He drew his gun again. Back to business.

"Just fucking do it!" she screamed at him. She hid her face behind bloody hands. Blood from her neck ran down between her tits and across the blank spot where her pubic hair should have been.

Lars put one in her head.

Another shot from the Glock punched the ceiling above him.

He spun and shot three times. Mr. Poker's chest punctured like a paper target at the gun range. Two in the heart. One outside the lines. That never happens.

Breathe in, breathe out. Get centered.

By the time he got to the door, security had arrived. Lars checked the peephole before he left and saw two linebackers in navy blue suit jackets with 9mms in their hands.

He stepped back beside a potted palm to the left of the door. They entered, smelling blood. He let them pass and then shot them both in the back. Train their whole lives for a moment like that and then they go and fuck it up. Their mothers would not be proud.

He got out without leaving any more bodies, but it still amounted to a hell of a mess. It made headlines. It made trouble. It made Lars look bad. It couldn't make him look as bad as he felt.

Word got out quick that he was *persona non grata* in Vegas anymore. Seems the local boys were offended Nikki Senior hadn't seen fit to hire one of theirs for the job. Of course all the talk was that if they had, this kind of thing never would have happened.

Calls went out to have Nikki Senior turn Lars over as payback. God bless that loyal bastard, he refused. He reminded the Vegas brass of several screw-ups in their own ranks over the years. Another great thing about having Nikki Senior on your side was his memory. His body may have been starting to crap out on him, but his mind still held an encyclopedia of family business, triumph or tragedy. Most times he got more mileage off the tragedy.

Lars left town without collecting his fee. The money sat in a bank safe deposit box just waiting for some enterprising young heist man to make off with it. A plus to doing business in Vegas is with so many targets on every street corner, no one even thinks about robbing a bank.

Lars slunk back to Albuquerque with his tail between his legs.

He studied his eyes in the rearview. The blue had gone darker. Still and smooth like the deep end of a lake. No sparkle.

Put me out to pasture, my time is up.

4

Trent walked into Lars's room without knocking. Lars arched his body in a downward dog pose on the patch of carpet by the foot of the bed.

"What the fuck is that?" Trent asked.

Lars took his time to straighten, exhaling and letting his spine move slowly and set straight. He stood up.

"Yoga. Don't you knock?"

"Damn. This desert has seriously gotten to you, dude."

"It keeps me calm and relaxed. It's good for the job. You could use some."

"Um, yeah, I don't think so. Let's go. We got snitches to kill."

Lars slid his feet into well-worn cowboy boots. "You eat breakfast yet? I was gonna make you some eggs, but I heard you snoring and figured you'd sleep until noon."

"Nah, just swing by a Starbucks on the way and I'll grab a latte. Maybe get it iced in this fucking climate."

Lars rolled his eyes, pulling on a plaid Western style shirt with pearl buttons. "You know what caffeine does to your trigger hand?"

"I know I'm real fuckin' cranky in the morning without it. What are you, a Mormon or something?"

"No. Just a professional." Lars continued to button his shirt, letting the silence build until Trent was too uncomfortable to stay in the same room.

The Mustang growled along pavement soft with heat. Trent had shed several layers since the day before and sat in the passenger seat in a white wife-beater and his mirrored shades.

The cassette player cranked out Van Halen's "Unchained," one of Lars's top ten guitar tracks of all time. Maybe even top five. Unconsciously, his fingers pinched around an invisible guitar pick and strummed power chords on the edge of the steering wheel, a patch in the finish worn away from years of riffing along with Eddie.

"What the fuck is this?" said Trent.

"Are you serious?"

"Yeah. Do we have to listen to this crap?"

The bridge hit. *"C'mon Dave, gimme a break" "One break comin' up!"* Even Lars had to admit this part came off a little cheesy, but he still thought it fit brilliantly into the rest of the song. "It's Van Halen. *Fair Warning* album. You seriously don't know this?"

"I know Van Halen. Spandex-wearing drunk fuckers. Can we at least turn it down a bit?"

Trent reached into his pocket and took out a paper folded into quads. Lars turned down the volume, feeling like a scolded child and wanting to fight back, to tell the punk it was his car, dammit. But he wanted to get on with the task at hand, so Lars swallowed his anger, breathed in, then out, and waited to see the names on Trent's magic list.

On Trent's lap, the sheet of paper listed three names and addresses written with ballpoint pen in crooked lines. He held the page down with one hand as the corners flapped from the air wafting in through the open windows.

"So where'd you get this info?" Lars wanted to know.

"I told you, a guy in the Bureau."

Lars had shaved that morning but one stray whisker, right on the tip of his chin, dodged the razor and now bugged him. He kept fingering the sharp hair and trying to pinch it between his fingers to pluck it out. Beat chewing his nails.

Trent watched Lars like a specimen. "How come you don't

wear sunglasses, man? It's brighter than shit out here." Trent spun his head all around as if to prove that it was bright no matter where he looked.

"You get used to it. I like to see the world as it is. That's something I learned way back. In this business you need to see everything as it happens. Your eyes need to be fast. Faster than the guy you're facing. Notice everything. You can't notice everything if you're seeing it from behind a curtain."

Trent obviously didn't like the schooling. He shifted in his seat, his back already sweating despite the tank top. He absently flicked his nose ring around in circles in a much practiced, self-soothing way.

Lars smiled knowing he got to the inexperienced kid.

They found the first address in a new subdivision with row after row of tan houses that looked as if they'd been stamped out of a giant machine. They passed two houses in foreclosure, the lawns brown and Chinese menus piling up in the doorway.

Lars knew this cheat sheet the kid brought with him stank of high-grade bullshit. After seventeen years, no way was the kid going to find Mitch the Snitch on the first day.

"There," said Trent, pointing to a house distinguishable only by the number painted on the curb. Stucco walls, brick-lined walkway, square of abnormally green lawn and a black guy climbing into an SUV. Not their man.

Lars snorted out a derisive breath. "Maybe he had plastic surgery. Got a reverse Michael Jackson."

"Fuck you," said Trent. "Let's go to the next one."

The brakes on the Mustang caught and Trent pitched forward, almost smashing his nose on the steel dashboard of the '66.

"Let's show some respect to your elders."

The guy in the SUV craned his neck around to see the muscle car that screeched to a halt in front of his mailbox.

The Mustang's engine glugged. As they sat still, sweat beaded on Lars's nose and on Trent's forehead.

Trent tried to be hard, not apologize to the geezer. Just to get the car moving and some air flowing again, he gave in.

"Fine, all right. Let's get going. You know where this next one is?"

"Yeah. I know. It's my job to know."

Lars gunned the Mustang and left twin lanes of rubber behind.

No one answered at address number two. They'd arrived during working hours. Trent suggested kicking in the door, but Lars told him they would wait. "It takes patience."

"That's no joke. Patience is all you got, man."

They ate lunch at a taco stand where they could have taken the opportunity to get to know each other better, but neither man felt like chatting. Instead their silence included Lars neglecting to tell Trent that the green chile sauce was the hottest one.

Spitting and slugging his Corona, Trent cursed the desert.

"Why the fuck would they eat something so hot when it's fucking hot enough outside?"

"It helps." Lars sipped at his lemonade. Trent wiped his tongue with a napkin and looked at Lars like he'd gone nuts. "If you raise your body temperature, the outside doesn't seem so hot. Why do you think they wear those big robes in Saudi Arabia?"

"I thought that was, like, religious shit."

"It's all perspective. When you work in the sun, the shade's cool enough."

"All right, sensei. Enough. I didn't come for lessons. I came to finish a job you couldn't." He spit again, ignoring the disgusted stares of a woman seated behind them.

Lars set his eyes like stones, dropped his voice to a similar granite tone. "How many?"

"How many what?" Trent sounded like a petulant child.

"How many for you?"

"Make sense, man."

"How many have you killed?"

Trent saw the stone seriousness in the deep lines of Lars's face. "Four."

Lars did not scoff, did not smile.

"Forty-three. And I've been out of the game for the better part of the last seventeen years. I'll stop the lessons. Only trying to do you a favor. But don't you go criticizing my career until you have one of your own to back it up." He picked up his drink, waiting to see if Trent had a snappy comeback. He didn't. Lars stared through the mirrored sunglasses with his bare, hard eyes. "Four isn't a career, it's a bad night out."

He sucked on his lemonade until the straw slurped loudly.

5

Trent was glad to be away from the old man. Nothing but silence had passed between them since lunch. Lars dropped him off at a big box hardware store to get a few supplies. A fan for his room, first of all, and a pair of tin snips. The kind of shit you can't carry on an airplane anymore. The snips were for the finger. Proof that Mitch the Snitch was dead after all this time. Right index and right thumb were enough to make a positive I.D. That he could pack in his carry-on.

The body parts were part of Nikki Junior's new rules and something Nikki Senior never would have agreed to. One man's trophy is another man's evidence, he said. Nikki Senior once even co-opted the Sierra Club's motto for ordering a hit, and Lars subscribed to the wise words: *Take only lives, leave only footprints. But don't even leave those.*

The parking lot crawled with day laborers. Trent hated them for standing out in the sun all day long and not sweating. Guess the old man had been right, you get used to it.

It wasn't the heat making his blood boil. It was the verbal ass-slapping he got like a bratty kid who wet the bed. Four was a decent, solid number. You gotta start somewhere.

Trent wanted to like Lars, wanted him to be a cool guy. He'd heard the stories. They called him a Johnny Cash killer. Killed a man in Reno just to watch him die kind of stuff. And holy hell—forty-three? *And* he's been out here shriveling like an apple in the sun for the past…fuck and goddamn.

Why couldn't he be cool? Why did he have to be Trent's stepdad all over again, with the lessons and the condescension and the "You can't smoke in here."

Trent picked up the tin snips and browsed the fan aisle, big business down here apparently. He'd never seen so many to choose from.

The day laborers milled around a McDonald's built right inside the store. Getting out of the heat. Smart. Layers of Mexican gibberish crowded his ears, making his fan decision more difficult. Trent's head spun with the humiliation of lunch, his disappointment that Lars wasn't the badass killing machine he'd expected and his fear that none of the three addresses his pal hooked him up with would pan out and he'd be stuck out here in the desert until he'd been cooked and wrinkled like Lars.

One of the Mexicans came out of the john. To Trent the man suddenly had a target on his chest. They all did. Little Spanish toys at a carnival. Pay your dollar and fire at will. One after the other, watch them fall.

Four. Let's be honest, what a fucking pathetic number.

Another Mexican went into the toilet. Trent slipped the tin snips into his back pocket and followed, grabbing up an extension cord out of a bin next to the fans, marked "$9.99."

The bathroom smelled of fresh piss. Must have been used a thousand times a day. After the management had to scold the day workers one too many times for pissing in the bushes outside—it frightened the customers—they allowed them to use the toilet inside. Let the minimum wage fast-food jocks clean it up.

The bathroom had two stalls, one larger for handicapped customers, and three urinals, one occupied by the man who entered before Trent. Trent pushed open the doors on both stalls to confirm they were empty.

He tore the wrapper off the extension cord and let a big loop of the orange plastic hang down. He stepped behind the man taking a leak and dropped it over his head.

Trent yanked back and took the man backwards into the

handicap stall, piss spraying as he went. In this shithole no one would even notice.

He tightened the loop around the man's neck, and another smell added to the bouquet. José had shit himself.

The man sputtered and gagged, but Trent locked the cord in a knot and twisted to tighten it even further. The man's dick flopped outside his pants but the stream of urine had stopped. His penis waved like a surrender flag.

He fought for every last sliver of air that made it through, but the tubes and duct work of the man's neck were collapsed. The only thing now was to wait until the last of the oxygen in his bloodstream made the lap around his body and then hold on longer as each of the organs shut down, tired of waiting for a new supply of the precious oxygen. Trent knew he didn't have all day before another worker came in to piss out his jumbo Diet Coke. Besides, the smell was enough to gag on.

He gripped one hand firmly on the knot in the cord and reached into his pocket to pull out a knife. A short, fat blade under three inches long—legal for air travel—with a handle that ran perpendicular to the blade, allowing him to grip it between his middle and ring finger. One two three he shivved short sharp shots into the man's kidney.

He let loose the cord and the man collapsed. The Latino bashed his head off the toilet bowl on the way down and the porcelain crushed his nose into his skull.

Trent lifted him up to sit on the pot and tugged his pants down around his ankles. Most of the blood leaked down into the bowl so to an outsider it would look like nothing more than a bad case of too many Big Macs.

Trent washed his hands before he left, picked out a fan with a swivel and a picture of a tornado on the side and went to meet Lars across the parking lot, at an ice cream shop where he waited inside the freezing cold air.

Let him ask me again how many.

6

Five o'clock came and the two adversaries rode in the Mustang headed for house number two. Lars wondered about the look of smug satisfaction the kid wore on his face when he picked him up, but he didn't ask. To Lars, Trent reeked of self-satisfaction all the time.

They drove back to the suburban street listed on Trent's handwritten info sheet. This time there was a car in the driveway.

"So what now?" asked Lars.

"We knock," said Trent, adding a "duh" with the arch of his eyebrows.

"So, you knock on the door with your gun drawn and hope he'll admit that he's in witness protection?"

"We've got photos. We'll know if it's him or not. I'll pretend to be selling Girl Scout cookies. You like that better?"

"Whatever you say, Shirley. This is your game now. You want me to wait on the bench?"

"Ha-ha. Come with me. I want to see the look on your face when you meet him after all this time."

Trent tucked the 9mm into his belt in the small of his back. Lars rolled his eyes. Not exactly where you want it in case of an emergency. It's classic redneck to say that you don't carry a loaded gun unless you plan to use it, and those good ol' boys are right. There's a damn good reason John Wayne never wore his six-shooter behind his back when he faced down the guy in the black hat.

Trent showed classic fake gangster moves lifted directly

out of rap music videos. Millionaire badasses who own twenty guns but have never fired any of them. If shots ever did ring out, they'd all be reaching behind them into baggy pants and firing sideways with one hand. Lars could stand upright with a target on his chest, walk right through a champagne and caviar party at a Hamptons' mansion and take out a dozen rappers before any of them got a shot close enough to part his hair.

Lars kept his gun, the silenced Beretta, down by his thigh, in his hand. Safety off.

Trent knocked.

A man answered. Balding, overweight, glasses. Mitch would have had to change quite a lot.

"Can I help you boys?" Southern accent. West Texas most likely. Mitch was born and raised in Philly.

Trent smiled. "Mitch, we're here to share the good word. Have you welcomed Jesus Christ into your heart?"

Baldy crinkled his brow. "I'm a good Christian, but my name's not Mitch. We already give at our church, boys."

"Mitch, do you believe in the afterlife?"

Lars flipped the safety back on with his thumb.

The fat man grinned, trying to be hospitable. "Are you looking for someone specific? I don't know any Mitch. I know you boys are doing God's work, but..." He shrugged his shoulders.

Lars put a hand on Trent's shoulder and gripped it hard. "Our mistake, brother. Jesus loves you." He steered Trent away from the door, using his body to block the gun from Baldy's view. The man who wasn't Mitch stood confused in his doorway. From inside a woman called, "Roy? Who is it?" He ignored her.

Trent kept up his character. "Go with God, Roy."

"You as well," Roy said out of politeness more than understanding.

Lars blasted the Mustang out of there, the deep roar of the

engine setting off alarms on minivans in driveways as they passed.

"So were you planning on taking him out just in case?" Lars accused.

"No. Not a bad idea though. If we take out all three of these guys, we don't leave any doubt."

"Oh, I'd have doubts about you. Why they brought you in on this one, for instance."

Trent turned to Lars and ripped off his mirrored glasses like a cop on TV.

"I'm here because you couldn't get the job done. I recently did a very high-profile job for Nikki. He knows I can get this asshole. And I can do it before I'm halfway dead like you."

"Junior or Senior?"

"What?"

"Nikki Junior or Nikki Senior?"

"Junior. He runs things now. Or didn't you even know that? Should I ask you who the president is? What year it is?"

"Just wanted to know who's cutting my rope, that's all." Breathe in. Breathe out.

"You should be more worried about who's tying your noose. The way I see it, they spent a lot of money to get this guy and you couldn't fulfill. I think a refund is in order."

"Is that right?" said Lars.

"Yeah." Trent put his sunglasses back on, that certain smugness returning to his face.

"When I get back, I'll see if that's what they want to do. I'll discuss it with Nikki. Senior. The man I take my orders from."

To anyone driving alongside them it looked like a father-and-son argument. Probably over how loud to play the car stereo and what decade the tunes came from.

More silence. They were getting good at that part. Two cacti in the desert. Quiet and still, but don't get too close.

House number three was routine. Neither one felt much

like going through the motions. Trent began losing hope in his plan to do in twenty-four hours what Lars couldn't do in seventeen years. This trip, with the proper outcome, could be the jump start his career needed. Kill Mitch, then kill Lars and return home the new cock on the block. Paychecks rolling in, respect from his peers, fear in their eyes.

Almost a thirty-minute drive. Out here where land is cheap, folks tend to spread out. This is the place where settlers first came to get the hell away from other people. The great land grab when homesteaders all raced their covered wagons west of the Mississippi for a free slice of the pie was all just people trying to get the fuck away from their neighbors in the thirteen colonies. Lars came to the conclusion years ago that the only reason this part of the world became populated at all was a steady stream of loners and misfits who colonized it in the 1800s. Even loners breed, though.

The Mustang slowed to a stop across the street and down two doors from a simple ranch-style house. Trent checked the house number against his list, wanted a cigarette, spun around his nose ring instead.

"Same routine?" Lars asked. He was turning over the reins. Only one week. If the kid didn't want to learn anything, fine. Play out his time on the clock and go.

"Sure. Why break up the band?"

They didn't need to. The front door opened, and a man stepped out and picked up a coil of green hose attached to a spigot in a flower bed beneath a bay window. He cranked the knob and began spraying the lawn. Now that the sun had moved below the tops of the distant mountain peaks, it was safe to turn on the hose and not burn your grass or waste water that would evaporate in seconds in the midday heat.

Lars carried pictures, twelve in all, for all these years. He studied them like snapshots of his own family. He sifted over and over them like memories saved from a fire. He knew that face. Pictured it with long hair, short hair, black hair, no hair.

Pictured it with a beard, mustache, goatee. Pictured him with twenty extra pounds, fifty, a hundred. Knew what he would look like with colored contact lenses, caps on his teeth and lifts in his shoes.

Mitchell Kenney. Mitch the Bitch.

Trent reached for the door handle. Lars grabbed his arm.

"Don't bother. That's him."

7

Well, I'll be goddamned. The kid turned out to be right.

Lars hated to do so, but had to hand it to him. The list paid off. He'd never say it to his face, of course, but damn if Trent didn't lay old Mitch right in his hands after all this time.

Lars faced an aggravating question. Shit. What now?

Shoot him here and his work is done, but Trent gets the credit.

He'd get the credit either way. He deserved the credit. Or at least his guy in the FBI did.

Bested by a kid. Lars shook his head. *I'll never hear the end of it.*

Lars regarded Mitch, the object of his obsession. He looked the same as the photos. Nothing special. A guy watering his lawn, a numbers guy for the mob. No difference. The neighbors would never believe it.

Any way this goes down I have to be the one to pull the trigger. The kid's got to understand that, right?

Trent giggled like a child who got what he wanted from Santa.

His gun came out and his fingers danced on the metal. "I told you. I *told* you, motherfucker!"

Lars didn't dance, didn't smile. He looked and saw a man. Not a target. Not a job. A guy doing yard work. It was the same Mitch the Snitch and yet it wasn't.

Trent reached into the backseat and fought with the plastic hardware store bag, trying to get his tin snips out.

"Wait." Lars kept his eyes on Mitch. "We can't do it here. Not now."

"Why the fuck not?"

"What if they want us to bring him in? What if they want to make it worse for him than just a quick bullet in the head?"

"They would have told us that."

"No one thought he would ever be found."

Trent dropped the tin snips on the seat. He spoke, exasperated, as if he'd been told he was grounded.

"No, *you* never thought he'd be found. I knew it. This is the whole reason I came out to this stupid shit-brown oven of a city. It's the reason you've been out here for half your damn life!"

"Look, we know where he is. It can't hurt to check in. We'll make the phone call and then we'll know what to do."

"Fine." Trent laid his gun on his lap and pulled his iPhone from his pocket. He tapped the screen to life, dashing Lars's plans for a stay of execution for Mitch.

"Who are you calling?"

"Nikki. Who do you think?"

"Junior or Sen—"

"Junior for fuck's sake. What is your problem?"

"I only deal with Nikki Senior."

Lars emphasized his point by clicking off the safety on his gun. It rested in his hand, not aimed at Trent but ready to go. Trent's 9mm still napped against his thigh like a Chihuahua.

"What is your hard-on with that old man?"

"He's my boss. And until next week, I'm yours. We go back to the apartment, I'll make the call, we'll know what to do."

The close quarters of the two-seater made the air sweat with tension. The bullets practically rattled in the guns, straining to get out, bulls in the chute. Trent needed to spit. Turning his head to fire one out the window wasn't an option right then, so he swallowed stale saliva tainted bitter with anger.

Lars breathed in through the nose, out through the mouth.

A dog barked behind the fence of the house they'd parked

in front of, and both men knew they couldn't stay there long without drawing attention. Trent slowly put his phone away. He could see the dog behind the slat-wood fence over Lars's shoulder. It was a beast, Rottweiler and something else mixed to create a slobbering fist of muscle that you wouldn't let your kids anywhere near. Grown men crossed the street when this dog walked by.

Mitch was obviously used to the beast making noise. He didn't look up from his watering. Other than the admirable restoration job on the Mustang, there wasn't anything significant about the car parked across the street and two doors down.

"Okay, you call the old man. I don't have his number."

"Not many people do."

"I still don't know why the fuck we're waiting."

"Respect. A lot of time has passed since I got the assignment. Maybe things have changed. I got respect enough to call it in."

Over Lars's shoulder the owner of the dog came out to see what his beast was barking at. The neighbor opened the fence a crack. The barking drowned out his asking, "What is it, boy?"

The dog saw an opening and tore through. It nearly knocked down its owner as it pushed past. Looking past Lars, Trent saw the Rottweiler rush the car, covering the expanse of irrigated sod in only five bounds of coiled legs. White foam gathered in its jowls before flinging out like twin vapor trails on a fighter jet.

Even knowing what was coming, Trent still flinched and backed away from the window when a hundred and twenty pounds of animal rage hit the car. The snarling black dog put both front paws up on the door frame and bit at the window over Lars's shoulder, smearing thick spit and clicking teeth against the glass.

Lars never moved. Never flinched. Never turned.

He kept his gaze on Trent to sell how serious he was. For the first time Trent felt he could see the cold killer Lars had been.

The beast's owner caught up to the dog and gripped him by the collar, a thick studded leather strap, and wrestled the Rottweiler away from the car. He shouted commands and the dog obeyed.

With contrition he turned to the car and the men seated inside. "Sorry about that. Hope he didn't scratch up your car there."

Lars turned with a smile and spun the window crank a half turn, opening the window an inch so he could be heard.

"No problem. I'm a dog lover myself."

He nestled the gun under his leg, pushed the gearshift into first and drove off.

8

Lars had zero intention of making any phone call to Nikki Senior. Did the kid think he was nuts? Lars is supposed to tell his boss he finally found Mitch the Snitch and his only thought turned out to be how much he didn't want to kill him?

Part of him thought Nikki would understand, let bygones be bygones. In the real world though, no chance. Grudges last with his employers.

Trent had gone out. Lars had no idea where. *Let him celebrate. Gives me more time to come up with a plan.*

Lars stuck on the vexing question: a plan for what? How do you plan to *not* kill a guy? Everyone spends all day long not killing countless people all around them. Takes no planning at all. The difference here was that Lars had a little punk along for the ride who wanted desperately to blow Mitch's fucking brains out, and Lars had developed a desperate need to not let the kid one-up him. Besides the fact that if he had the chance to do the job and didn't...then the kid or someone like him would spend seventeen years hunting Lars down. And he'd been looking forward to some peace and quiet.

Lars had never done any formal accounting of how much he'd stashed in banks over the years, but he knew it totaled enough that he wouldn't have to worry about work ever again.

Maybe I could hire Mitch to run some numbers for me. Lars made himself smile, quickly squashed it. No time for jokes.

He let his eyes wander over the tiny mountain ridges of the popcorn ceiling. He did a little math. Seventeen years meant about sixty-two hundred days alone in rooms, silent with nothing to do but think about killing Mitch Kenney. Had to be a few leap years in there too, plus the days since his exact seventeen-year anniversary. Call it an even sixty-two-fifty. Never in all that time were his thoughts so busy, so noisy. Inside his skull the final note of a Nirvana concert played. The instruments smashed, broken guitars left screaming feedback into Vox amps turned up to ten.

There's no way out of this. I have to kill him. Christ, it's what they've been paying me for.

Pull the trigger—job complete. Simple as that. The kid still gets credit for finding him. After that they could talk all the shit about Lars they wanted. He'd be gone. Trent would tell tales of how he'd lost his edge. The Vegas job would come up.

Fuck 'em. My record speaks for itself.

The busy thoughts swirled, formed an idea. He could take the kid out. Bury him in the desert. Play dumb.

No. They'd find out. They always do.

His thoughts shattered, spun and re-formed into a new, clearer vision.

Honor. Respect. His word. He took the job. Cashed the checks. Lived the life. So did Mitch, only he got away without paying for his indiscretions. This was the life they chose.

Lars had to do it. He promised he would. Promised Nikki Senior. If nothing else, Lars remained a man of his word.

The noise faded, clouds receded. The new idea solidified diamond hard. Something he could hold.

I damn well need to make sure I'm the one to pull the trigger. Can't let that little shit rob me of that.

9

Earl Walker Ford might work for the FBI, but don't call him Special Agent. He figured: if everyone is a damn special agent then we're not so special, are we? But it was routine. Someone coined the phrase back under J. Edgar Hoover and it stuck. Much like the Situation Reports Ford dreaded.

Gather the middlemen, which he was fully aware included him, and have them give a rundown to the upper management, who filed it away and sent it to Washington, where Earl Walker Ford would bet his left nut no one ever read it. Still, he showed up to all Sit Rep meetings on time and prepared. It was why the Bureau loved him.

As a black man in the Bureau he found himself being courted for promotion over the years, but he could always smell the undercurrent of affirmative action, or at least the subtle stench of "Please don't sue us. Take the promotion. Make us look good."

To Earl Walker Ford the only thing worse than giving the Sit Rep would be taking it. He was fine being nothing but special, and since his transfer to the Witness Protection Service, the job had been smooth sailing. A favorite joke within the department was to call the Witness Protection division the FBI's day care program. *Let them laugh*, thought Ford. *No one's taken a shot at me in ten years and my office is air-conditioned.* Yes, babysitting has its perks.

Ford and four of his colleagues had one hour to deliver the update on all outstanding witness cases to their superior, Special Agent Barry, a veteran who ran out of patience with bureaucracy around the time of the first Bush administration. Sit Reps were supposed to take place monthly but Agent Barry only got around to them every three months or so and only after his secretary reminded him that delaying the reports was technically a violation of an act of Congress.

Agent Barry let out a bored sigh and set aside another file he was equally convinced no one in Washington would ever see.

"Ford, what have you got?"

Earl Walker Ford ran down the plentiful nothing going on in his districts, ending on the New Mexico/Arizona territory. "Same old, same old on district five. Slow as a desert tortoise."

"We have a replacement for Agent Corrigan yet?"

"Not yet, sir. Whitney's been the temp man in charge."

"Still? It's been two years. We can't get the budget for a fucking replacement?"

"Three years, sir," Ford corrected.

"Goddammit. Whose cock do I have to suck in Congress to get me an appropriation? Fucking Homeland Security shit-bags are draining my budget."

Earl Walker Ford and his colleagues nodded along to the broken record.

"Any word on your Vegas shooter?" asked Agent Barry.

"Vegas, sir?"

"Yeah, the guy you said was from back east. I remember that case 'cause at least it had some shots fired. I like a little action in my reports." Agent Barry pointed to his subordinates around the room. "Remember that, gentlemen."

"No, sir," said Ford. "The shooter, Lars I believe was all we could get off him, had been off the radar. We thought he was dead. There hadn't been any word of him in quite a few years. I put in my report that the ID was a best guess. The hotel video was good, but not great."

"Yeah, I remember all that shit. He hasn't surfaced again, huh?"

"No, sir." Ford regretted even putting that in his report six months ago. He hated the idea that he might have to do some actual legwork just to satisfy an itch his boss had for some alleged shooter with an East Coast pedigree. If there was actually a case there beyond tall tales about a hit man named Lars the FBI collected from a half dozen witnesses over the years, Earl Walker Ford would act on it. He'd love to be the golden boy who brought in a notorious gunslinger who'd been pulling triggers since before he was at the Academy. Who wouldn't? But the best part about being a middleman is the lack of action. And that air-conditioning. Made the Houston office bearable.

"Well, whoever it was I wish he would show himself again. We need a little jolt around here."

"Yes, sir." Ford handed over his report. Typed, double-spaced, destined for obscurity.

Agent Barry took it and added it to the pile, sighed again. "Brewer, what have you got?"

10

Trent eased the door to the apartment open and turned around to hush the girl. Kristi? Crystal? He couldn't remember. Smoking hot body though.

Two beers and six shots of tequila made it tough to walk through the darkened apartment without bumping into every piece of shitty cream-colored furniture in the place. She laughed every time he stubbed a toe or clipped his hip on a side table, like he was the king of comedy.

Midway through the room she sat down on the couch, lifting her short black skirt as she did, and said, "Where are we going anyway? Come on and fuck me right here on this couch already."

"No, no, no, baby. Come on. My room is better. You don't know who's been on this couch." *Probably you*, he thought, mentally reminding himself not to forget to put on a condom.

She giggled and grabbed his hand as he led her to his room.

Before they left the bar, she'd promised him a few lines of coke, but it turned out to be cheap home-cooked meth, the kind that is more plentiful than sand in the Southwest. He did them anyway, the powder burning in his nostrils.

Speeding from the crystal, he fucked hard and fast and lasted all of a minute and a half. Not that she noticed.

When they caught their breath and he pulled out, she got up to go to the bathroom and he watched her walk away, her perfect ass catching a flattering side light from the bedside lamp. Her skirt bunched up around her hips, her thong sat in a ball on the pillow next to Trent, and she hadn't been wearing a bra all night long. Those things would have stood straight in a hurricane.

When she shut the door, he reached for his smokes and lit one. He got out of bed, reached up to slide open the window over the headboard. It opened onto the back parking area, with a view of a Dumpster and the identical apartment building next door, but at least it let some of the smoke out so he wouldn't get too much of an ass chewing from Lars in the morning.

He couldn't believe the way the old man hesitated. Making excuses, bringing Nikki Senior into it. Lars was so scared shitless of being outdone by the new blood that he froze up and put on the stall.

Yeah, good luck, old-timer. Tomorrow you'll both be dead.

No matter what his father said, Nikki Junior wanted Mitch the Bitch dead. Lars too, on principle.

Trent pulled off the used condom hanging shriveled on the end of his shrinking dick. Looking like a post-molting snake skin, he deposited the generic-brand condom in a glass next to the bed with a half inch of warm Root Beer in it and immediately flicked ash on top. The sight grossed even him out, and he pushed the glass away behind the phone.

Depending on what Lars said in the morning about his talk with Nikki Senior, Trent had several contingency plans. All of them culminated in killing Mitch inside his own house, preferably while his wife watched, then taking out Lars and snagging the keys to that sweet ride.

Then again, something could be said for doing Lars first, taking his car and doing Mitch second. It might even be worth saying fuck it to the return airfare and driving the Mustang back east. A nice little road trip vacation.

Ugh, not with her.

The girl came out of the bathroom, the toilet still gurgling, body still smoking, the face showing signs of too much booze and crystal. She walked crooked. She wiped her mouth, and Trent got the feeling she'd vomited while she was in there. The tequila shots or was she bulimic? Who gave a shit?

"You got to go now, baby."

She started to crawl back into bed. "I kinda thought I'd be spending the night. Maybe a little round two action."

Trent exhaled smoke up to the open window.

"Sorry, baby. Not tonight. Big day tomorrow."

She ran fake fingernails across a tattoo of the Black Flag logo inked above his heart. "Are you sure, baby? You can do anything you want to me."

He stared at the ceiling. Chugged smoke and dropped ash in bed.

She licked his nipple. "You can fuck me in the ass, baby."

"Yeah, you're really gonna have to go now."

She sat up sharply. "What the fuck, dude?" She didn't remember his name either.

"I told you. Work in the morning. Rain check on the ass fuck though."

"As if." She snapped up her thong from the pillow and started angrily gathering the few things she had with her. "You at least have cab fare?"

"No. You can always blow him. That should be worth a trip along the scenic route."

11

Lars had been out cold. Laughter and the banging of a head-board sprung him from his hard-fought sleep.

That little fuckwad brought a girl back here. Thank God he's a quick draw in the sack and I didn't have to hear them squeaking bedsprings all night.

Every now and then Lars regretted not taking up smoking. Lying awake in a lifeless room trying to stave off thoughts of a man you had to kill seemed like the exact moment a cigarette might feel pretty good.

Lars pictured the man across town sleeping away his last night on earth and not knowing it, while the little pecker next door was dipping his wick with a barroom slut. Lars hoped she had crabs.

Mitch might have done something stupid a while back, but he's a human being after all is said and done.

Lars confronted that head-on when he finally saw Mitch in the flesh. He couldn't say he hadn't been thinking it for a while.

Once, in Sedona, Lars came damn close to him. He had good intel, plenty of lead time. Lars snooped around and got the make and model of his car. Tailed him one afternoon for hours. He had Mitch the Bitch in his sights.

Walked right past him coming out of a bank. Perfect scenario. Give him one behind the ear, take his money, and it goes in the books as a robbery. Lars held a hand on his gun, silencer screwed in place. He could smell Mitch's aftershave, he'd been so close.

Lars kept on walking. Too crowded, he reasoned.

What he excused away as being cautious and careful was really stalling. Even then, more than five years ago, Lars didn't want to kill him.

What had Mitch done but cover his own ass because he didn't want to go to jail for stuff the guys much higher up were into? Lars knew the way these FBI interrogations go. All Mitch had was the key to the books, and they still threatened him like they had him pegged for multiple murders *and* gambling *and* prostitution *and* racketeering. Scare the shit out of him, make him cop a deal.

Lars couldn't believe any of those high-ranking mobsters in the wood-paneled offices wouldn't have done the same thing to save their asses. When the Bureau offers you a new life, it's awfully hard not to take it.

Mitch had a wife, too. They'd been married less than two years when he got pinched. A real looker. Second cousin to someone in the family, and unlike the rest of the females in the clan, she ended up without the mustache, wide ass and eczema.

Life in prison kind of throws a wrench into your plans to start a new life together.

So he left the family behind, but they couldn't leave him behind.

Lars always had a problem with how much the family guys lived in the past. They talked of the old country even though most of them had never been there, and they talked endlessly about so-and-so and what's-his-name, who were the *real* gangsters. Guys dead twenty, thirty, forty years.

Now that's me, realized Lars. *Christ, that's what Trent sees when he looks at me. A relic. That's what Nikki Junior is doing—trying to update.*

In Sedona he'd hung around too much, let himself get seen. He wanted to be seen. Wanted Mitch to run. Wanted to be called home and taken off this assignment.

Lars wanted to leave the past in the past.

Best he could do now is to fade away and hope they stop telling stories about him, or at least stick to the good ones.

12

They parked the Mustang in front of Mitch's house at five after eight in the morning. Trent had yet to take off his sunglasses, so Lars couldn't see his bloodshot eyes. He'd been itching for a smoke the whole ride over and shook one out of his pack.

"You know the rules," Lars said.

"Just one. My hand is shaky." Trent held out his hand to demonstrate.

"Not in the car."

"Fine, I'll step outside."

"Let's discuss the plan first." There was no rush, but Lars liked seeing him sweat.

Trent tucked the cigarette behind an ear and stared straight ahead, waiting for the lecture.

"It's my contract, so it's my shot." Lars waited for the protest, but Trent kept quiet. *Let the old man have his shot*, he thought, *then I'll have mine.*

Lars continued, "You can take all the credit in the world for finding him. That's fine with me. But we do it my way. We wait for him to come out, we don't go busting in the door. And he's the target, not the wife. Only him. No collateral. Got it?"

"Can I smoke now?"

"Sure."

Trent stood by the back bumper and chugged out smoke signals. Lars rested his gun on the wheel of the '66 and thought about the first thing he would do when this job ended. He couldn't think of a damn thing.

In the past seventeen years the heat had grown on him, and the idea of leaving the desert seemed wrong. He hadn't researched any place to live, and he didn't want to pull all his money out and go plunk it down for a place that he would end up hating six months from now.

The dry air is supposed to be good for you. Maybe he'd stay awhile longer.

The smoke was welcome to Trent's lungs, but it did little to ease his headache. He knew the gunfire wasn't going to help either, but it would be over soon enough and he'd be able to go get some Tylenol or something stronger.

In the light of day he wished he'd taken up the girl on her offer of seconds around the back door. That's pretty standard bro code—never turn down a girl who offers to take it in the seat.

He smoked the cigarette down to the filter and was trying for one last deep inhale when Mitch stepped out onto his front porch.

Trent hustled back into the passenger seat and snatched his gun from his belt as he sat down.

"Settle down there, cowboy," Lars said calmly. "If I tell you to stay here, are you going to?"

"You don't want backup?"

"Backup is you waiting in the car. If you step out with me, that's a posse."

"I still get the finger." Trent made a snipping motion with his fingers.

"You can have all ten."

Lars thumbed off the safety on the Beretta and gripped the door handle, ready to end this hunt. Ready to start a life of leisure.

Then the front door opened again. A girl stepped out, maybe sixteen years old.

"Oh, shit. Dude's fuckin' the babysitter." Trent smiled and slapped his knee.

Lars hesitated. Again. That was no babysitter. She slung a backpack over her shoulder, wore a school uniform of tan skirt and navy-blue polo. Long straight hair, ten extra pounds, a hunched over awkward-phase gait. She and Mitch politely ignored each other in a way only a father and daughter would.

Mitch had a daughter.

Lars blinked. No collateral damage.

Trent turned to Lars. "You going or what?" Lars remained still, staring as Mitch and the girl routinely climbed into the mocha-colored Lexus SUV. This wasn't in the reports. How could they miss a daughter?

"Dude, you going?" Trent lifted his mirrored glasses and looked at Lars like he was an old man lost at the mall. Lars clenched the door handle, but did not move it.

Over Trent's shoulder the doors to the SUV closed.

"Okay, fuck it then, I'll go." He cranked back the slide on his 9mm and reached for the door.

"No!" Lars snapped out of it.

"What do you mean, no?"

"The girl."

"So?" Trent reached again for the door. Lars hooked his left hand into the crook of Trent's elbow, keeping his right on the gun.

"She's not a part of it."

"So I won't kill her unless she gets in my way. Now let my fucking arm go or I'll shoot you first."

Lars let go. Trent pushed through the door.

There it was again. Hesitation. It cost him before. If he continued to hesitate now, it could cost that girl her life. Mitch he could justify, but not her.

Lars left his door wide open as he exited the car and moved out around the striped hood. Trent walked swiftly across the lawn toward the SUV, gun down by his side.

"Wait!" said Lars.

Mitch opened his door and peered out over his shoulder, saw Trent. "Can I help you?"

Trent raised the gun. "Get out of the car, motherfucker." The girl screamed. Trent aimed the gun at her. "Shut the fuck up. Don't move, don't get hurt."

Mitch wasn't moving, so Trent grabbed a fistful of his dress shirt and pulled him down onto the grass.

Lars reached them. "Wait, wait."

"You still want it? Go ahead. Do it." Morning sun flashed off Trent's sunglasses in concentrated laser-beam blasts. Mitch looked up from the grass, and Lars could see that he knew exactly what was going on, that he'd been waiting for this moment as long as Lars.

"Daddy?" The fear in girl's voice cut through Lars.

"H-Hold on a minute," Mitch said.

Trent erupted, turned to Lars. "No. Fuck this guy. You've been holding on for seventeen years, man! Now finish the job!"

Lars's world slowed down. He looked around him for an answer to why he couldn't pull the trigger. Mitch's pleading eyes, the girl in blue still buckled into the front seat of the sensible family car.

Overhead a jet burned white lines across the blue. To Lars it looked so slow from down on the ground. With distance everything is slow. Up close it's so fast. Too fast. He wanted it to slow down.

Trent danced from foot to foot like he was barefoot on hot sand. It made Lars edgy.

A child. A little girl. How could he take her father away? Lars knew Nikki Senior would understand if he knew. He wouldn't want Lars to kill a man in front of his own child. He'd understand. It's one of the rules. Never in front of family. Never involve the kids.

This is a goddamn moral crisis is what it is, thought Lars.

He longed for the good old days when a bullet solved a problem, not created one.

Lars looked back down to the grass, ignoring Trent's anxious hopping, the girl's confused crying. He locked eyes with the man who had been the preoccupation of his last seventeen years. Mitch the Snitch. Up close and very personal.

Mitch kept looking at Lars. At the gun, really. His eyes were moving so fast between them Lars couldn't really tell. Mitch had started crying, though. That much was obvious.

"How did you find me?" Mitch asked.

I didn't, Lars wanted to say. *Blame the kid.*

Trent would have rather waited for Lars's silencer. The noise would play hell with his headache, but fuck it, this little scene was getting ridiculous.

Trent fired two shots into Mitch's belly.

The fading sound of the shots was overtaken by a scream from inside the car. The girl sat with her seat belt still on, her head dropped into her hands.

Mitch writhed in the grass, an ant with its legs pulled off.

Gut shots. Fucking amateur, Lars thought. Unless you're trying to send a message, it's the wrong way to kill someone. High chance of surviving. Still able to pull a piece and shoot you. Painful as hell. The kid showed no goddamn respect for the work.

Lars grew angry at Trent. *He can have the kill. I don't want it. Maybe I did all those years ago, but I don't now.*

Lars wondered if Trent even knew enough to go ahead and put one in Mitch's brain. Make sure he doesn't get up again.

He wondered if Trent even cared to learn what could be fatal to him on the next job, the one that's not a guy on a suburban street driving his daughter to school.

He wondered why Trent's gun was now aimed at him.

13

Between them in the grass, Mitch barely made a sound. He squeezed his eyes and grit his teeth to fight the pain in his belly, but he didn't cry out. Being strong for his daughter.

Trent held his gun out at the end of his arm, point-blank, at Lars. The engines of the Lexus and the Mustang harmonized in idle. In the yard next door, lawn sprinklers kicked on.

Lars could see himself reflected in Trent's sunglasses. His lined face a contrast with the now familiar self-satisfied grin Trent wore below the shades. Lars saw a man defeated. Replaced. Aged out of a business in which he used to be the best. In that reflection, staring back, stood a man who'd given up.

He didn't like what he saw.

Lars's focus changed. The most important thing became to keep Trent from killing the girl. A surge of power ran from the Beretta, up his right arm and into his chest. Adrenaline blasted through his veins and he felt twenty years old again.

As Trent thrilled in watching the confusion swirling on Lars's face, he mulled over several dramatic last lines. The girl threw a wrench into anything he had rehearsed, so he improvised.

"I wanted the rest to be for you, but I guess I have to save at least one for her." He jerked his neck backwards in the girl's direction. "Nikki Junior thanks you for years of service."

With youthful reflexes Lars ducked left, fired as he sank to the turf and hit Trent in the shoulder of his shooting arm before he could squeeze his trigger.

Lars rolled and in one continuous move got back on his

feet, headed for the SUV.

Trent went down to one knee, which landed on Mitch's hip as he fell. Trent ricocheted off and fell flat on his back in the grass beside Mitch. From his position on the lawn Trent fired two shots roughly in Lars's direction, but one smashed through the bay window in the front of the house and the other clipped the front panel of the SUV.

Lars kept moving and leapt up into the vehicle, avoiding the running boards. He pulled the door shut and kept low as he wrenched the gear lever on the steering column down into R. The girl sat frozen still. Her beige skirt and navy blue shirt matched nicely with the tan leather interior of the Lexus.

"I won't hurt you. Stay down." He wasn't sure she was going to trust him. He wouldn't have.

Trent screamed. As quiet as Mitch was, Trent was the opposite. He yelled enough for both of them. He switched his gun to his left hand and took three potshots at the SUV racing down the driveway. One shot clipped the luggage rack on the roof and the other two sailed high, off to pierce the vinyl siding of some suburban home a half mile away and confuse the hell out of the owner.

The passenger door opened and the girl dove out of the car, the loose seat belt slapping against the door frame as it ratcheted back into place. She hit the pavement, skinning her knees in the same spot where she'd skinned them many times before on her roller skates. She ran, foolishly, for the front door and the illusion of sanctuary she felt it offered.

Lars ground the car to a halt, punched open his door and was met by three blasts of Trent's gun echoed by three metallic thumps in the frame of the Lexus. He retreated back to the driver's seat and slammed the door.

Watching through the windshield like it was a widescreen TV, he saw the girl sprint for the house. Trent spun on the ground and moved himself up to a low crouch, arms out like a defensive lineman. The girl squealed a short, frightened sound and dodged left. Trent countered her move, his wounded arm dipping low alongside. She shifted right, advancing on him the whole time. Lars watched as Trent threw himself at her, letting out a scream that started low in his throat and ended on a high note of pain. Trent reached out and managed to get the hand from his uninjured arm around her left ankle, and she pitched onto the ground, all forward momentum stopped as if her feet had been caught in a rabbit snare.

Trent was quick to stand and grab a fistful of her long brown hair and start dragging her, caveman-style, to the garage.

Lars took aim through the glass but was unsure he could hit a moving target through an obstacle with so much adrenaline in his system. Hesitation again.

Trent pulled the girl up to standing by her hair. He pushed her, hard, into the garage door and raised the gun to her forehead. The girl whimpered.

He paused, wanting so badly to think of something cool to say. Not that anyone else could hear it. He blanked, no *Die Hard*-worthy words coming to him. A shock of agony ran through him, and he grimaced through the pain of dragging the girl with a bullet hole in his shoulder. Too long of a pause. Pull the trigger already.

The girl's eyes squeezed shut. Trent pulled. Two metallic clicks. Empty clip.

The butt of a gun came smashing down on Trent's head. Lars had left the SUV too late, but he'd been given a second chance and he knew it. He wasn't going to mess up twice.

Trent let the girl's hair go and staggered. Lars hooked a cowboy boot around the punk's ankle and kicked up, sending Trent to the driveway. Lars knew he should kill the asshole. He knew it. At any other point in his professional life he wouldn't have thought twice about it. But there, in that front yard, the thought of killing someone, anyone, made Lars sick to his stomach. He drove a boot heel down into Trent's shoulder wound and the kid cried out again.

Lars took the girl's wrist and pulled her back to the Lexus. Dazed, her scalp in pain, she let herself be pushed back into the passenger seat.

Lars had left the driver's side open, so he slid in easily and slammed the gear into reverse with the silenced gun still in his hand. He kept his head down, not looking in the rearview as he stomped the gas pedal down.

Lars bumped into the street and cut the wheel, reversing directly into the twin-striped hood of his precious Mustang. It didn't stand a chance.

The SUV's rear bumper, complete with trailer hitch, demolished the front end of the vintage car. Unceremoniously Lars rammed the Lexus into drive and squealed tires as he left the scene.

Trent struggled to keep the gun still in his right hand, the pain of his ruined shoulder rocketing down to the tips of his fingers and shaking the gun so that getting the new clip in was nearly impossible. He found the opening and rammed the gun down on the driveway, the pavement slamming the new load into the grip. He ripped off two shots at the retreating SUV, but he knew they were pointless even as he pulled the trigger.

Trent let out one more scream to the heavens, not out of pain, but frustration.

He clawed to his feet, the headache now gone, replaced by a white-hot flame of rage inside his brain. Bested by a walking antique. And how to explain it? The man had gone rogue. He wasn't in control. How could Trent be expected to defend against that?

At least the hit was done. Almost.

Mitch moved slower now but kept up his insect writhing, his spit-sucking through gritted teeth, his eyelids shut to the reality of it.

It wasn't much, but it was all he had right then, so Trent put two bullets into the skull of Mitch the Snitch.

Trent felt only slightly better.

Across the street a curtain pulled shut as the person inside saw Trent look their way. Cops would be there soon. The Mustang was undrivable.

Trent pulled out his iPhone, and it calmed him like a security blanket. He ran a finger along the face of it, smearing his own blood across the screen.

He dialed Nikki Junior. Time for backup.

14

Lars rode two wheels of the Lexus up onto the curb to make a right on red around a woman in a minivan.

Damn I'm gonna miss that car, he thought. Of all the thoughts swirling through his brain, memories of his beloved Mustang came bubbling forward.

Breathe in. Breathe out. Breathe in. Breathe out.

He slowed, scanned the road ahead for signs to figure out where he was. In the dozen blocks since leaving Mitch's house he hadn't exactly been paying close attention to the route. He realized they'd been driving west, but to where, he had no idea.

Riding along in my automobile. Baby beside me at the wheel. No particular place to go. Chuck Berry's version was happier.

In those first few seconds after they pulled away from the house, he'd tried to get all the pertinent information from the girl.

"Where's your mom?" asked Lars, wondering if he had to go back and stop Trent from killing her too.

"They're divorced. She moved away." The girl was still crying, but the confusion and the force of his words made her answer like he was the principal and she had been very, very bad. With each question she flinched like more gunshots were going off.

"What's your name?"

"Shaine."

He gave her another look as he wove through light traffic.

He put the name to her face, and it came out: Plain Shaine. Lars felt sure she got it all the time. Look who's coming down the street, it's Mitch the Bitch and his daughter Plain Shaine. He saw the potential to grow into a lovely young woman, but she gave off none of that sixteen-going-on-thirty-makes-you-want-to-fuck-them vibe so many girls today seemed to radiate. Rat-brown hair, nose slightly off center, front teeth a little too big; her thighs poking out from the school uniform skirt should have driven a man nuts, but those two slabs said "Lay off the pizza, girly."

Lars had a choice to make: keep on driving and get as far away from Trent as he could, or stop, hunker down and figure out a way to get rid of Shaine.

He knew crossing state lines meant kidnapping. He also figured he probably had that charge in the bag already. He couldn't exactly drop her off at the police or child services or anywhere she could immediately ID him.

He tried to think, drumming his hands on the leather-wrapped steering wheel, wishing for some thinking music. Stevie Ray Vaughan was his choice for big decisions. You could get lost in the intricacy of those solos, and it was easy to let your mind chew on big issues.

He needed to hole up. Do some planning. The apartment wasn't safe. He needed a hotel. Lars was tempted to go get his money right away, but about the only thing safe in his life at the moment was the cash locked away in a bank safety deposit box. It could wait until morning. He'd stop off and grab a donut and a few dozen stacks of tightly wrapped hundred-dollar bills and then get out of town. With or without her. No, without, definitely without.

But that could mean many things. He'd never left a witness to his work. He didn't quite know what to do with one, like someone had dropped off a newborn on his stoop with a note pinned to her chest: "SHE'S YOUR PROBLEM NOW." Only this girl was no baby. She could talk. For all he knew she had the FBI on speed dial and that could bring down a world of hurt.

His training said: eliminate all witnesses. Now that the excitement of Mitch's front lawn faded, Lars allowed himself to contemplate following the rules. Maybe the girl he'd worked so hard to save was a liability.

The bile in his stomach rose. Lars squashed the thought.

He pulled to stop sign, snuck a glance at her. Stoic. Cold as ice. That's sixteen for you. Quiet, introverted. Lars thought she looked like she's read Sylvia Plath and dog-eared some pages, maybe underlined a few passages in *The Bell Jar*. He figured it was better than a hysterical crying mess.

Must be shock. That or she's a great candidate for life as a hit man.

She'd done nothing wrong. She didn't deserve to die. Fuck the rules.

Lars lingered at the stop sign. A car behind them honked. Lars gunned the engine, hating to be caught daydreaming at the wheel.

The jerk of the car roused Shaine. "Do I get to know who you are?"

"Lars." He made a turn toward the airport and all the hotels nearby.

"Lars," asked Shaine, her head down and fingers digging at hangnails, "what's going on?"

15

Lars explained it to her. Told her the whole damn thing. Left in just enough details to make it informative, but not overwhelming. She sat and took it all in silently. She calmed quickly after he assured her again he wasn't going to kill her. Shaine was unsure at first, but she'd seen the way Lars shot Trent and then clocked him on the head, so she knew the man she was with wasn't the one to fear.

Shaine ran out of tears. The crying turned to steely resolve now.

"I always knew something was up with my dad. Didn't think it would be this."

She pushed away the memory of the gunshots, the screams of that man, the one with the sunglasses and the tattoos who wanted for all the world to kill her dad, and it seemed like he did.

Her dad was probably dead. Push it aside. Forget it for now. Shaine put it all in a locker and swallowed the key. The cuticle on her forefinger began to bleed. She held it in her mouth to make it stop.

Lars wasn't sure what to say. He hadn't had a conversation with a teenage girl since he was a teenager.

"Is that right?" he managed.

"He was always nervous. Mom left because of it."

"When did she leave?"

"About three years ago."

The hard shell was making more sense. Divorced parents, moved around a lot, dad with a secret. Puberty was hard enough without this crap.

"Lars?" she began, timidly. "I think I want to get out."

"We'll be at the hotel soon. Then I can figure out a plan."

"No, I mean, I want to get out. I don't want to go with you. You said you weren't kidnapping me or anything." He had said it. A way to calm her as part of his explanation of events. "So I think I want to get out."

Lars thought about it. Things would be easier for both of them if they split up. Risky, he knew, but he was beginning to think Shaine could handle herself.

He slowed the SUV and pulled over between an abandoned car lot and a Mexican produce market. Miles away from the police. If Shaine wanted to stir up trouble, she'd have to wait awhile to do it. Lars could be long gone by then.

He had to give her a choice. She deserved that much.

"I'm not forcing you to come with me," Lars said. He got nothing from her but a stare, a slight pleading behind her eyes but without any confidence. Lars play-acted the hard man. "Take a walk if you think you can do better on your own. Frankly, I don't need the baggage."

He could see the wheels spinning in her head. He watched her run down all the options—from going straight to the police to the very real possibility she would take one in the back as soon as she stepped outside the car. Not the kind of thought a sixteen-year-old should ever have.

Lars waited for her to decide, uncomfortable with the feeling he wanted her to stay, but the tug at his gut was undeniable. The risk she could make trouble for him was small. Hiding out was his life's work. If he couldn't outrun a sixteen-year-old, he really was past his prime. She had no such experience. If Trent or any other punk with a trigger finger got the job from Nikki Junior to take her out, it would be the easiest hit they'd ever have.

The smooth-toned bell sounded when Shaine opened the door. The Lexus quietly sending an alarm signal against her decision.

She wouldn't take her eyes off Lars. She was doing her best to judge a man over whether or not he would kill her for making the wrong choice. It was not a decision Saint Albray's Academy prepared her for.

The heat came at her like a wall she had to pass through, like a force field trying to keep her inside the car. She backed out, nearly tripping as she set a foot out behind her and missed the running board. Her feet crunched in the dirt in front of the old GM lot.

She shut the door.

Inside, the air-conditioning blasting white noise, Lars felt like he'd just let a puppy out to fend for itself on the city streets. He clenched hard to keep himself in the seat, reminding the logical part of his brain that it could only help his escape to not have to worry about her.

Shaine took two steps back and then swished her head side to side, checking out where she was and where to go next. She started walking east.

Lars stayed in park. He watched her go in the rearview. He moved the gearshift into reverse, which brought up the backup camera, and he saw her walk away in the distorted fish-eye angle.

She took an even dozen steps and then stopped. She didn't turn around. Lars's pulse quickened.

Through the backup camera he watched as Shaine crumpled to her knees. He saw her shoulders lift and fall in heavy sobs. Her skirt picked up dust from the gravel-filled parking lot. Her arms dropped away at her sides.

"Shit," Lars said to himself. He watched her for a few moments more, then opened the door and got out.

He approached her slowly, hearing her cries rise in volume. He didn't want to startle her or make her afraid. She was the most vulnerable thing he'd even seen. One time, driving along the Merritt Parkway back east, he'd hit a deer with his car, before the Mustang. The doe leapt directly onto his hood and put a big crack in his windshield when she bounced off. He pulled over and, after he'd checked the car, went to see if the deer was dead. She lay in a motionless heap on the shoulder, and as he turned to get back in his car, he saw a tiny fawn step out of the woods, walk over to sniff its mother and begin pacing around in circles by where the corpse lay.

Watching Shaine was worse.

"Hey," said Lars, quietly. She contained her crying. "Look, Shaine, I'm not the one you should be running from. In fact, right now, I might be your best chance of survival. That guy back there? He wanted to kill you. Did you see the gun in your face?"

She started crying again. Lars lamented his total lack of psychology.

"Hey, I'm not trying to scare you. I'm trying to help you. I was trying to help your dad."

She turned to Lars. "Then why did you show up with guns at my house? You were there with that other guy to kill him."

"I tried to explain. I don't think you really know what a chance I'm taking. How pissed off some guys are gonna be when they find out what happened. I was wrong, you need to stay with me. It's still not a kidnapping or anything, it's for your own good. You need to get back in the car and we need to get away from this place."

"And go where?" Shaine looked up at him from the dirt. Her eyes, wet and red, pleaded for an answer.

"I don't know yet. But if you try to run on your own, you'll never make it. With me, we've both got a shot."

Lars crouched beside her in the gravel, leveled his gaze at her, tried not to accidentally give her a hard-ass hit man stare. Tried to throw in a little compassion. It felt foreign on his skin.

Shaine's tears slowed. Her posture slumped.

"Can we go now?" he asked.

Shaine nodded. "My dad? He's definitely…"

The answer stuck in his throat like sand. "Yes." Lars wanted to be blunt. No point in sugarcoating anything now. He decided not to expand, though. He didn't feel the need to explain how badly Trent wanted to kill Mitch. What it would mean to the young punk's reputation. Or how Lars knew the anger and frustration in Trent would boil over and undoubtedly Mitch ended up getting a few extra bullets meant for Lars. Maybe the kid finally wised up and used a good old fashioned headshot for a change.

The tears started again. This time Shaine leaned forward and put her face, tear-soaked and sobbing, on his shoulder.

Lars reached a hand around to pat her shoulder, feeling awkward. Looking worse.

A short, round Mexican woman exited the produce market carrying six plastic bags of fruit and cactus. She stopped to watch the couple in the dust. Lars gave her a shrug-shouldered look, hoped she wouldn't think anything too strange about the scene. She stood and watched for a moment more, enjoying the soap opera of it all, then moved away on stiff hips, rustling her bags as she went.

Lars helped Shaine stand up. He wished he carried a handkerchief he could offer her, then remembered his trusty red bandana. He handed it to her and she wiped her eyes. The fabric was nearly threadbare, softened by years of living in his back pocket. Lars watched her dry her face and realized the bandana was older than she was.

"You okay?" he asked.

"I guess so. I'll be fine."

"There's nothing wrong with crying." Solid advice from a man who hadn't shed a tear in over thirty years.

"Yes, there is." Shaine stood, slapped her skirt to clean the dust from the parking lot. She turned to Lars, transformed. She was Clark Kent with his glasses on. A subtle change, but one that made the person standing there a moment ago unrecognizable. The crying had its moment. That moment had passed. She handed him back his bandana.

Lars was beginning to like this girl.

The passenger door opened with another ding of the bell, a little less like a warning the second time.

She sat down and pulled on her seat belt. They said nothing.

Lars put the Lexus in gear and pulled back out into traffic.

After six traffic lights, Lars spoke.

"We need to hole up for the night. Figure out what to do. Okay?"

"Okay."

"Anyone asks, you're my daughter."

"Fine."

Lars checked them in to a decent hotel. Got adjoining rooms but only one key card.

Shaine shifted nervously in the lobby while Lars registered them. He could feel the doubt coming off her like the thin scent of baby powder she wore. He could tell her a thousand times he could be trusted, but nothing could erase the suspicion.

For a moment Lars worried about what the pudgy man in the sweater vest checking them in would think. A middle-aged man, a teenage girl sulking in the corner. No baggage. Lars tried to read his face for signs that he might immediately go call the cops as soon as they adjourned to their third-floor rooms.

Instead, the clerk gave Lars an eye roll that seemed to say, "I got one too. They can be real bitches at that age, can't they?" Lars smiled. It seemed appropriate.

Up in their adjoining rooms Lars opened the common door and invited Shaine into his half of the suite. They ordered room service and ate while sitting on separate beds.

"So where is your mom now?" he asked.

"I don't know. After she left, I never saw her again. She bolted."

There went his plan A to return Shaine to her mother and then disappear.

"That sucks."

"I guess so."

She finished off her cheeseburger.

"Any other family?"

"No. I never met my grandparents. Don't have any cousins that I know of. I told you my dad was weird. He never talked about family. In seventh grade, when we did our family tree, he made me copy one off the Internet and change all the names to characters out of Stephen King books."

It made sense. Mitch left his old life behind. His family, his friends, his name. Shaine was born to a blank sheet of paper.

"Do you think I can go back and get some clothes? All I have is this uniform and I hate it."

"No way. Your house is going to be crawling with cops right now. They'll have it sealed as a crime scene for at least a week."

"Well, what am I going to do about a new outfit?"

Lars stopped by an ATM on the way to the mall. He took out the daily max, three hundred dollars. He hated being out in the SUV, but stealing a car with Shaine in tow didn't seem right.

When they got to the mall, he parked around back in the employee parking, next to the shipping bays and Dumpsters. Before they went in, he switched license plates with a Volvo behind the Victoria's Secret.

Shaine embarked on some shopping therapy, bright colors to mask the pain. Lars followed ten paces behind her like a real father would do. He sat uncomfortably in chairs and on couches while she tried things on. She ran through the three hundred in about forty-five minutes.

Shaine looked genuinely happy. Nobody can repress feelings like an already damaged teenage girl.

16

Six hours later and Trent hit a third shot of tequila to fend off the pain. A thin Mexican with a thick mustache and a perspiration problem hunched over Trent's shoulder stitching up the wound where he'd taken out the bullet. This guy was the best the East Coast could do on short notice. He spoke no English and introduced himself by dropping the name of Marco Carbone, a big man back east, and repeating, "Doctor. Doctor Luis. Fix you. Fix you," several times as he pointed from his own chest to the bloody wound on Trent's shoulder.

Trent knew the type. Lost his license, lost all his money, probably gambling, so now he does quick patch jobs for the family. No questions asked. To Trent's dismay all he carried in his bag was a shot of novocaine, which didn't do much to dull the pain when he dug around inside the hole like a teenage virgin trying to find a girl's clit. At least with Lars gone he could smoke in the apartment. He'd been chain smoking all afternoon and he was on the last cigarette in the pack.

Trent hadn't been able to get in touch with Nikki Junior but found a few guys who made some calls to some people who knew some guys who called in a favor or two. He had a doctor, for what he was worth, and lined up two guys for muscle. He also had the names of the banks Lars got his money transferred to and the aliases he used to open the accounts. Two in Phoenix, one in Vegas, one in Denver. Only one in Albuquerque.

"You almost done, Doc?" Trent said to the man stitching his shoulder. He hadn't seen a diploma or anything, so the fact that Luis was a doctor Trent took on faith.

Dr. Luis ignored him. The dark rings of sweat under his arms spread out across his short-sleeved Oxford shirt. An out-of-fashion tie stayed in place with a tie clip but a fat drop of sweat was about to come loose from the fringes of his giant mustache.

Trent's iPhone blasted the custom ringtone he had set for Nikki Junior—machine gun fire. He swiped a finger across the screen to answer, "Yo."

"Jesus Christ, I just heard. What the hell happened?"

"The guy is bat-shit crazy, that's what. He started whining and crying, saying he didn't want to kill him. Then there's this girl and he—"

"What girl?"

"I don't know, like, the guy's daughter I guess. But Lars, he starts saying no collateral damage—"

"Mitch had a daughter?"

"I guess so. Yeah."

"So did you clip her?"

"No. The fucker shot me and then took off with her. I got Mitch though. Dead as disco."

Nikki Junior stayed silent on the other end of the line, trying to piece it all together. Trent reached the butt of his last smoke.

"So where did he take her?"

"I don't know."

"Is he going to kill her?"

"I don't think so. He was trying to save her or some shit."

Nikki Junior clicked his teeth. Normally this is where his dad would step in and solve the problem. New territory for Junior.

"Can you find him?"

"I don't know. I think so. I got guys and we got his bank accounts. If he wants any of his precious money, we'll know about it."

"Okay, that's good. Marco got you hooked up with some meat?"

"Yeah, two big guys. Fully loaded. Seem good."

"Okay. Hey, he shot you? Is that what I heard?"

"Yeah. No big deal."

Trent grit his teeth as Dr. Luis tied off his last stitch. He dripped sweat onto the fresh, less-than-straight line of blue thread.

"Jesus Christ," Nikki Junior said. "This guy is so much more trouble than he's worth. Okay, okay, keep me posted, but find him for fuck's sake. And don't take as long as he did, all right?"

Trent could tell Nikki Junior was annoyed, but he didn't seem to blame Trent, so that went down as a small victory.

"When I find him—when, not if—what do you want me to do with the girl?"

"How the fuck should I know? Shoot her in the head, dump her in the river, fuck her in the ass for all I care. I don't even want to know about her. She doesn't exist."

"Right on. I'll take care of this."

"Okay. Anything else you need, you call Mikey or Marco."

"Will do. We'll catch this fucker, don't worry about that."

"That's what Lars said to my dad when I was still sucking my mom's tit."

The line went dead.

Trent dropped the phone next to him on the couch. Dr. Luis was packing up his bag. He paused to wipe his brow with a yellowing handkerchief.

"You don't have any Marlboro reds in that bag of yours, do you?"

Dr. Luis set down a small pill bottle on the coffee table. He gestured to the bottle as if Trent was deaf or stupid.

"Yeah, yeah, I get it." He picked up the bottle. Codeine. "Well, it'll have to do."

17

A single sheet of paper was delivered to the in-box on Earl Walker Ford's desk. A fax from the Albuquerque sheriff's office.

"From district five. One of yours," said the man dropping the page off. He didn't stick around to wait for a reply.

Ford read the fax. A dead man turned up in the FBI database as one of theirs, fingerprints a perfect match. Earl Walker Ford let out a deep sigh. There hadn't been a witness death in over eight years. The bastards were supposed to stay hidden and quiet. Now Ford would have to work. He hated work.

He stood to retrieve the file on the man named in the fax: Mitchell Kenney.

Ford had no aspirations to the front office. He hated giving bad news like this to Agent Barry, but once he palmed the burden off, he was done with it. Better to be the bearer of bad news than the keeper of bad news. Earl slept soundly for every night of his twenty-one years on the job.

He knocked strong and businesslike on Agent Barry's door.

"C'mon in!" he heard.

Agent Barry sat behind his large oak desk in the usual position: head down looking at paperwork. When he looked up at Earl, he held the usual expression on his face: like he was on the verge of a headache.

"You remember Mitch the Snitch?"

Agent Barry scratched his chin. "Mob guy? Taxes or something?"

"Yes. Last relocated to Albuquerque five years ago."

"Okay. What about him?"

"He's dead."

Agent Barry closed the file on his desk. He leaned back into the deep recesses of his oxblood leather chair.

"Please tell me it was a heart attack."

"No, sir. Shot and killed on his front lawn this morning."

"Robbery? B and E?"

"Possible. His car was stolen." They both knew it wasn't possible at all. "Possible but not likely."

"Who's his handler?"

"Whitney's been on the case, working out of the Denver office. He's on vacation. He's been informed and he's on his way back."

"Shit, that's right. The temp guy. Where's he on vacation?"

"Lake Havasu I believe."

"Damn shame. Been frickin' forever since I been fishing. Well, do we know anything?"

"Not much, sir."

"Okay. Give it a once-over. I guess we got beat this time."

"Yes, sir."

Earl knew that the chance of finding anything solid on this stood about the same as finding the mugger who stole your purse. If the Mob really wanted someone dead that bad, they usually got their way. This one was sloppy by all standards, but circumstances on a hit like this were rarely clean and easy.

"Wasn't he an old-timer?" It was coming back to Agent Barry.

"Yes, sir. Seventeen years hid."

"Why now?"

"I'm afraid we don't know that, sir."

"Hmm." Agent Barry shook his head once, gave an "oh well" look to Earl Walker Ford, reopened the file on his desk and continued on with his work, like skipping over a crossword answer you know you'll never get.

Ford waited for further instructions. None came.

"I'll ask some questions, see if I can dig anything up on this. We have several assets with knowledge on the family."

Agent Barry didn't look up. "Yeah, yeah, sniff around a bit. See what stinks."

"I'll do that, sir."

Earl Walker Ford turned to leave.

18

Lars finished his initial stretches and put his palms on the hotel room floor, ready for his first yoga pose. He couldn't help wonder why they always did up the rooms in a faux Southwest look. Didn't everyone get enough of that around here? The ugly Navajo woven rug he bent over had a tag that said MADE IN CHINA. Who were they fooling?

He wasn't any closer to a plan despite the hours since they checked in. Shaine remained happy enough, thanks to the TV.

What the hell am I going to do with this girl? I've got to find her mom somehow, Lars thought. *Of course anyone I would have made a phone call to for help is now probably trying to find me and kill me since I fucked up a hit and shot one of the family. Even if the kid was a douche, he was a made douche and that don't go over well.*

So far the plan consisted of getting his money out of Albuquerque tomorrow, hopefully before they froze the accounts. Since he'd been dealing almost exclusively with Nikki Senior for all these years, he doubted anyone else had his payment information. Lars always assumed everyone back east forgot about him long ago. He didn't like the idea of being reintroduced this way.

Man, I really screwed this up good. Way worse than Vegas. Who ever thought killing two girls would be less of a cock-up than keeping one alive?

* * *

Two nights ago Shaine complained to her dad that she lived "the most boring life in the entire world." She wasn't the first teenager to make the claim, but if they ran a boring life contest, she might have had a shot at the title.

Mitch kept things buttoned down since he went underground, the only world Shaine ever knew. He didn't socialize. They never went to the movies. Rarely went out to eat. Picking up and moving in the middle of a school year was hell on her social status. You can't jump on board that moving train. Kids have friends; they don't need a new one who shows up uninvited.

Shaine made her few girlfriends slowly in Albuquerque, and she didn't miss them at all. This life made more sense. After all, she'd already lived her entire life on the run. You can keep the details from kids, but you can't help them noticing the smell of fear in the air.

Lars interested her. He was quiet. He tried to stop that other dude from killing her dad. But why? He tried to explain, but he left out so many details it all sounded like the Cliffs Notes version of some Shakespeare play. All bullet points and no story.

The hotel room was decent. Adjoining rooms on the third floor. She had been expecting some roadside motel with cockroaches and a vibrating bed. And he bought her all those clothes. She was living every teenage girl's fantasy of having her father replaced by a much cooler guy.

Thoughts like that made her remember. Her dad was dead.

She kept expecting to cry. She wanted to, but she'd had her purge and now the well was dry. She felt neither happiness nor sadness. Just confusion. He was gone and she didn't know what to feel. Her mind stayed occupied with the idea that she should feel something, until she talked to herself about it for so long she forgot what it was she should be sad about.

Oh yeah, Dad's dead. Murdered by the Mob. Her dad? It seemed unbelievable. It added to the confusion. First she saw her dad gunned down on the lawn, and then ten minutes later she found out he used to work for the Mob and he was a rat. She learned a man had been chasing him down since before she was born. Fantastic. Remarkable. In death, her dad was ten times cooler.

Another rerun of *Friends* ended, and she couldn't stomach an episode of *Two and Half Men,* so she stood and went through the door connecting their two rooms.

Lars was on the floor with one arm in the air, his back arched, shirtless and his eyes closed.

"Are you doing yoga?" It was derisive, in a cadence only a sixteen-year-old is capable of.

Lars exhaled deeply as he brought himself to sitting. Only when he was firmly on the floor did he open his eyes, determined not to be jolted from his calm state.

"Yes. I was."

"Weird."

"You ever try it?"

"No," she said like he asked if she ever tried eating raw pig testicles.

"You should. It's good for you."

He stood and slipped on a T-shirt with a worn AC/DC logo. She stayed in the doorway. He caught her eyeing the shirt.

"Loudest concert I've ever been to," he said.

Shaine raised her eyebrows.

"*For Those About to Rock* tour. It was insane. Madison Square Garden. Motorhead opened."

He was speaking a foreign language, but she knew some of the words. "I've heard *Back in Black.*"

"Great album. A desert island disc for sure."

"Hmm. Maybe," she said, mentally tallying her own list: Arcade Fire, the Subways, Kings of Leon.

"What can I do for you?" He continued to deep breathe.

"I dunno. I'm sick of watching TV."

"I didn't think teenagers could get sick of TV."

"Well, with no DVR I have to watch the commercials, and that pretty much sucks, so..."

"Oh." He tore off the plastic wrapping on a short glass by the minibar sink and filled it with water. "You want to...talk... about today."

"No. I think I got it all."

"I'm sorry again."

"What for? You said that guy would have killed me. You saved my life."

"Yeah, but I couldn't save your dad."

She stared at the bad Indian rug.

"I'm not going to have sex with you."

Lars almost did a spit take with his water.

"No, no. God no. I don't...It's not like that. I would never...That door locks, so..."

"I'm just saying. Don't get any ideas."

"I didn't. I wouldn't. You're sixteen for God's sake."

She kind of liked seeing him squirm. A killer blushing in front of her.

"Yeah, well. A lot of guys would try."

"Sure, yeah. But not me. Don't even...don't even think it again."

Kidnapping would be easier than this, thought Lars. All he had to do was tell her to shut up and keep her hands tied and a gag in her mouth.

Shaine crossed into his room and sat on the corner of the bed.

"Can we order dessert from room service?"

"Sure, yeah. Call 'em up." He hated sounding like the hip uncle, but he would have bought her a car to get her to change the subject at that moment.

She bounced across the bed over to the phone on the night-stand and pressed zero.

"Yeah, can I get a chocolate sundae to room three-twenty-five?" She put a hand over the mouthpiece. "You want anything?" He shook his head. "That's it. Cool, thanks." She hung up.

Lars refilled his water and breathed in through the nose, out through the mouth.

"You don't look like a killer, y'know." She wasn't looking at him.

"I guess today was my retirement party."

"How long did you say you were looking for my dad?"

"Seventeen years. Give or take."

Shaine picked at the few remnants of pink nail polish on her stubby fingers.

"I knew something was off about my dad. He acted like someone was after him. I'm kinda glad to find out it was true. I thought he was turning into a weirdo."

"Yeah well, just because you're paranoid…" He shrugged his shoulders and downed the second glass of water.

"What?"

"Doesn't mean they're not after you. It's a saying."

"Oh."

Lars felt as if she wanted to open up. Like if she had a diary, she'd be writing in it instead of talking to him. She stayed quiet, picking at her nails. He wasn't the first male to not know what was going on inside a sixteen-year-old girl's mind.

He made it a point never to get to know his victims personally. This was a hard-and-fast rule. You don't know them, don't know the family, don't know the name of their dog. It all got in the way. He stood and studied the back of her head, seeing for the first time what happened after his job was done.

This wasn't exactly a textbook case, but it was all he had to go on. The guys he was used to killing knew the drill. If they had a wife, she knew about the good chance that something could happen. The usual reaction was anger. Even the tears were angry tears. More often than not, the survivors weren't pissed at Lars but at their dead husband or boyfriend or son who'd chosen a life that put him in front of a bullet.

A sharp pain seized his right calf. Muscle cramp. He'd aborted his yoga routine too quickly.

Lars cried out and bent to one knee. Shaine stood up, not knowing what was going on, ready to yell rape. She saw him in pain.

"You okay?"

"Cramp," he gutted out as he tried to straighten his leg.

A knock at the door in her adjoining room.

"Oh shit, that's room service. You gonna be okay?"

"Yeah. Go ahead. I gotta work it out."

She backed out through the connecting door with genuine concern on her face. Once she was gone, Lars really let the pain show. He started rubbing and trying to move his leg.

Idiot. Always drink the water before the workout, Lars thought. *This thing has got me all messed up.*

He tried to remember if he'd taken his weekly drink yet in the last seven days. *Fuck it. I'm off the clock for the first time in a dog's age. I'm having a damn drink.*

He found a single-shot bottle of Jack Daniel's in the mini-bar. He didn't care how much it cost.

19

At 10 a.m. Lars pressed the entry button on the SUV remote. He had let Shaine sleep in, but she still dragged. He thought he could see the first stages of actual grief over her father's death, though it was hard to tell under the thick layer of teenage angst. Dressing up in her new clothes had brightened her mood a little.

She waited on the sidewalk as Lars brought the car around. Across the street stood an Episcopal church. She noticed the sign first. Those replaceable block letters always with an inspirational saying, like a worm on a hook to the lost souls passing by.

This one read: GIVE GOD WHAT'S RIGHT—NOT WHAT'S LEFT.

She appreciated the humor, and an idea suggested itself. When Lars had pulled out of the hotel parking garage, she leaned in the passenger side. "Do you mind if I go across the street for a second?"

Lars looked up and saw the church, a mid-sixties brick triangle. Not exactly St. Patrick's, but he didn't want to stand in her way if she needed a little divine guidance.

"Sure, sure. Hop in."

Lars pulled a U-turn and parked in front of the church. He made no attempt to get out with her. If he so much as set foot in the place, holy water would boil and the statues would break out in stigmata.

"You coming in?" Shaine asked.

"Uh, no. If you don't mind. You do whatever you need to."

"Oh." She stayed in her seat. "I was kinda hoping you'd be able to tell me what to do."

"Me? Oh, hell, I don't know what to do in there."

Shaine looked out at the building. "I was just gonna light a candle or something. Seemed like a thing to do. I dunno. Maybe it's stupid."

"No, no, you should. I think that's nice." What was he going to do, tell the girl that lighting a candle for her dead father was a waste of a match?

"Okay. I guess I'll be right back."

"Yeah, I'll wait here."

Shaine opened the door thinking she had no idea what an Episcopalian believed in. Her image of all churches was a version of the Vatican. Choir music, men in robes waving smudge pots, confessionals with waiting lines.

This place had more of a community center vibe. A short-haired woman approached her in a purple shirt with the tell-tale little white collar on it. A woman. This was no church she'd even been in. She reminded herself she couldn't remember ever being in a church at all.

"May I help you?" the woman asked. She seemed slightly annoyed, like she forgot to leave the door locked during non-business hours.

"Um, I'm here to light a candle for someone."

"A candle? For who?" Her manner was brusque. So much for all the peace and love crap.

"For someone. Does it cost money or...?"

"We don't really have candles. We put some out on Sundays. You're thinking of the Catholics." She said the word like Shaine had ordered a New York strip steak in a vegetarian restaurant.

"Oh, well. Never mind I guess."

"If you'd like to write down a prayer on one of these sheets here, we'll add it to the bin." The woman minister pointed to a small pile of cut-up sheets of printer paper and a stack of stubby pencils with no erasers. Shaine guessed mistakes weren't allowed on prayers. On the floor next to the stack of paper rectangles stood an upturned water cooler bottle half filled with folded papers. God's to-do list.

Shaine's eyes lifted from the jug to the minister again. She gave Shaine a practiced sour-lemon smile perfected by a thousand celibate nights.

"Y'know what? It's okay. Thanks."

Shaine left, happy her dad never made her go to church.

When Shaine got back to the car, he didn't ask her how it went inside.

"This car is too hot," Lars said. We can't take this into town, we'll get made. We need to ditch it."

She waited, one foot on the running board, for instructions. She grinned a little at the criminal lingo, even though it took her a minute to get that he wasn't talking about the car's temperature.

Stealing a car was riskier than staying in the Lexus. Lars only assumed the police had an APB out for this car, but if he stole one they surely would. It was a good long while since he'd hot-wired a car, too. Not since back east. There was serious doubt if he could even do it anymore. Cars had changed. Lars hadn't.

He weighed the risk and reward, decided a new car could wait. Once he had his money, the first stop would be a used lot. Maybe he could even find another Mustang. But that would be replacing the irreplaceable. Like if your girlfriend died and you went to a hooker with the same name. Close but...not quite.

"Okay, fuck it, get in." He opened the door. Shaine finished her climb into the passenger seat. His words came back around like a boomerang and he felt bad. "Sorry, meant to say screw it. Or...aw, forget it. Pardon my French."

"I don't give a fuck," she said, then tried to dial in the radio.

20

It wasn't a major bank branch. Not a national chain. Better to stay off the big boys' books and go local. This place catered mostly to the immigrant population, so they were used to money going in and out of state and across borders down to Mexico. Lars's monthly wire transfers didn't stand out.

There was a chance he held the distinction as the bank's largest depositor, but that didn't raise any red flags. Someone had to be. They survived like most banks, especially in a down market: don't ask questions as long as he pays the transfer fee, processing fee, handling fee and out-of-state fee.

The street bustled as people walked quickly between air-conditioned buildings and veered close to misters spraying cool water at the edge of a coffee shop patio. Even this early in the morning the heat seemed to come up from the ground as much as from the sun above, rising in a thick gum that had been lying dormant underground all night. The desert worked like that. Snakes curled up for hibernation each time the sun went down, but once the blinding light returned to the landscape it got dangerous all over again.

Shaine had been raised in the desert. She showed the casual indifference of a local to the blazing temperature.

Lars's back shifted under his shirt, clammy and moist from the sun and the stress. If the teller told him his accounts had been frozen he would have a decision to make: walk away and leave it behind or take what was rightfully his by force.

"Okay, you want to go shopping or something while I take care of this?"

Yes, she kind of liked this old guy.

"Sure. Drop me at the mall."

"Well, that's a little far. There's a shopping center up ahead about a mile. I'll drop you there and pick you up in a little bit."

"That place is so ghetto."

"Well, it's that or wait in the car." She sat still, waiting him out. "Like a dog."

"Fine."

Shopping was shopping, even if the store selection was not quite Rodeo Drive.

Lars bumped the SUV over broken speed bumps in the shopping center parking lot, and looking at it again, even he thought the place was a little ghetto. The stores all flashed neon signs of names he didn't recognize, most offering factory close-outs or slightly damaged merchandise. The storefronts were tagged with graffiti, and the rent-a-cop at the entrance looked like he needed to be sandblasted as badly as the building itself.

"I shouldn't be too long if everything goes okay," he said as she climbed down onto the curb. A big *if.*

Every other shopper there was Hispanic. They turned to look at the white girl like she'd been dropped off naked.

Shaine's head dropped in her patented don't-look-at-me walk, usually reserved for high school hallways.

"Oh, wait. Here." Lars handed over a hundred dollars cash. She took it but kept it hidden, convinced if the other patrons saw the wad of cash, she'd be mugged and left for dead in minutes.

He wanted to park close to the bank so once he was done he could get back in the car and go, especially if something went wrong. He resisted and parked down the street half a block away, out of sight in an alley between two buildings.

He joined the flow of sidewalk traffic, another mild-mannered citizen making a withdrawal. A one hundred-eighty thousand dollar withdrawal but still...

21

Trent sat on the vanilla-colored couch thinking about the future while spinning his nose ring. His iPhone buzzed. He hadn't set a custom ringtone for the two musclemen Mikey had hooked him up with. He reached for it by habit with his right arm and pain tore through him from the bullet wound in his shoulder.

"Fuck me," he spat. He dragged a finger across the screen. "Yeah?"

"It's Chet." Trent couldn't remember, was he the one with the shaved head or the one with the muttonchops?

"What's up?"

"He's here."

"Seriously?" Trent sat up, wrenching his arm again, but he bit back the cry of pain.

"Walking in right now."

"You sure it's him?"

"Matches the picture, your description. Plus, he was walking like he just bought a load of porn. Looking around, trying to be inconspicuous."

"Is he with the girl?"

"Alone."

"Do you see the car? Is she in the car? If he's not with the girl, maybe it's not him."

"Trent, it's him. What do we do?"

Definitely the bald-headed one. He was ex-military. All business. Mean as herpes. Scary as hell, too.

"Get him."

"Will do."

The line went dead. Trent lit a cigarette, sorry as hell it wasn't him pulling the trigger on the bastard. Shootout in a bank, at least maybe he'd get to see it on the evening news.

22

So far so good, thought Lars. The female teller helping him had been nice. Nothing too unusual about a guy wanting to check his safe deposit box. Lars enjoyed when they called him Mr. Oswald. Most of the tellers were too young to even think of Lee Harvey, but the old joke still made him laugh.

She shut the door, leaving him alone with the long steel box. Number 173. He knew it well. *Come to Papa*, he thought as he eased the lid open.

Eighty thousand dollars cash. Lars took a moment to admire the sight. It never got old seeing that much green in one place. Lars blessed the banks for bundling such crisp new bills. It wouldn't be as impressive all stuffed in a backpack in loose cash. The neat rows and wrapping bands were a big part of the appeal. Eight stacks in green-and-white wrappers, all marked with that beautiful, symmetrical number—ten thousand—on them.

Like he did every time he entered the safe deposit room of any bank, Lars wondered what else could be in the rows of boxes. More cash. Jewels. Love letters. Dirty movies of ex-wives. Cocaine. He heard that almost ninety percent of all one-hundred-dollar bills have some cocaine residue on them. That meant seventy-two thousand dollars in his bag had coke on it. Incredible.

Eighty grand in cash now filled five zippered freezer bags that Lars had nestled into his nondescript canvas duffel bag. Next came the hard part.

Lars knew his next transaction held the greatest potential

for attracting attention. *Yes, I'd like to withdraw a hundred thousand dollars please.* Get ready for some cross-eyed looks.

Maybe leave it. Maybe this is enough. I still have money in Vegas, in Denver, in Arizona. Maybe...

Nope. Fuck it, he thought. *It's mine. This is the rent on my life for the past two decades, almost. Paid to live in a sweat-box. Paid to live in the sand. Paid to live like a hermit.*

Lars pressed the buzzer, waited for the teller. She returned, all business, ignored his flirting. "PILAR" read her name tag. Nice ass, if you like 'em big.

Out to the window. A young guy, mid-twenties, now stood next in line at Pilar's window. She brushed the new guy back with her faux polite bank-speak.

"I'm sorry sir, this gentleman was here first. I'll finish up as quickly as I can and be right with you."

He shot a look to Lars, who ignored it and took his place at the window.

"Will there be anything else?"

"Yes, can you change these for me?" He set down two hundreds he'd peeled off a stack. He knew how hard it was to use a hundred-dollar bill in these days of debit cards.

"Twenties okay?" she asked.

"Fine."

Pilar counted out ten twenty-dollar bills and with a smile said, "Anything else?"

"As a matter of fact, yes."

Lars dropped the number of the withdrawal he wanted to make, ignoring her reaction and concentrating on the tingling sensation he felt, not from the mid-twenties guy, but from two men by the door.

If I was that security guard, I'd keep an eye on them, he thought. *Baldy's got an eye for danger and Muttonchops there has an itchy trigger finger. Come on, lady, cut me my check and let's go.*

Chet nodded in the direction of the farthest teller window.

Lyle scratched at his chops as he nodded. They moved slow, not attracting attention. Alarms can go off real quick in a bank, and that brings a world of hurt down mighty fast.

Lars waited for the look of shock to fade from Pilar's face. "All of it?"

"I'm leaving the country. For an extended period. Work."

"I'll have to get my manager to cosign a check that large, sir."

"I understand. Thanks for your help, Pilar."

"Yes, sir." She walked back past the vault and knocked on the manager's door.

He knew what she thought. How does an old guy like you with a green-and-white Western-wear shirt in need of an iron and jeans that look like they've been dragged through the Grand Canyon end up with a hundred grand? And why the hell do you need it all at once for?

Two windows down loitered two Mexicans in cowboy hats and boots. They laughed and spoke in Spanish, boots shedding dirt on the marble floor. An aging woman with leathery skin filled out a slip at a solid stone island in the middle of the floor. The table was topped in white marble veined with grey and stood tall for easy filling out of deposit slips. The high ceilings gave the building the grand appearance you want from a bank. The bulletproof Plexiglas walling off the tellers from the customers gave a sense of security to the staff, but an unease to those trapped outside its protective cover. If you stood on the customer side, you were left vulnerable among the madmen who warranted putting up the barricade in the first place.

Bank robberies have been a time-honored tradition in the Southwest since the days of Jesse James. For this reason, and his own gut instinct, Lars kept the two muscly thugs in his periphery.

Chet and Lyle stepped up slowly, in a purposefully casual meander and straddled Lars, Chet to his left and Lyle to his right, pretending to fill out forms. Lars clenched. He willed Pilar back to the window. She wasn't receiving his signals.

"One of you boys have a mint?" asked Lars. He turned to Chet, the more dangerous-looking of the two. Something about a shaved head always gave off a formidable vibe. Lars didn't turn his back to Lyle, simply rotated his neck to see Chet. Chet shook his head.

"No? I think I have one in here." He hoisted the zippered bag to the counter and unzipped it only enough to dig his hand inside.

Pilar returned.

"Here you are Mr. Oswald. We're sorry that you're closing your account with us today."

"Oh, you can keep it open. You never know when I'll be back."

He took the check with his left hand, his right still inside the bag, resting on his gun. Chet spoke up.

"Going somewhere, Mr. Oswald?"

Lars exhaled, centering himself. Then the shots started.

The first one ripped through the side of the bag and into Chet's arm, the one Lars knew held a gun under his jacket. Why else have a jacket on in this heat? Security guard should have spotted that.

Lars spun and lifted his leg high in a kick to Lyle's face. Limber is a good thing to be. Means you can reach the nose on an average-sized man with your heel and drive that sucker straight back into his brain. Lyle dodged at the last second, but Lars still got a solid connection and felt the bone crack, even through his boot.

Pilar screamed and hit the floor.

Second shot came from Chet. A wild ricochet that bounced up off the marble and then again off the Plexiglas before embedding in the oak door of the manager with a polite knock.

Lars clamped a fist around the bag and pumped his legs, on the move. He stuffed the check, half-folded, into his breast pocket and tried to snap the fake pearl button closed but gave up when it proved too hard to do on the run. He lifted the bag in front of his face and heard Chet's second shot echo off the high ceilings. Something struck the bag and punched it into his forehead as he ducked around the island and slid to the floor.

He landed next to the twenty-something with an attitude, who now appeared wide-eyed and respectful.

"You a cop? Off-duty or something?" the young guy said, thinking he had landed in an action movie.

"Something like that," said Lars. He flipped his bag over and saw the hole surrounded by a ring of burned canvas. A slight smell rose from the singed plastic of the freezer bags and the scorched paper around a neat hole bored into a stack of cash. Check off another thing tight bricks of money were good for—stopping a bullet.

The two Mexican brothers scrambled toward the door, their boots struggling to get a grip on the marble. They passed right by the woman, old enough to be their *abuela*, and left her for bait. Lars pressed his back against the cool stone of the island, breathed in and out once. A pen on a chain dangled in front of him.

Lars looked to the glass front doors. He could see the reflection of Chet and Lyle both on the floor beneath the teller windows, neither quite recovered from his wounds but both looking madder than hornets. Hornets holding Glocks.

"So what do we do now, bro? Call for backup?" The twenty-something vibrated with adrenaline.

"Well," Lars gestured toward the security guard, who had taken a position under his chair by the entrance, "I don't think he's going to do the trick." The aging guard tried crawling under it completely, but the chair offered little shelter so he held it out in front of him like a lion tamer as he shielded his path to the door, mumbling the Hail Mary in Spanish as he went.

Lars thought it took a little long, but finally the alarm bell rang. Not exactly a crackerjack team to be looking after his hundred and eighty grand.

The twenty-something clapped his hands. "Whoa-ho. Here comes the cavalry!"

Like a smart bomb locking on target to the sound, a bullet flew from Chet's gun and blew apart the young guy's head. A shot meant for Lars.

Lars covered up, but a bit too late. A fine spray of blood hit him like the misters along the sidewalks keeping New Mexico cool, only this spray landed warm and sticky on his skin.

It made him hesitate. Again.

On his left side came Lyle. He put a heavy foot down on Lars's right hand holding the gun, pinning it to the floor beside a spreading pool of blood from the twenty-something. Lyle brought his gun to rest an inch from Lars's forehead. Those muttonchops lifted as he pulled his cheeks back into a grin. He had meth-head teeth, rotten and small from grinding during long nights speeding. His breath reeked, or it could have been the week's worth of food residue in his chops.

Lars couldn't tell if this character was saving the kill for Chet, who seemed to be in charge, or if he wanted the last thing Lars saw to be his laughing mug. It was Lyle's turn to hesitate.

Lars reached with his left hand to snatch the pen swinging on the chain and drove it sharply into Lyle's neck. The mutton-chopped smile quickly disappeared.

Being right-handed, Lyle brought his gun hand up to the pen in his neck, and by reflex or stupidity he fired off a round no more than an inch from his ear. The shot struck the ceiling, and a fine snow of plaster floated down.

Lars could tell the pen hit Lyle's voice box from the ragged cry of pain, like Tom Waits after a bender. Blood oozed out of the tube, mixing with blue ink. The chain swung as Lyle staggered. Lars raised his gun and launched three rapid-fire shots into Lyle's chest. Perfect grouping, up and down in a straight line over his heart like the light tree at a drag race. Ready, set, gone.

No collateral damage kept running through his mind.

Lars leapt out from behind the other side of the marble island and fired two shots over his shoulder as he did, not intending them to land, only to keep Chet in check. He lunged forward three steps, grabbed the old woman by the neck of her dress and dragged her backwards behind the marble slab. She writhed on her back and moaned, looking sad and scared. If she had looked up at him and said, "I've fallen and I can't get up!" he wouldn't have been surprised.

He slid her through a slick of red that oozed from the twenty-something's head, but she didn't seem to notice. She was too busy saying her final absolution to notice she lay side-by-side to a dead man.

The alarm bell rang on. Lars knew time was an issue. He hadn't started the firefight, and everyone in here would attest to that, but eighty thousand cash and a cashier's check for more wouldn't exactly escape notice when the cops showed up. Lucky for him, the cops worked opposite of the snakes in the hills—the hotter it got, the slower they became.

"Quit fighting it, Lars! If it's not me, it'll be someone else!" Chet said.

Cue the hero music. The primal scream, the fearless charge into the open. The bank manager.

Out he came from behind the protective wall of Plexiglas, a shotgun in hand like he'd been waiting to get robbed since the first day he moved behind the oak door. Whatever pep talk he'd been giving himself since the shooting began worked, because he entered the lobby clearly out for blood.

The shotgun led the way by two feet as the bank manager charged into the open. He ripped off a booming shot at nothing and kept up his scream until Chet's first bullet hit him in the chest. He cut off like a record being scratched. Blood appeared on his blue dress shirt and his tie flew up into his face as he pitched forward, driving the barrel of the shotgun into the marble floor.

As the manager fell, facedown, Chet fired another one right through the top of his skull. The manager hit the floor and the solid stone did to his nose what Lars's foot couldn't do to Lyle's.

Lars was sorry the manager tried to be a hero, but it opened a door for him.

He spun out from behind the island and fired his same rapid three shots into Chet. He grouped the bullets around Chet's heart.

The old woman continued to moan on the floor, making music with the ringing bell. The two brothers were long gone. The security guard clung, frozen solid, behind his chair.

Lars stood with the bag of cash in hand and went to Pilar's teller window.

"Pilar? Are you okay?"

"Yeah. Are they gone?" she answered from the floor behind the bulletproof wall.

"In a way."

No other tellers could be seen, all hunkered down, hoping like hell the Plexiglas would hold.

Lars made it quickly to the door. He paused to move the chair away from the security guard's face. He'd never seen such terror in someone's eyes before. The name tag read: "MANNY."

"Congratulations, Manny. You foiled your first robbery. Nice shooting."

Lars slipped out the door.

23

When the hell did pay phones become an endangered species?
Lars thought. He finally spotted one at the far end of a mini-
mart parking lot. He pulled in, threw the Lexus in park and
realized he had no change.

The automatic doors opened when Lars stepped on the
minimart doormat. He could feel the security cameras leering
at him like the eyes of a balding businessman at a strip club,
and Lars was taking center stage. The duffel bag remained
gripped tightly in his hand.

"Can you make change?" he asked the mid-twenties counter
jockey. The kid seemed more interested in getting off shift and
making it to band practice than in doing his seven-bucks-an-
hour job.

Lars reached into his pocket and pulled out a twenty he'd
gotten in change. He allowed himself a little self-pride in his
forward thinking. Cashing a hundred at a minimart was as
easy as sucking a watermelon through a straw.

The kid eyed it and gave Lars a look. "You got anything
smaller?"

Lars wanted to hit him upside the head with the duffel full
of hundreds, but he breathed out slowly and said, "No. Sorry.
I just need two dollars in quarters."

The kid rang up "NO SALE" and counted each coin, each
single and two fives out painfully slow before handing them
to Lars. He felt like dropping a hundred-dollar tip on the kid
just to see his reaction but thought better of it.

Lars stepped back out through the automatic doors, pockets jingling.

He dialed the number by memory, a number he hadn't called in ten years. Still, Nikki Senior would always be his lifeline. That's a number you don't forget.

It rang three times. Lars knew how he would start, but where it went after that no one could say. Just be honest, he'll understand. Explain how badly things had gotten fucked up. Maybe throw in a reminder or two of his years of faithful service. Couldn't hurt.

The voice on the other end picked up. It was Nikki, but a different Nikki. A time warp. He'd dialed back in time to the Nikki who hired him.

"Hello?" the voice repeated. "Who the fuck is this?"

Nikki Junior. Answering his father's private line. Things were worse than Lars expected.

"Where's your dad?"

"Who the fuck wants to know?"

"Listen, Junior, call off the dogs. Your little plan didn't work. Let's call it quits and you'll never see me again."

"Lars? Is that you, you son of a bitch?"

"Just back off, Nikki. No more stunts. You got it? Call Trent back to Jersey. You guys go about your business and I'll go about mine."

Lars could hear Nikki Junior stand up, could almost hear his face getting red through the phone. "You don't tell me how it's gonna be. I'm gonna tell you, you washed up piece of—" Lars slammed the receiver down. So much for a reasonable dialogue.

Still on the run. Time to pick up the pace a little too.

The sound was almost worse than the pain, the constant high-pitched whine. Even when the needle wasn't digging into her skin, the sound was still there, reminding her of the dentist.

The outline had gone quickly, but now that he was filling it in with that blue color that seems to only exist in tattoo ink, Shaine closed her eyes and bit her lip.

He figured it better than a fifty percent chance she was underage, but he didn't care. It had been a slow morning, and Myles liked nothing more than a girl out to piss off her daddy. She wasn't much to look at, but he frowned disappointment when she wanted it on her arm and not her upper thigh or, even better, her ass cheek. At least it wasn't another tramp stamp. Myles never felt good about skankifying the nation's females, but if that's what they wanted, then that's what they got.

He leaned in so close, Shaine could feel his hot breath on her arm. It didn't help the pain any. A last flurry of tiny looping motions with the needle and he was done. Finally the drill bit noise ended and she unclenched her teeth.

"There you go, little lady. It's on there now. Hope you aren't having any second thoughts because you're shit out of luck."

"No. I like it." She twisted her neck to look in the mirror at the raw redness and growing swell of her upper arm and the deep blue of the Chinese character that now graced her flesh.

"Good. 'Cause taking them off is a hell of a lot more painful than putting them on."

He slathered the fresh tattoo in Vaseline and taped a gauze pad over it.

"Keep it moisturized, keep it out of the sun, and if I had to guess from over thirty years doing this, keep it away from your parents for a few days. At least until it heals. They won't freak out so bad when it don't look like an infection."

"But it won't get infected, right?" she said, suddenly worried, but not about what her dad would think.

"Not if you take care of it. All our shit's clean. Can't say as much for the world outside these doors. Keep it covered and do like I say, and it'll still be with you in your grave."

She gingerly rolled her sleeve back down over the gauze.

"We said fifty, right?"

"We did indeed. Not including tip." Myles smiled. Tip enough would be to lift that shirt and flash those titties. She paid cash. Fifty for the tattoo, twenty for him.

"Thank you ma'am. Come again."

"Thanks."

A tiny bell tinkled over the door as she left the shop.

Lars spotted her about two minutes before he would have gone to find security and have her paged. He'd already run through a dozen scenarios where she ditched him and went to the cops, so when he finally saw her, he went a little limp. One less thing to worry about.

"Where the hell have you been?" he asked.

"You never said where to meet." She had him there.

"Well, come on. We've got to go." He took her arm with his right hand, his left holding tight to the bag of cash.

"*Ow!*" She peeled his hand off her. A Mexican woman and her three kids turned to them, eyeing Lars suspiciously.

"Sorry. I didn't even grab you that hard."

The short sleeve of her top leaked through with a rust color Lars recognized as blood.

"What happened to you?" He grabbed the arm again and she yelled again. Two more onlookers joined the staring contest.

Lars lifted the sleeve and reacted as any good father would.

"A tattoo? You got a frickin' tattoo?" The peanut gallery relaxed, satisfied this was merely a family dispute, and went about their business.

Shaine made no excuses. Copped no attitude, just stared him down.

"Come on," he said.

Inside the confines of the SUV he made her show him. She undid the gauze to reveal the single Chinese character about three inches high and an inch across. As tattoos go it was innocuous.

"What is that, something you picked out of the book? You never pick one out of the book. A thousand other people have that. If you're going to do this to yourself, at least pick something meaningful."

"It says 'Father.'"

Lars froze. Shaine sat still, firm and proud. It may have been the stinging of the fresh needlework, but he thought he saw tears start to gather behind her eyes. Silently he reapplied the gauze pad, smoothed it over and made sure the tape held securely before rolling her sleeve down to cover it.

Shaine turned her eyes forward. He started the car.

"If you have anything in here you want to keep, gather it up now. We're going car shopping."

He put the SUV in reverse and started backing out from behind the loading dock where he'd parked.

"Lars?" Her voice was tiny, a little girl's.

"Yeah."

"Is that blood on you?"

He thought he had gotten most of it. He checked the rearview and saw where smears of maroon stained his shirt collar and flecked his hair amid the stray wires of gray. He licked his finger and wiped them away. He did not answer.

"What's in the bag?"

"I told you. Money."

Shaine turned to the backseat, where the canvas bag sat like a toddler behind them.

"The whole thing?"

Lars stopped. He put it in neutral. He turned to her.

"Look, we haven't really talked about it because it didn't need saying, but we're in a world of trouble here. I do what I do...did...but beyond that I'm out of my depth. I'm going to do what I can to keep you safe." Lars almost put a hand on her knee, but stopped himself. "You didn't do anything wrong, even if your dad did. I don't even think he did anything all that wrong anymore. Nothing any good man wouldn't have done to defend his family. We have some money and that's a start. It doesn't solve all our problems, not by a long shot. I need you to trust me. My first way of earning your trust is not to lie to you. I don't know exactly what's next. They're on me faster than I thought. That's not a good thing."

Shaine listened attentively, taking mental notes.

"Look, keeping us both from getting killed is priority number one. Once I feel like we're safe, then we can work on priority number two, which is finding you a place to go. I got a while before I'll feel really safe, don't you?"

Shaine nodded but also knew she felt safer with Lars than with anyone she had ever been next to in her life.

"Okay then. Let's go get a new car and stop driving around in this flashing neon sign. I'll feel a little better then. I need you to promise me you won't go doing something dumb like getting any more tattoos without asking me first, okay?"

She nodded.

"I'm not the fashion police. I won't make you stick to a curfew, but we have to have rules. The only one that matters is that I call the shots. Okay?"

She nodded again.

"Okay then." He put the car in gear and drove to the exact letter of the law. Only a few miles to go for a used lot. He wasn't going to get pulled over on a traffic stop with an abducted underage girl, blood on his shirt from a quadruple homicide and eighty thousand in cash and an unregistered gun in the backseat. No, thank you.

Lars could use a good stretch. *I'd part with one entire bundle of that money for an hour of quiet and a yoga mat,* he thought.

He knew an area where a line of car lots all gathered up and down both sides of the road. He thought about the weird way they cluster together like that. Lars knew who else did.

Vultures. Hyenas. Any kind of animal that feeds off the carrion of another will congregate by instinct the same way. One used car lot gets built, and you can bet, without even realizing it, the others will come.

"You're not scared," Shaine said. It wasn't a question.

Lars rolled it around in his head before answering. "Maybe scared's not the word, but I got a lot on my mind."

"But, you're not scared. Not like my dad. He was scared all the time. I could tell. We had a dog once, after Mom left. He thought it might help me adjust. It didn't last. That dog barked and barked every time my dad came into the room. It smelled the fear. We had to get rid of it."

"Being scared's not such a bad thing. There's a time and place for it."

"Yeah, but, it's no way to live."

Lars became fascinated with the way she clammed up as quick as she started talking. Must be something really interesting out that window, the way she stared. He couldn't decide if she was looking at the past or toward the future. Hard to tell which was more bleak.

24

At first he thought maybe a cricket had gotten into the van. The chirping continued too regularly and electronically. Cell phone.

Ed was alone in the coroner's van, strapping down the last of four bodies pulled out of the bank. The other two vans already headed back to the morgue, along with Ed's supervisor. The chirping continued.

He unzipped the bag and found it hard not to stare at the pen spiking out of the guy's neck like that. At least it was something different. Heart attacks and natural causes made the work dull most days. With the body bag open, the sound was louder, and he followed it to the front pocket of the guy's jeans.

Not sure what else to do, he answered it.

"Hullo?"

"Lyle! Where the fuck have you guys been?" barked Trent. "Chet's cell comes up busy. What's going on there?"

"This isn't Lyle."

"What? Who the fuck are you? Where is he?"

"He's in a body bag, man. Hate to tell you, but I work for the county coroner's off—"

The line went as dead as Lyle.

Trent knew he should have gone with them. He should have sat in a car across the street and been there in case Lars made it out alive. He could have gassed it and run him over. Would have felt good to smear that guy all over the sidewalk.

Stupid gunshot wound.

Stay here and rest, Chet said. *We'll take care of it*, Chet said. Well, Chet's dead.

Trent leapt off the couch and burst into Lars's room. He opened drawers, searched the closet, checked under the bed, looking for anything to give him an edge. He needed to know where Lars was going or if he was coming back for him.

If Lars could take out those two meathead bastards, then Trent was a sitting duck.

He found nothing. The guy lived like a hobo. He had five T-shirts, three pairs of jeans, an extra pair of cowboy boots and a jean jacket. No photographs. No books. No diary. A few CDs: Cheap Trick live, AC/DC, early Iron Maiden. Lars lived out of a suitcase for seventeen years, like he might be going home any day, like he was waiting for a ride to the airport.

Trent thought he might be overreacting. If Lyle and Chet were dead, there was nothing to say Lars wasn't as well. Maybe the bank was one big bloodbath and it was good he missed it because he would have caught another bullet and not been so lucky.

He turned on the TV and flipped channels on the remote, looking for news. *Wheel of Fortune. Judge Judy.* Boom, breaking news.

Bank holdup turns deadly. Four dead. The bank manager, the two robbers and one unidentified customer. His head was so badly mutilated that the medical examiner would have to run fingerprints and dental records. Could be Lars. Could be.

No one knew anything more, details at eleven.

He should call Nikki Junior, tell him what happened. But for the moment, Trent bypassed the iPhone and picked up his gun instead. His phone offered comfort in most cases, but some situations call for a good firearm by your side. If Lars did decide to come back, Trent couldn't defend himself with the latest app.

25

The only Mustang on the lot was an '88 and that wouldn't do. Lars kept running his eyes over a mid-eighties Camaro, but it was too impractical, so he found himself sitting behind the wheel of a late-nineties Honda Civic four-door. It was bland, but purposefully so. No one would give them a second thought. As soon as he got rid of Shaine though, the thing was going to the junkyard.

Driving off the lot, they passed by the parked Lexus, Shaine watching through the window as it vanished behind a cinder-block wall, the SUV nearly the last remnant of her old life. Lars made her keep the school uniform even though she tried to leave it behind. He told her when, not if, someone picks up the Lexus, it would look bad to have her clothes crumpled in the backseat.

Lars hit the I-40 headed west, the land of opportunity and home to the rest of his money. As usual the odd couple drove in silence, she looking out the window, he trying to think of something to say. Spending the vast majority of two decades alone doesn't improve your small talk skills. Lars would have been deadly at a party. Throw in a sixteen-year-old girl who watched her father get shot and his conversational well came up dry from square one.

The late afternoon heat came seeping out of the blacktop, and thankfully the AC worked well in the Honda. Some people came to this part of the country for the beauty, but Lars never saw it. The only time he found the landscape tolerable were times like this, with the sandy dead flatness whizzing by at seventy-five.

As was becoming a habit, Shaine started a conversation in the middle, leaving Lars to catch up.

"So this job of yours..." She let it hang in the air, hoping he would pick up the rest of the story.

"Yeah?" *Christ,* he thought. *She's been sitting there thinking about this for an hour. Where is this going to lead?*

"Killing people."

"Um...yeah."

"I'm guessing you don't go to school for something like that."

He tried to decipher whether she was busting his balls or merely noticing the elephant in the room.

"No. Not exactly. It's more like an apprentice type thing."

"You learn from someone else, you mean?"

"Yeah. Someone with more...experience."

It was almost becoming a real conversation.

Shaine eyed Lars up and down, looking for something she couldn't name and not seeing it. "You don't seem the type. If there is a type. You're too..."

Lars waited for her analysis of him. "Too what?"

"I don't know. You don't look like a killer to me. You're not dangerous."

Lars smiled. If she only knew. "Not unstable" is what she really meant. Lars had control. He didn't seem like he could fly off the handle and shoot up a post office. That's about all most people thought about killers. Introverts. Weirdos. Outcasts. Not aging rockers with a yoga obsession. "I guess thanks, then."

"And you say my dad worked for the Mob too?"

"Well, he did accounting for the family. They don't like to say Mob. That's something that J. Edgar Hoover named them." Zero recognition to the name. Moving on. "He never... are you asking if he ever killed anybody?"

"My dad? Fuck no. I know he could never do that. We had mice once and he couldn't even buy mousetraps. He hired an exterminator and we stayed in a motel for three days."

"So you're...interested, is that it?"

"I am riding in a car with you for what I assume will be several hours. We already spent the night in a hotel together. I have a right to know who is kidnapping me."

Lars took his foot off the accelerator.

"Woah, woah, woah. No one is kidnapping anyone here. You say the word and I let you out at the next exit. I don't think that's very smart of you, but if you want it, I'll do it."

Shaine cracked a smile. "Relax, Lars. I didn't mean it. You're taking care of me, I should have said."

"Yeah, well, big difference there."

She chuckled. "I want to go to the beach." Topic change. Much more time with this girl and Lars would get whiplash.

"Sure, who wouldn't? We're in the wrong state for that."

"I know. I've never been. Never seen the ocean. It totally sucks. I want to go."

"I won't lie to you." Lars smiled, relaxing a little. "It's amazing. Everyone should see the ocean."

"You've been? Of course you have. You've lived some-place other than the desert. I bet you were allowed to go out to movies when you were a kid, too."

"Allowed to. Couldn't afford to."

"Atlantic or Pacific?"

"Both."

"Which is better?" Shaine turned to him in her seat, feeling refreshed to talk about something other than Mitch and the business at hand. It was good not to look out the window at the rushing brown nothing outside.

"Pacific. No contest. Warm water, sandy beaches. East Coast beaches, at least the ones I saw, are dirty and rocky and cold as shit. Sorry."

She laughed that he still watched his language with her.

"Where were you? Los Angeles?"

"Mexico." He smiled when he thought of it.

"Wow." Her face lit up like Lars had showed her a ten-carat diamond. "What was it like?"

"Beautiful. Warm. Exotic. I think of it and I picture sunset on the beach doing yoga. The way the sun turns orange and gets all wavy at the edges and sinks right into the ocean like a fat guy into a hot tub. I swear you can hear the world say, 'Ahhhhh,' and let out a big deep exhale."

"Oh my God I wanna go so bad!" She balled herself up and pictured what it must be like, grinning. "Were you on vacation? Did you meet someone? Tell me you met someone and fell in love on the beach at sunset."

The rest of the memory returned to Lars. He tensed in his seat, thought about turning on the radio, scanning for some Bad Company or Bob Seger. Nothing too loud or fast.

He chastised himself. *Mexico. Nice going, dipshit. You can't tell her about Mexico. All caught up in the sunsets and the waves that I forgot about what really happened down there.*

"Yeah, yeah, vacation. No, I didn't fall in love. There was a girl, but..."

"But what?"

"It wasn't meant to be. You'll find out someday."

"I hope so." Her head hung, sad, the Mexican sunset light gone from her eyes. Lars could tell she knew she was a little homely. Maybe it was one of those duck and swan things. She'll grow into it. "I want to have my heart broken. Does that make any sense?"

Not to Lars, but he kept his lips shut.

"I've never had a boyfriend." Shaine dug at her cuticles again. Self-loathing turned to self-mutilation. "I've been in the loser squad since we moved, and my dad barely let me out of the house, so it wasn't easy. I don't know, I guess it's easy for any girl to get laid if that's what she wants. It's not, by the way, what I want. But I'm smart enough to know that I need to get my heart broken a few times before I can find the right guy. So I'd like to get on with it, y'know?"

Damn. No one Lars knew at sixteen was that smart. For someone who'd never been anywhere in her life, Shaine spoke like someone worldly. Hard to believe Trent was so close to putting a bullet in her head.

Lars shook his head at another thought. *Fuck, it's hard to believe I would have done the same thing up until a few days ago. How could I do that job for so long and already, just a day later, it feels like another person?*

The quiet returned. With Lars offering nothing to the conversation, Shaine resumed staring out the window. She got that look in her eye Lars had been accused of getting. The looking-inward stare.

I know she's not playing I Spy out the window. Thinking about life. Right now, she's got a lot to think about. Hey, at least it got me off the hook for the Mexico story.

26

The trip came the year before Lars took the job hunting Mitch the Snitch. Nikki Senior sent him down Mexico way because a local drug lord got tired of being the hired help, started getting a little too close to Nikki Senior's business. Turned out the Mexican had a brother who moved up to the tri-state area to act as go-between to his brother back in Baja.

Lars went down to deliver a message—"Dear hombre, fuck you. Stop pissing in our pool. By the way, I killed your brother and now I'm going to kill you. Tell your friends."

The job went fine. Lars took care of the brother in Jersey, boarded a plane to Tijuana the same day, got in clean, showed up, did the job, said his lines and put two in the back of his head. Clean and professional. What they pay him for.

Then Mexico happened to him. He figured, *As long as I'm here, and ahead of schedule, why not stay on and take it all in?*

Lars holed up in a little town about twenty kilometers north of Cabo. Quiet and slow. The kind of place made for escape. It didn't matter that he didn't speak a lick of Spanish. A man with money in his pocket is a welcome sight down there. For hotel clerks and vendors, but also pickpockets and whores.

Ah, Lucia. Lars smiled at the thought of her. She couldn't have done much business in a small town like that, holding out for tourists. The village wasn't on any travel agency brochures. Hell, everyone else in town was probably related to her.

Shaine continued to watch the scrub brush barrel past. Lars drove on toward the rising hills, unaware of the grin on his face as he replayed the first few moments of his lost week with Lucia. The steady rush of I-40 traffic almost reminded him of how the slow waves massaged the shore as he and his Mexican beauty walked on the sand.

The night they met was supposed to be his last in town, and to celebrate, he brought Lucia back to his room. While Lars lay on sweaty sheets humming along happily to the purr of the overhead fan and caressing the graceful swell of Lucia's hip, he decided to stay an extra day.

He spent the next day drinking with Lucia, forgetting the daily charge for her time. Hoping the meter ran out the night before and that she stayed with him because she wanted to, not for the money. They sipped the sweetest concoction he'd ever tasted. She said it came from a local plant, fermented down and aged six years. It could have been a line the locals tell gringos to sell their bathtub gin laced with kerosene, but it went down smooth all the same. That night, spent and sweaty in the same hotel sheets, the idea of payment never came up.

On his second extra day in town he met up with her early. He planned to spend an hour making love then take her out dancing and then return to the hotel for more lovemaking. Lars started making big plans for that night.

After the first session of lovemaking, they weren't eager to get out of bed. Neither needed food. They had each other, he told her. She told him the same, in broken English.

A gringo in town stood out, though. A man spending cash sparked gossip. Opportunists wanted a piece of him. And word traveled fast.

As it turned out, the men Lars killed had another brother. Eduardo. Lars might not have known about him, but Eduardo found out about Lars and exactly what he'd been doing since arriving in Baja.

A brother. Lars should have guessed. He hadn't met anyone down there with fewer than six children. Goddamn Catholics and their "Be fruitful and multiply."

The traffic outside the Honda didn't sound like ocean anymore. The grin faded from Lars's face. He hated to remember the next part, but once it started, he couldn't stop it flashing in his brain.

He and Lucia were about to embark on another flight of ecstasy when the door to the hacienda burst open. From there the details got fuzzy. Lars did recall he'd never reacted as quickly before or since.

Because of all the pickpockets, quick-fingered bellhops and sneaky maids, he kept a gun under the pillow, even with Lucia in the bed. Eduardo burst in and the sound of violence triggered an instant response. Lars's Mexico state of mind vanished quickly, and thinking back on it, he felt damn glad it had.

Eduardo brought three men with him. They held machetes and Eduardo a gun.

Lars didn't need a translator to know the stranger was shouting about killing his brothers. Lars rolled and Eduardo's six-shooter tore up the bed, sending chicken feathers flying higher than they ever did on the bird.

Lucia screamed. She covered up in the white cotton sheets. That was the real crime. She had everything you hear about in a Mexican maiden; the dulce de leche skin, the breasts heavy and high, made for feeding a brood of a half dozen but even better suited for the bedroom, the long black hair that looked good combed through or tangled, the perfume of jasmine and sea salt. That's how he chose to remember her.

Helpless, she made an easy target. Eduardo chased Lars's shadow with the revolver as he rolled across the tile floor getting a firmer grip on his own gun. Two of the machete-wielding helpers stormed the sanctity of their bed.

White sheets became red. Her screams were loud and pleading, then were replaced by quiet. The men grunted and sweat in their work, not unlike Lars had done with her only an hour prior.

Lars shot. First at Eduardo. Two in the chest, one in the face. Then at the man behind him charging with his machete, the blade still dirty from working in the fields. Lars gave him two in the heart.

He fired on the closer of the two men standing over Lucia. Lars hit him in the ear as he brought down the machete again. How many times had they already hacked? He couldn't count. Enough that they were short of breath from the effort and sweaty on a not-very-hot evening.

Lars shot the second man on the bed, Lucia's blood still dripping from the Latino's blade. His head came apart to decorate the wall by the door. It was futile. Lucia lay cleaved in two. Lars ran his eyes over her quickly to keep the image from settling on his brain. He stopped counting at three pieces of her.

Lars turned and did not look back.

I shouldn't have stayed the extra day. Even now, years and hundreds of miles away, his heart ached.

He left through the veranda and caught a taxi for Cabo that night. When he returned back east, he got a special thanks and a bonus from Nikki Senior for taking out Eduardo. "One fewer cockroach in the kitchen," the boss man said, laughing. Lars didn't smile, just took his cash and left.

Mexico. I still remember the sunsets, but that's not all I remember. Shaine doesn't need to know that.

27

Trent tapped the screen, answering his iPhone. "Hello?"

"So when were you gonna tell me you fucked it up? You wanted me to see it on the news or something?"

Nikki Junior tended toward sarcasm when he wanted you to know he was angry.

"You heard?"

"From the man himself."

"What? Lars? He called you?"

"Who he called was my father; who he got was me. So now I'm calling you to ask what the fuck happened."

"I don't know yet."

"But you will?"

"Yes."

"And soon?"

"Yes."

"Trent?"

Trent swallowed, waited for the rest. "Yeah?"

"Don't make me call you again."

The line went dead.

28

Earl Walker Ford knocked on Agent Barry's door again and was disappointed to hear he hadn't gone home for the day yet.

"Come in!"

Earl stepped in to find Agent Barry shrugging into his jacket, briefcase closed and on his desk, ready for exit.

"Sorry to bug you with this last-minute."

"What is it?" Agent Barry folded over the collar on his jacket, setting it right.

"Bank robbery attempt. Four dead, the two suspects and two bystanders."

"They stopped it?"

"Yeah, nothing was stolen."

"Good for them. And us. See you tomorrow." Agent Barry patted Earl's shoulder as he passed by on his way out.

"There's one thing…"

Agent Barry stopped, turned back to Earl and waited to hear.

"A bank teller says a man withdrew a hundred thousand dollars in cash and cleaned out his safe deposit box about thirty seconds before the shooting started."

Agent Barry's shoulders sank. He turned. "So they did get something."

"No, it was a legitimate withdrawal. And he was the one who shot the two robbers."

"The guy who took the money?"

"His money, sir."

Agent Barry looked at the carpet. It held no answers. He reminded Earl of those kids at a spelling bee who are stumped and they know it.

"Not much there, Earl."

"No, sir. But something."

"Yeah, well, look into it. See what you dig up."

"I will."

"Thanks, Earl. See you tomorrow."

Ford let Agent Barry leave. He decided to sit on the intel he'd gotten from the Newark office that afternoon. Just some backroom rumors, nothing that would stand up in court. Word was Nikki Senior was on his way out. The next generation was stepping up, trying to assert itself.

Interesting information, but Earl Walker Ford wasn't on any Mob-busting task force. His job was babysitting, he reminded his New Jersey friend.

"What's this got to do with Albuquerque?" Ford wanted to know.

It seems a young gun may or may not have been dispatched to the city in the sand. A person of interest in a job a few months back. A kid who doesn't mind bragging to a room full of people, uninterested or too dumb to care if one of them might be an FBI informant.

"That's a lot of maybes," Earl Walker Ford said.

"Ain't that the whole job?"

29

A few phone calls to the right people and Trent had details from the coroner's report faster than the district attorney. The mystery man from the bank shootout was not Lars.

Trent worked his iPhone all day, making contacts, dropping Nikki Junior's name to get favors. It turned out that if Lars had been doing his job properly, there was a lot to know about Mr. Mitch Kenney and his daughter, Shaine. Starting with the fact that their name was now Kendall. Those FBI guys, so creative.

Time to call Nikki Junior and tell the boss what he'd found.

"Do you know what fucking time it is? There's a time difference you know!"

Trent sat straight up, his shoulder pulsing with pain.

"Oh shit, sorry, Nikki. I forgot. I haven't been out here that long and—"

"What is it that's so important?"

"Oh, okay. I found out the girl's name. It's Shaine."

"Big fucking deal. Where are they?"

"I don't know yet. But soon. Mitch was a little paranoid, for good reason. He rigged her cell phone with a GPS. It's like a tracking device for kids. That way he could always tell where she is. Sick shit, right? I'd kill my mom if she did something like that to me."

"You'd kill your mom for a baloney sandwich. So what does this mean?"

"I got a guy working on it. Total nerd. Loves this shit.

When he can get the number for her cell, we'll have a bug on her twenty-four-seven, as long as her phone is on."

"How do you know they're still together?"

Trent opened his mouth, but nothing came out. He was stumped. Finally he stammered out an answer.

"I—well, I don't but—I assume they are because where would a sixteen-year-old girl go on her own?"

"She'd go down on my dick if she knew what was good for her." Nikki Junior yawned and popped out a crick in his neck. "All right, it's better than nothing. Keep me posted, but not so fucking late next time."

"Yeah, sorry. Okay."

Trent hung up and immediately reset the time on his phone.

30

The sun setting over the desert is truly beautiful, even Lars had to admit. He smiled, glad to be driving west.

Long smears of pink and lavender hung inches above the mountains as the sun grew bigger and more orange the closer it got to the horizon. Shaine stopped looking out her side window and studied the changing colors through the front windshield.

Lars imagined a world without oceans, where he could drive west for the rest of his life, chasing sunsets. They passed a sign welcoming them to Arizona. Without the oppressive rays of the sun, the desert began to cool, so he turned off the AC and rolled down the windows, letting in the dry air. He breathed deeply, inhaling the tranquility of dusk and the emptiness of the landscape.

"How come you didn't kill me?"

Just like that, Shaine snuffed out the peaceful glow of a desert sunset like she blew on the orange tip of a matchstick and darkened the world.

"You weren't in the contract."

With the light show gone, she turned to him.

"Is that it? That's the only reason?"

"It's a job. It has parameters."

"So you've never killed anybody that wasn't in your contract?"

Lars shifted in his seat. He hadn't noticed it before, but he really needed to use the bathroom. "Yeah, well, shit happens."

"Yes it does. It really does."

To head off any more questioning, Lars asked, "Are you hungry? I could eat."

"Sure."

He guided the Honda off at the next exit and into a truck stop with fast food, gas and showers for the truckers.

Before they ordered food, they both took a bathroom break. Lars relished the opportunity to stretch his legs. When they split to go to their respective gender-assigned restrooms, Shaine pulled out her cell phone, thumbed it on and hit the speed dial. She hadn't brought her charger so the calls had to be quick, but she was going to take every opportunity to make them, then power down, until her battery ran out.

The desert darkened quickly. They sat in the car eating fast-food burgers and fries, parked in the far end of the lot, on the edge of an expanse of nothing.

Shaine sipped on a milkshake that was so hard to get up through the straw she gave up, took off the lid and gulped it, using the straw as a spoon.

Lars couldn't get comfortable in the bucket seats of the Honda.

"I'm going to go stretch."

He got out and sat on the hood of the car. The metal had stayed warm from the engine, but the night air was cool coming in off the sand. Stars dotted the sky, and the glow from the truck stop outlined the shape of a low mountain nearby.

Lars reached and stretched and twisted his body. Shaine watched from the front seat, curious. She drained the last of the milkshake and went to throw away the wrappers and empty ketchup packets from their meal. On her way she had a thought.

When she got back to the car, she interrupted Lars's meditation.

"We could go see my uncle Troy."

Lars opened his eyes. He turned to her, silhouetted by the

neon glow of the clustered fast-food joints and gas station.

"Who?"

"You asked if I had any relatives, and I remembered Uncle Troy. He's not a real uncle though."

"But he's someone you know?"

"Yeah. He used to come over all the time when Mom and Dad were still married. They were, like, best friends."

"You know where he lives?" Lars slid off the hood, his backside feeling the cool air again.

"Sort of. He moved to Burbank. In California."

"Okay, okay, we can work with that. Uncle Troy it is."

"Should we call him?" Shaine held out her cell phone for Lars to use.

"No. It's a little much to explain over the phone. Plus, if you say you're with me, he might think something…seedy. I don't want to show up there and find the cops waiting for me in the welcome wagon."

Shaine agreed and pocketed her phone. They had a destination. Two more banks along the way, in Sedona and Vegas, and Lars would have most of his money, with a little stash still leftover in Denver for safekeeping.

After he dropped her off in Burbank, Los Angeles would be a great place to find himself a better car.

31

Another shot of Black Label did little to stop the dull pain in Trent's shoulder.

"You got anything better than this?" he asked the bartender.

The Neanderthal man looked back at Trent from a few paces down the bar. He was twice Trent's age and doubted the punk kid knew good liquor from homemade corn mash. Those fifties he flashed sure looked good though.

Trent had plenty of money. As handsomely as Nikki Senior paid Lars for the job, Nikki Junior paid nearly as well. The plan wasn't for it to go on so long, so a short investment of fifteen grand was, to Nikki Junior, a one-time investment. Long-term overpayment was one of his father's habits he was trying to break. Spending money on men because they did you a favor thirty years ago simply wasn't a good business model. Nikki Senior had become a one-man pension plan for too many old-timers. That, and a long list of other things, would change under the new regime.

The bartender reached under the bar, not out among the watered-down hooch that lined the wall behind him, and brought out an all-black bottle.

"Negra Suprema. Best tequila you can get. And you can't get it in the States. Made in Cuba. Harder to get than the cigars." He smiled at the kid, showing years of tooth-cleaning neglect.

"Hit me," said Trent, without asking the price.

The bartender poured from the ordinary bottle of tequila a

buddy had brought back from Mexico. The black bottle made it look expensive and mysterious. True, it wasn't readily available in the States, but mostly because better tequila was sold by the case at every liquor store in America. It was good enough but not the thirty-dollars-a-shot good he was about to charge the kid with more tattoos than sense.

After less than a week in New Mexico, Trent had come to the conclusion that liquor was the only thing worth buying in this state. He didn't want any fake Indian artifacts, and after that, what else did they have to offer?

"Holy shit, you again!"

Trent spun on his stool to see Crystal? Kristen? Christine? What was her name again?

"Come back for more, huh?"

She grinned at him. Her eyes were pink and bloodshot, her pupils dilated, speeding on meth for what looked like a few days.

"Oh, hey. How are you?" He didn't care about hurting her feelings, which made being cold easier.

"You were a real shit to me, you know that?" She still grinned a goofy ear-to-ear that told him she wasn't really mad and also that it was not out of the ordinary for her to be treated exactly that way.

"Yeah, sorry. Work, y'know? Stress."

"Oh, it's all right." She sat on the stool next to him, stinking of sweat, her clothes dirty and her hair unwashed.

"Buy me a drink!" She slapped the bar. The bartender stood poised and eager to pour another Negra Suprema and add it to his tab.

"Y'know, I was on my way outta here..."

"Oh, come on. You might get me drunk." She slid closer to him. "You might get lucky." She ran her tongue along her teeth. He had a flash memory of how good her blowjob had been. He shot the tequila and signaled for two more. The bartender smiled, with cartoon money bags in his eyes.

Ten minutes later Trent stood behind the building getting his dick sucked next to a Dumpster. He refused to kiss her when she tried, but with his eyes closed this counted as some of the best head he'd ever gotten.

The smell of the garbage covered over the smell of her anyway.

The iPhone vibrated in his pocket, which hung halfway down his leg with the rest of his pants.

She didn't notice or didn't care, so she kept on sucking as he fumbled to get a hand down to retrieve the phone.

He reached it by squatting, which pushed forward his hips, and she made some well-rehearsed moaning noises. She didn't have a clue.

"Yeah," he answered. She kept going.

"Hey, Trent. This is Jake, man." His friend with the computer skills.

"What's up?" He tried to pull away, but she only clung to him harder, and it felt too damn good to stop now.

"Hey, I found that girl's phone, man. It popped up on the grid outside of the Petrified Forest, man."

"It did?" Trent lost all interest in the blowjob.

"Yeah, only for a little bit. The call lasted thirty-three seconds. Then she powered down again. But once I got the records I found three others like that. All in places headed out on the I-40."

"They're going west."

"Yeah, looks like it. Should I keep an eye on it, bro?"

"Yeah. Fuck yeah. This is awesome, Jake. Keep it up. I got some serious scratch coming your way if this pans out."

"Yeah man, don't forget about me."

"Cool. Thanks, man."

Trent hung up. Her head kept bobbing back and forth. He stepped back and pulled out.

"Oh, yeah, come on baby, gimme that load all over my face."

Trent grimaced. He never quite understood dirty talk like that. If a girl is really into it, then it's fine, but when they say shit they think you want to hear, it did nothing for him. No girl really wants a load in the face. Trent's attitude was that he was going to finish however and wherever he wanted, and what she had to say about it was moot.

"Oh, stand up."

She opened her eyes, confused. "What's the matter, baby?"

"Nothing. I gotta go."

"Yeah, but, don't you want to finish?"

"No. See ya." His erection started to fall.

"What the fuck? Are you doing this same shit?"

"What do you want? A fifty? I'll give you fifty."

She stood up, angry. "I'm not a whore!"

"Yeah, if you were a whore you'd have made me come. You took too long and now I gotta go. Step back so I can pull my fucking pants on."

She stepped back. She may not have been a whore, but she had been a cheerleader, and she wound back with a high kick she'd practiced a million times and planted her foot, wrapped in a plastic shoe, right on his exposed balls.

Trent buckled at the knees, grunted a wet sound and fell to the dirty alley pavement.

She turned and didn't look back as she slapped open the back door to the bar and disappeared inside.

Before the door closed, the bartender came through as if he'd been sitting by, waiting for the action to stop. He held a piece of paper in his hand. The barkeep stepped up and stood over Trent, who moaned and cupped his balls in both hands, and read off the numbers on the tab.

"You owe me three hundred and twelve dollars. You want to settle up now or you want to come on in for a nightcap?"

32

Shaine slept, but Lars pressed on driving. The awkwardness of the previous night's stay soured him on making too many stops with her in tow. Out here in the high desert there wasn't much but truck stops and wayside motels that would give Norman Bates the creeps.

Plus, the night was beautiful. One of those pitch-black new moon nights where the landscape is as dark as the sky, so the stars begin on a blurred horizon then get thicker as they go up and over your head, making you dizzy.

Lars usually loved night driving. The slightly unnerving sensation of black all around you. Lars figured it must be what it's like to drive at the bottom of the ocean.

But now the sensation felt unnatural. He'd known exactly what his day was going to look like for so long that the black, the unknown, stretching before him filled him with half freedom and half fear. He grasped for the word to describe how he felt. Untethered.

Fuck the bottom of the ocean, he felt like an astronaut out on a spacewalk who suddenly realizes the cable connecting him to the ship is broken and he's floating away.

Christ, I'm talking myself in to a mini panic attack. Mitch is dead. My purpose for being is over.

The knowledge that he could go anywhere and do anything frightened him. It had been so damn long since he'd been a free man, the tingling feeling was foreign. Lars forced himself to do yoga breathing. In. Out. In. Out.

He'd known some guys over the years who'd done long

stretches in prison. All of them got used to the regimen of prison life quickly. Even the guys on a two-month stretch had an adjustment period when they got out. But the guys who went longer—years, a decade or more—they had it hardest back on the street. The worst part of all was being in charge of your own free time.

Driving through the ink of an Arizona night, Lars didn't have to worry about getting back to the apartment, didn't have to think about where the next lead on Mitch the Bitch would come from, didn't have to make time for target practice to keep his skills up. All he cared about was getting to the bank in Sedona during regular business hours, a quick stop in Vegas for more cash, and then making it to Burbank to dump Shaine.

Lars started to want a little more structure.

He took stock of the moment: On the 40 headed west. He had a destination and a time table; they would make Burbank day after tomorrow. It seemed vaguely like a plan. A purpose. He didn't have a job anymore, though. That part was messing with his head.

Then he thought of it.

Wait. Her. Keep her alive. No collateral damage. That's a job. That's a goal.

I can work with that.

The steady thrum of the road beneath the tires and Shaine's steady breathing lulled Lars into a foggy state somewhere between waking and sleep. He pulled off a rest stop and closed his eyes, ended up sleeping four hours before jerking awake. Took a second to remember where he was. Shaine was still asleep. She stirred, turned in her seat and resumed her steady breathing. Lars got back on the road.

The sun rose early. Light began to spill over the eastern horizon at twenty after five, and by the time Lars entered the Sedona city limits at five-thirty, the red hills and outcroppings were already posing for their postcard.

He let Shaine sleep through the night before, turning off the I-40 and down the 17 past Sedona to Phoenix and back up again. He made the round trip twice, all the while craving the sound of the stereo. The best way to drive at night is to roll the windows down and turn up the volume on "Born to Run." Has there ever been a better driving song? Lars knew the answer—no.

Despite the silence and the monotony of the white lines, the more miles in the car the better. Even though he was driving around in a big loop, it satisfied the part of him that wanted to run as far away as he could.

He pulled into the parking lot of a Denny's and got out, stretching. He did a few sun salutations, a downward dog. Shaine woke up slowly, taking a moment to remember the past few days and realize why she was in a diner parking lot with some weirdo doing yoga in the rearview mirror.

Oh, that's right: dead dad, killer who saved me, going to see Uncle Troy. Got it.

She rolled down the window. "Are we eating here?"

Lars stood up slowly, straightening his spine as he went. "You wanna?"

"I guess. Not many options around here."

"We can go into town and wait for something to open up. Lots of cute places nearby. We got money."

"Let's do that." She stretched in her seat. "No point in living like fugitives even if we are."

33

Three thousand miles away Nikki Junior knocked on the door to his dad's bedroom. In the expansive Tudor mansion there was room enough that Junior hadn't seen his dad in several days, despite living under one roof. Nikki Senior spent most of his time holed up in his bedroom, permanently attached to the oxygen tank that fed pure oxygen up his nostrils through two clear plastic tubes.

Nikki Senior would still have had a kick to him if it wasn't for his damn lungs. His mind remained sharp and his disgust grew over what his son was doing to the business.

"Dad?" Junior asked as he peeked around the door.

"Come in," wheezed Senior.

The room smelled stale, with a heavy film of dust motes swimming in the air, the flat screen tuned to ESPN, where it had been for days.

"Hey, Dad. I thought you'd want to know Mitch Kenney is dead."

A slow smile crept across Nikki Senior's face. The deep grooves growing in his jowls smoothed out as he beamed pride.

"That old son of a gun. He finally did it."

"It wasn't Lars, if that's who you mean."

"Who else would I mean?" The smile was short-lived.

"I sent someone. A new guy on the crew. Very good."

"Why the hell would you do that? I've had Lars on that job for ten years now."

"Seventeen, Dad."

Nikki Senior had a stricken moment of realizing how little

he noticed the passage of time anymore.

Junior went on, "And in all that time he couldn't get it done. My guy made the hit in less than a week."

"You don't replace a man on a job without asking me first."

"I had to, Dad. Do you know how much money we spent on Lars all these years? He's been jerking us around out there living a vacation in the desert. He was playing you for a fool."

"Bullshit. He's a good man. The best."

"Maybe he was. Was, Dad. Not anymore."

Nikki Senior wheezed in and out. The slack of the oxygen hose knocked a bell-ringing-beat out on the side of the pale green tank every time he moved.

"When he gets back here," Nikki Senior started, "you put him on a good assignment. You don't waste talent like that."

"He's not coming back, Dad."

"What do you mean?"

Junior paced across the end of his father's bed, back and forth, a duck in a carnival shooting gallery.

"He blew it. He messed up the hit. Tried to save Mitch the Snitch from getting hit. Then he took off with Mitch's daughter. She's sixteen, Dad. God only knows what he's doing to her right now."

Nikki Senior raged. "I don't believe you!"

"It's true, Dad. I've got multiple teams out looking for him, but he split into the desert with the girl. Some people... y'know, you can't tell."

Nikki Senior sat up in bed, stirring the dust in the room to a swirl.

"Bullshit! That man was loyal. He could be trusted. You send out a replacement for a man of his caliber and it's an insult. No wonder he went crazy. I tell you one thing though, he's not no kiddie diddler. Not Lars."

"Hey, I only know what I know. He took the girl and ran off. Maybe they went camping at the Grand Canyon, I don't know. I do see the news enough to know what it most likely means."

Nikki Senior fell back to his pillow. "If only you'd let me talk to him first."

Junior stopped his pacing. He stepped beside the bed, next to the wheeled cart of the oxygen tank.

"Look, Dad, I'm here telling you this as a courtesy. I thought you'd like to know. I don't have to come in here to have my ass chewed out. I'm not a kid anymore." Junior reached down and turned the handle on the tank. It tightened and the sound of flowing air constricted.

Nikki Senior dug deeper for breaths.

"I don't know why you can't see that my way worked. I made the hit happen and saved us a shitload of money. Now we don't pay that useless old man another dime. And if he ever comes back here looking for a job...I'll kill him myself."

He twisted the nozzle again. It shut completely. Junior kept cranking until he felt the threads start to grind.

"I don't care how many people he's killed. And I don't care how many years you've been in charge anymore, Dad. I'm officially calling the shots. From right here and right now. It would be great if word came from you that you're stepping down, but it's not necessary."

Nikki Senior sat up again and threw back the bedsheets.

"You take over only when you learn to show respect!" The mere act of getting up, and the air it took to spit the words, left him gasping. His ruined lungs, racked with emphysema, were giving out even if he had a lot of fight left in him. Senior fell back into bed.

"Lars is off the deep end, Dad. He's old news." Junior leaned in close and spoke quietly. "And I know when someone's time is up."

Junior cut a swath through the dust motes as he exited.

Senior used what strength he had left to turn the nozzle on the tank. Sweet oxygen flowed again and Senior breathed deep. In through the nose, out through the mouth.

34

She had the eggs Benedict, he had the chorizo omelet. The orange juice was fresh, and each plate came garnished with plump strawberries and wet slices of cantaloupe and watermelon. After breakfast Lars ordered a slice of chocolate cream pie, for the hell of it. They stayed over two hours. It was worth the fifty-dollar check.

Over the long meal they talked intermittently, but all conversation was about the food itself. Shaine didn't drop any bombshells. Lars got nervous every time she opened her mouth to talk about how fluffy the eggs were, worried she might segue awkwardly into asking about his work again. But they ate happily and talked of nothing. Their relationship had grown into a mutual don't ask, don't tell policy, like most fathers and daughters.

Both Lars and Shaine rubbed full bellies as they parked in front of the bank, an upscale stone-and-marble facade flanked by a women's wear store with headless mannequins in the window and an estate jewelry reseller. The morning grew warm but not oppressive, and the people on the street moved slowly in the way they do only in a resort town. Sedona had built a reputation as a place to stop and smell the roses, or at least the lavender and honey milk bath with seaweed wrap.

"You stay here," said Lars.

"Leave the keys."

"Why? You going somewhere?"

"The AC," she said in that "duh!" tone of voice. "You wouldn't leave your pet dog locked in a car sitting in the sun, would you?"

"I don't know. I never owned a dog. Stay put, okay? This won't take long."

"Like the last one?"

She still didn't know the full extent of what went on in Albuquerque, but she knew enough. And like the price on the dresses in the window display in front of them, if you have to ask, you don't want to know.

Lars stepped out, leaving the engine running, and surveyed the sidewalk for trouble. He scanned for anyone who fit the bill of the two meatheads who ambushed him at the last bank. He pretended to browse for estate rings, checked out listings in the window of a real estate office and took an inventory of each and every person on the street and in the shops. Lars decided he was safe, so he entered the bank.

Shaine watched from the front seat, wondering if he lost his way during the long trek across the sidewalk to the giant stone building that said BANK on the side. She knew he was being cautious about something, but she had no idea how worried to be. He went inside, so things had to be okay.

As soon as he moved out of sight, she powered on her cell phone. After a welcome screen and a scan of the area for a cell tower, she saw three bars. She hit the auto dial and listened. She held the phone to her ear for another thirty seconds and then hung up and switched off her phone.

With that out of the way, she was left to sit like the dog she'd warned Lars about. Bored, she turned the air down a few degrees. The sun baked the top of the car. She checked her teeth in the mirror on the rear of the visor. They shone white and clean.

She poked around the pockets of the car, found a tarnished old penny wedged in between the center panel and her seat. She opened the glove box.

Lars's gun. Silencer attached. It sat on top of the Honda's user manual.

* * *

Lars entered the bank. Cool, casual.

Okay, nothing funny going on here. Let's just get in and get out. No surprises this time.

"May I help you sir?" "Joy," read her name tag. A good sign.

"I'd like to make a withdrawal."

"Okay, sir, your check card or your account number?"

Lars could rattle that number off in his sleep. Whenever he opened a new account, he made it his business to commit the number to memory. He used a technique he learned in a book, and it worked like gangbusters. Lars hadn't been in Sedona for more than four years, and he didn't even hesitate when she asked. Popped it out like it was his name, which he couldn't use here because this account was registered to alias number three.

Joy asked for his I.D. and he fished in his wallet, looking for the right one. It would be a bit of a red flag if he said one name and handed her a license for another. Always a risk, which is why Lars always remained cautious.

Made it easy that he needed his old Arizona license. The same one he came across the state line last year to renew.

Joy's brow crinkled as she studied her terminal screen. Normally the expression would have been real cute on her, but instead it made Lars nervous. Joy looked less joyful by the second.

"I'm sorry, sir, but that account was closed yesterday."

Shit. They got here first. Maybe they did it by wire from back east.

"Perhaps it was your wife..."

"Yeah, that must be it. She never trusts me to get things done off my honey-do list, so she musta done it herself. That's so like her."

Keep smiling so she keeps smiling back. Joy's got some crooked teeth.

"Y'know, so I can say I did it, mind if I take a look at the safe deposit box, see if she cleared that out too? Do you mind?"

"Not at all, sir."

Shaine sat watching the gun for almost three minutes, waiting for it to jump out at her. When it didn't, the pull of it became too much to resist. She lifted the pistol out of the tiny glove box cave. She held it with two hands, low so anyone passing on the sidewalk couldn't see. It felt heavy and more like a machine than she would have thought. She expected it to be hot to the touch, still steaming from the last shots fired.

She turned it over in her hand, ran a finger along the barrel of the silencer, traced the curve of the trigger.

Lars thought Joy should quit this job and become a hostess in a high-class hotel, she'd been so eager to please. She shot him that crooked-tooth smile before she closed the door on Lars and his safe deposit box. He knew when she handed it over that the box was too light. He had to see for himself though.

Here we go. Fuck. Not a red cent. Just a note: "YOU'RE DEAD, FUCKER."

No signature. As if Lars had to guess. He felt sure Trent or Nikki Junior didn't write it, but he was sure they had composed the sentiment.

Okay, one alias blown. Did they get to Vegas yet? Only one way to find out.

The metal started to warm to her body temperature through her hot and moist palms. She tried to imagine aiming it at someone. She tried to conjure the feeling of pulling the trigger and firing. She couldn't picture what it was like to walk on the moon either.

Slide a finger in this slot (she did) *and look them square in the eye* (unless you're aiming at their back), *or do you follow the path of the bullet like keeping your eye on the ball in sports?*

She barely passed her driving test after failing the written three times. She couldn't imagine mastering a piece of machinery like this one.

Shaine never got the lesson in squeezing the trigger, not pulling it. Nor had she gotten any lessons on how little pressure you need to put on the trigger.

When the bullet exploded out of the barrel she jumped not at the sound, only slightly above a whisper, but at the way the gun bucked in her hand—exactly the way she imagined it might when it sat coiled up and sleeping in the glove box.

A tiny finger-wide hole opened in the window beside her and then the window of the clothing shop shattered. If the mannequins had heads, she would have shot one off.

What the fuck was that? thought Lars, reacting to the glass shattering sound outside.

Joy's question, "Did you get what you needed, sir?" would have to go unanswered.

If they did anything to that girl, I'll never stop seeking blood.

Lars stepped out of the bank, calm but urgent. He surveyed the scene. Shaine remained in the front seat of the Honda where he had left her. An alarm blared at the women's wear store next door, and tiny diamonds of safety glass littered the sidewalk. A small crowd gathered, ignorant of the fact a bullet had caused the window to break. No one heard a bang.

Their eyes met. She looked guilty. At least she wasn't covered in blood.

Lars slid back into the driver's seat.

"What happened?"

"Can we go?" Three of her cuticles were bleeding. Her leg danced as her foot tapped on the floor mat, anxious synapses firing, wanting to run.

"You okay?"

"Yeah. I'm just an idiot. Get out of here."

Lars dropped the Honda into drive and pulled away from the sidewalk gawkers wondering if a meteor had fallen to earth.

"I'm not mad," Lars said, "but what the hell happened? I didn't hear a shot. Was that my gun?"

Shaine nodded, looking over her shoulder.

"You fired my gun?"

"Not on purpose."

"Oh, well, that makes it better."

They drove in familiar silence as Lars navigated the car back to I-17 north.

"You want to tell me why you had my gun and how you shot out a window, not on purpose?"

Shaine shrugged. "It was there."

Hard to argue that rationale. It worked well enough for the people who climb Mount Everest.

Wind whistled through the hole in Shaine's window.

"You're lucky you're sitting so close to that. The bullet is still going so fast it didn't even break. Score one for Honda. Strong windows."

Lars remembered similar stories of him and his friends, years younger than Shaine, lifting guns out of their dad's drawers and going out shooting at cans, frogs, abandoned train cars. How many times had one of those boys been one false step away from taking a bullet? Too many.

"Can we agree that you won't do that again?"

She nodded. "You're not going to punish me?"

"What am I gonna do, ground you?"

A smile released a steam blast of nervous energy.

"Tell you what, your punishment is that we have to listen to whatever radio station I pick, okay?"

He set the radio to scan and after three Latino stations, one hip-hop and one all-news channel he landed on a Cheap

Trick song. He stopped the scan and turned up the volume; he'd found home. Robin Zander sang, *I want you to want me. I need you to need me.*

"I'd have killed to be at this concert. Listen to that crowd. Singing along and it's not even their native tongue. Fucking awesome."

Shaine couldn't stop grinning.

Lars exhaled, letting the music bring him down off the razor's edge he'd been walking since he heard the breaking glass of the storefront.

He realized, mid-breath, the relief he felt overshadowed the anger that Trent and Nikki Junior had cheated him out of a hundred grand. Probably because he expected as much. The gunshot came as a total shock.

I'm a goddamn idiot for leaving her behind. Fuck, for those few seconds I thought my whole life was going to be spent getting revenge on everyone and anyone responsible for killing her. Already in my head I'd killed the shooters, Trent, Nikki Junior, their families, mother father sister brother, aunts and uncles, family pets.

Jesus Christ. When they killed my dad, I didn't feel even half this. Sure he was a bastard. Sure it saved me the trouble of doing it myself, but...man.

Right when he thought it couldn't get any better than Cheap Trick at Budokan came the song that used to be his anthem. The simple barre chords Angus played. Bon Scott's screech always with a hint of the rogue smile. "Dirty Deeds Done Dirt Cheap." Growing up, the hard boys all used this as a theme song to getting made. Kind of sold themselves short though, the dirt cheap part. Oh well, not too many songs about criminal activity to choose from.

When Lars started singing along, Shaine shook her head, one step away from an "Oh, Dad."

35

A melted bag of ice cubes drooped limp over Trent's crotch. Even though the cooling effects had long since dissipated, he kept the bag there so he didn't have to see the unnatural purple color of his testicles.

He lay on the couch, no pants, watching reruns of seventies' sitcoms on cable channels dedicated to nostalgia for an age before he was born. He spun the ring in his nose around in circles, his adult version of sucking his thumb. It soothed him, and also kept him from digging at his nostrils incessantly, a problem which led in his teens to more than a few bloody noses.

Trent's iPhone chirped. He muted a family dispute that would all be solved by half past the hour.

"Yeah?"

"Got another hit on that cell phone. Sedona this time. Maybe they're going for Mexico. TJ or some place."

"Nah." Trent shifted and took the bag of water away, careful not to look down. "He's got money stashed. Sedona makes sense as the next stop, but we took care of that."

"You want me to keep tracking them?"

"Yeah. I guess it's time for me to hit the road. Before they get too far ahead. Hey, can you get me a line on a car?"

"I don't know. Rent one. Fuck, steal one. It's cheaper."

"I need something specific."

"I'll call Rico. He can hook you up. What do you need so I can tell him?"

"I want a Mustang. A '66 Mustang. I want to fuck with this guy all I can before I kill him."

36

Lars stood in the lot of the rest area, waiting for Shaine to finish up in the ladies' room. He read the information placard that told all about the desert around them. One panel explained how the area had been Native American land and how brave the people were to carve out a living in such difficult terrain. It left off the part about being forced here by lying white men who pushed them farther and farther into the scrub brush whenever it suited them.

Another panel told Lars about the desert wildlife. He read about the Gila monster and some kind of tortoise that only existed in zoos these days.

Shaine stepped up next to him. Lars shared some of his newly learned facts with her.

"Did you know the baby rattlesnake is more deadly than the adult? Apparently they have no restraint, and if they bite you they will shoot all of their venom at once, where an adult will hold some back in case he needs to strike again. I didn't know that."

"Can we make a stop anytime soon?"

"What do you mean? We are stopped. You hungry?"

"I need tampons."

She wasn't looking at him when she said it, and he was grateful. He turned his attention out over the desert, seeing nothing.

"Um, yeah. Sure. We can stop. Let's…let's get going, I guess."

They returned to the car in silence. Lars turned the key but didn't put it in gear.

"So you need what, a grocery store? A drugstore?"

"Either one. Even like a 7-Eleven would work."

"Okay, yeah, good. Let's go then."

They continued west on I-40, despite all the billboards trying to lure them north to the Grand Canyon.

In the bathroom of the Super K-Mart, after inserting her new tampon, Shaine washed her hands and turned to the mirror to apply a fresh coat of Vaseline on her tattoo. The swelling had gone down, but the area around the blue ink still throbbed red. She wanted desperately to scratch, but the soothing balm of the petroleum jelly eased the urge.

She thought briefly about powering up her phone again, but she didn't. Twice in ten minutes was too much. She needed the battery to last.

Shaine caught her own eye in the mirror and gave herself a "You idiot" look, nearly slapping herself in the forehead. Why hadn't she thought of it before? She could buy a charger here. She covered the tattoo with gauze and checked her cash. Only eight dollars left. Lars only doled it out in small amounts. If she had thought to start pocketing extra from the first, she might have had enough, but her new clothes seemed a higher priority at the time.

She reasoned with her reflection. *Go ask him for more money.* He hadn't said no yet. For a hired killer, so far he'd proved a damn good road trip buddy. She constantly wondered what it would be like to bring out the old Lars, the killer Lars. She kept quiet. Didn't push it.

When he didn't freak after she shot out the window, Shaine began to believe in his reform.

No sense testing his generosity. If she asked him for money to buy the charger, he might ask questions about why she needed it. Better to start pocketing a little change here and there and she'd have the rest in no time. She couldn't let him be the only one with a few secrets.

37

Trent saw the Mustang as soon as he turned the corner. The tip had been right on. Aside from the color it looked exactly like Lars's old pride and joy.

Getting out of his rental, he felt no guilt abandoning it there in a neighborhood he felt confident would have it stripped down to the frame in forty-eight hours.

Two Latino men in white tank tops sat in weathered lawn chairs inside an open garage, awaiting the gringo who'd called to ask about their car for sale.

The smaller of the two stood but did not remove his sunglasses.

"You Trent?"

"Yep. And this is the car." Trent drew a finger across the hood, which caused withering stares from both men.

Trent started over. "You're Ramón?"

"Yeah. So you want it?" Ramón didn't seem keen on haggling.

Trent stood back and played at making a tough decision.

"It's a '66?"

"You know anything about cars, man?" Ramón asked, knowing he was dealing with a muscle car virgin.

"Sure, sure. So what did we say on the price?"

"Ten thousand. Firm."

The bigger man, still seated, let out a snort to emphasize the pair's reluctance to negotiate. Trent had other plans.

"Tell you what," he said as he looked the car up and down, acting overly casual while reaching behind his back.

"How about I take it for free?"

Trent turned with his gun drawn and leveled the barrel at Ramón, getting a small sense of glee at seeing his own reflection bowed wide and distorted in Ramón's sunglasses. The gun looked fucking huge. Trent felt like he was posing for a Tarantino movie poster.

Ramón stood almost a foot shorter than Trent, and since his pal remained sitting, Trent felt ten feet tall. Ramón did not panic. He and his friend froze. A light desert wind blew, and Trent heard it sail past his ears while he waited for something to happen. He deeply regretted not getting the keys first.

The threat of a gun in your face is greatly diminished if it is not the first time it's happened to you, and Ramón was a man with experience.

From inside the house two more men came through a door into the garage and quickly crossed it. They each held a sawed-off shotgun sniffing the air in front of them, metal pit bulls on the hunt.

By the time they reached Trent, he'd raised his gun over his head in surrender and tried pleading with them.

"Whoa, whoa, no need for that. This is a negotiation here."

No longer under threat, Ramón stepped up and grabbed Trent by the throat, pushing him down on the hood of the car face-first. Trent's nose ached as it was mashed into the hood. The two shotgun-toting friends took up position on either side of Trent.

"You pull a gun on me, motherfucker? Or are my eyes going bad?"

"Hey, hey, hey," Trent sputtered. Finally at a loss for words. Ramón pushed harder as Trent's face burned from the heat of the hood sitting in direct sunlight. His forehead pressed against the twin racing stripes. "I came here to buy a car, man. What, you can't take a joke?"

Both men worked the pump action on the shotguns. Impending death in stereo.

Ramón did all the talking. "Oh, I can be real funny, mother-fucker. Real funny."

On either side of Trent's temples a shotgun barrel came to rest. The metal cooled his head for a moment.

In the street, a kid rode by on his bike. He didn't even look up.

"So," growled Ramón into Trent's ear. "You gonna take it or what?"

Trent paused. Ramón turned Trent's head for him, pressing his cheek and ear down on the overheated metal of the hood. With his ear to the steel, he swore he heard sizzling flesh. Trent's eyes scanned his reflection in the three pairs of sunglasses glaring down at him. He was a scared kid being robbed of his lunch money. No movie Tarantino would ever make.

"You mean the car?"

"Yeah the car. What the fuck else?"

"Oh, um, yeah. Yeah, I'll take it."

Ramón released him. The shotguns came away.

"Ten thousand. Cash."

Trent swallowed hard. "Yeah, yeah, sure."

He went for his pocket to get the keys for the rental and noticed he still had the gun in his hand. He quickly stowed it back in his belt and fished out the keys, holding them up for all to see he was not a threat.

In the backseat he took his backpack and dug into the outside pocket for his spending money and removed five hundred of it and dropped that back into the pack, leaving ten grand in his palm. He slung the pack over his shoulder and turned to go back to Ramón. He stole a glance at himself in the rearview. His face was red in spots like he'd fallen asleep while lying out on the beach. For the first time since he landed in New Mexico, the desert air felt cool on his skin.

He walked the money back to Ramón, who handed him a key ring with a single key on it.

"All yours."

"Um, thanks. Sorry about—"

The butt of a shotgun cracked Trent across the face. He fell to the ground, the key skittering under a tire. He tasted blood.

The driveway pavement felt almost as hot as the car, but Trent was powerless to stand while waves of pain and shock kept him pinned to the ground. The man behind the other shotgun stepped up and leaned over Trent. Sunlight shot through the lenses of his sunglasses, focusing a dot of heat on Trent's cheek. He knew how it felt to be an anthill tortured by adolescent boys.

The man shifted the shotgun to his left hand and with his right reached down and pinched Trent's nose ring between his thumb and forefinger. Pulled.

Trent yelped like a Chihuahua and the quartet of men laughed. The nose ring would be kept as a souvenir.

It took ten minutes for Trent to get into the Mustang and start the engine. In that time the men downed two beers each.

The Mustang didn't have the same purr as Lars's baby, even Trent could hear it.

His iPhone rang. He dragged a finger across the face of it and answered, his voice nasally and clogged with blood. Mikey from back east barely recognized him.

"Trent? Issat you?"

"Yeah. Da fug you wan?" he slurred, then snorted a plug of coagulated blood up his nose and down the back of his throat.

"We cracked the other bank account. It's in Vegas. This dude's got more banks and aliases than..." Mikey drew a blank.

Trent coughed, cleared his throat, sniffed again, his nose clearer now. "Vegas, huh? Okay, thanks, Mikey. Gimme some names in the area. Put the word out we're paying big."

"Hey, we should put up signs like when you lose a dog.

Put the old man's picture on there, pin 'em to telephone poles and shit. Have you seen this man?" Mikey laughed at his own imagination. Trent exhaled a clotted wheeze.

"Just get the word out and dig me up the best guy. Not like those last two yahoos."

Mikey got defensive. "Which ones? My Albuquerque guys?"

"Yeah," Trent said. "The dead ones."

38

Earl Walker Ford repeated his mantra as he stood outside Agent Barry's door. "Don't put me on a plane to Albuquerque. Don't put me on a plane to Albuquerque."

"I said come in!" Agent Barry yelled from inside. Ford gripped his single sheet of paper and entered.

Agent Barry's impending-headache look had been replaced by a more sour the-dog-just-shit-the-carpet face. Ford had no idea how he would react to the news.

"Found out a little more about our East Coast young gun," Ford said.

"Oh yeah?" The subtext: this better impress me.

"Trent is his name. He shows up in New Mexico, and faster than you can wrap a burrito, Mitch Kenney is dead. Coincidence?"

"No such thing." The look changed to interest, like he was hearing good office gossip.

"Could be he's our shooter."

"I'm thinking, Ford." Oh shit, here it comes. "Maybe you should get on a plane out to Albuquerque."

"We highly doubt he's there anymore, sir. He's a bit of a cell phone junkie, so we can track him through that once we dig it up."

"Who's we?"

"Sasso in the Newark office. He's trying to get cell info on him as we speak."

"Dare I say it, Ford?" Agent Barry broke out in a sarcastic

grin. "Interdepartmental cooperation? I thought that was an oxymoron."

"We're exchanging information as needed, sir."

"Well, shit, keep it up. I don't like losing a witness on my watch. Even if the guy had outlived his usefulness."

"Kenney, sir?"

"Yeah. He wasn't giving us any more, was he? Whatever kind of accounting he did when he went away I bet is all different now. Plus most of the guys he dealt with are dead. None of those old-timers are left. I miss the old bastards. Those guys who all wanted to be like Sinatra. Crime was smooth for a while there. It made us look cooler by association."

"I'm sure, sir." Ford folded his sheet of facts.

"Oh well, let me know if you get a line on the shooter. Then you can hop a plane out there and check it out. Be good to get back in the field, huh?"

Good like a rectal exam from Captain Hook. "I'll let you know." Earl Walker Ford missed the old days too. When a witness got bumped, you buried him in an unmarked grave and forgot he ever existed.

39

Lars knew he could never be a trucker. He'd get bored as shit.

Even now, when he felt pretty damn sure they were being followed, or at least he knew someone seemed to know damn well what his next stop was gonna be, the long haul driving sucked.

And fucking tampons? How could this vacation from hell get any worse?

Shaine held the gun low on her lap so no other traffic could see it. Flat highway like this gave people the freedom to turn and gawk at whoever passed by. Truckers were forever peeping into cars from above on the off chance they might catch a freeway blowjob in action.

The silencer extended out between them, aiming at Lars's gut. She'd managed to slip the gun out of the glove box without him noticing. She saw that he drove with a furrowed-brow concentration a lot of the time, like he was thinking of a calculus equation. When Lars slipped into that mode, and quite often his lips moved to his inner dialogue, he was fairly oblivious to what she did in her seat. As long as she kept her head turned out toward the desert, now being taken over by the more dramatic mountains that made up the ass end of the Rockies, she could do almost anything and not cause him to look her way.

She didn't know enough about Lars to attribute it to the seventeen years he had spent alone; she figured he'd always been like that. There were many lingering questions about this man. Time for some answers.

Lars noticed the gun. He tried not to react.

"Can I help you with that?" he asked, calmly considering the perils of a gun resting in the hands of an amateur whose only previous experience consisted of beheading a mannequin.

"We should talk."

"Oh, now you want to talk? You haven't exactly been chatty Cathy on this trip y'know. All you have to do is ask. No need for the gun."

"I figured if we were gonna talk I should learn your language."

A fat bug with a hard shell cracked against the windshield and exploded in a green burst of goo.

"Pull over."

Lars did as he was told.

The Honda bucked wildly as they turned off the interstate and took an access road north toward the hills. The kind of road that leads to absolutely nowhere, but somehow someone decided there needed to be access to it.

Sufficiently away from the traffic, which gave off a wash of noise like a distant river, Lars braked to a stop.

"Let's get out," said Shaine.

"You don't want to stay in here in the air?"

She answered by opening her door and backing out into the sun. Lars followed suit.

Lars could see Shaine had kept the safety on. He knew she used the gun solely for dramatic effect. She failed to account for his total ease around guns. Not many people have it. Hours are required in the presence of firearms, and Lars had those hours and then some. His gun—any gun—as everyday to him as her iPod was to her. At least the little hijacking brought a diversion, a break from the skull-crushing monotony of the highway.

"So, what do you want to know?"

Shaine let the gun fall to her hip. Now faced with getting her answers, she suffered stage fright. She was blank on what to say. "I don't know. Why, I guess."

"Why what? That's a big question."

"Why my dad. Why your job. Why anybody has to die."

Lars sat on a tan rock that came up to his hips. He took off his sunglasses and squinted across the high mountainous desert.

"Damn good question."

When no answer came, Shaine joined Lars on the rock. The threat of her using the gun had never been real. She knew it. He knew it. Easier just to forget it ever happened. Theirs was a strange form of communication.

"You did it a long time, huh?"

"Only thing I ever knew how to do well."

"Last year, at Saint Albray's they made us take a test to figure out what career we were best suited for. I got real estate or homemaker."

"That's not so bad."

Shaine raised her voice. "Are you fucking kidding me? Real estate? How fucking boring is that? Have my face plastered on a bus bench so some little shits can draw big tits on me and black out my teeth? Take newlyweds around for their first house and then take them both separately a few years later when they're divorced? Sounds grand. And I swear if you are a female every single test says 'or homemaker.' It's fucking sexist."

"Yeah, well, you learn by doing, I say. You can't figure out what you want to do by taking a test."

Shaine turned to Lars, the gun swinging absently in her hand. "How did you know? How old were you?"

At least she hasn't asked how many, Lars said to himself. *But, Christ, I'm not going to sit here and tell her all about my first time. Not a chance in hot hell.*

Barney Felton's sister. That's where it all started. Barney and Lars were barely fifteen, she'd just turned seventeen. The guy she dated went off to join the army. Soon as he left, a bunch of his so-called friends started sniffing around looking to console the lonely and lovelorn maiden. One friend, Benji MacDonald, got a little too close.

Barney's sister wanted little brother to tell Benji to back off, inform him in the way they did in the neighborhood back then. With a baseball bat or maybe a bike chain. He'd get the hint.

It turned out Barney was a pussy. During the confrontation, he said some stupid, and completely nonthreatening, shit and Benji didn't scare at all. Took his weapon of choice—a length of chain link with a padlock on the end—and beat Barney silly with it. Then he went to see Barney's sister and got what he'd been missing.

Barney's sister was someone Lars wanted to fuck, even at the confused and confusing age of fifteen. Hell, everyone in the neighborhood did, but you don't go taking without permission. Not when it leaves her with two loose teeth and burns on her hands from where Benji had tied her wrists with her own panties.

"That shit ain't right," Lars said to Barney. His best pal's sister. Closest thing he had to his own.

Barney asked for help. "Fuck yeah," Lars told him. "I'm in." They cut their fingers with Barney's pocketknife and mixed the blood when they shook hands. Better than a legal contract in the neighborhood.

Two nights later Lars was there with a gun stolen from Barney's dad, no one thought about traceability back then, and here comes Benji out of his parents' puke-green house with the rusty swing set in the front yard.

"Benji, you fucking moron," Lars said. Not his best choice.

Lars couldn't aim worth a shit yet, so he walked right up to him. Close enough to gag on his Aqua Velva. *Pop pop pop.* Three in the head.

The third one missed. A combination of Benji dropping so

quickly and the fact that so much of his head went missing from the first two shots.

Lars didn't do it to get paid. He did it because it needed to be done. He knew better than to try to justify that to Shaine.

If he was being honest, he'd admit that part of him held out hope Barney's sister would reward him with a little taste of what Benji had taken for free, but that never happened.

I got my payment in the form of a reputation. Priceless. So if she's gonna sit there and ask me why anybody has to die— that's why. Fucker deserved it. That was my test. Only one choice of career for me.

Lars shifted his weight on the rock, shaking loose the memory from his head.

"Y'know, I've done a lot of things I'm not too proud of anymore. I'll stand by a lot of my jobs. And I know if it wasn't me doing it, someone would have. And don't start giving me that life is sacred bullshit. If that's true then explain AIDS or nine-eleven. Life is cheap. And I'm living proof that it has a price tag on it."

Shaine contemplated that thought.

"Mind if I have my gun back?" Lars asked.

She grinned a little and let him take it from her hand.

"When you took out that mannequin," Lars said, "was that your first time firing a gun?"

"Yeah. First time. No longer a gun-shooting virgin. Still a virgin though."

"You want to learn about guns? I hate to say it, but it might come in handy someday. The guys that are after us can be kinda persistent." Lars smiled. Shaine smiled back.

"Sure."

Lars slid off the rock, smearing red clay on his jeans.

"Come on. Let's go over here."

Shaine followed as Lars stepped into the scrub brush and

found a spot about fifteen feet from another low rock.

"Hold on," he said.

He went back to the car and pulled a plastic soda bottle from the backseat. The two sips left at the bottom came out warm. Lars placed the bottle on the rock and returned to Shaine's side.

The breeze blowing kept the heat down as Lars switched off the safety and taught Shaine how to use a gun.

Eighteen rounds later, she knocked that bottle off the rock.

40

Trent had difficulty driving with his left eye nearly swollen shut and the cut on his cheek open, raw flesh showing through the wound. The bleeding stopped after ten minutes of direct pressure, but the slightest breeze sent an ice pick directly to his nerve endings. He kept to the far right lane, staying only two or three miles above fifty-five for fear of any more wind coming in through the many cracks in the window seals and door joints.

The engine didn't sound good either. If Lars's Mustang sounded like...well, a Mustang, this one sounded like a horse that needed to be taken out back and shot.

Nikki Junior's custom ringtone blasted out from Trent's phone. He lifted it from the seat next to him.

"What's up, Nikki?"

"I won't ask if you found him yet, 'cause I'm starting to think I'd know it before you did." Trent took the insult and swallowed it, even pasted on a fake smile in the solitude of the car. "I'm calling to tell you to pick up the pace, kid. You might have feds on your trail."

Trent weaved over the white line, tires bumping on reflectors.

"What? Feds?"

"There's been some inquiries is all I know."

"About me?"

"About you."

"From who? How do you know this?"

"They have a guy, we have a guy." Nikki's tone said "*Just business, kid.*"

"What do you mean 'a guy'? Like an informant?" The pavement seemed to be rushing at him faster.

"Look, kid, it's better for us to know they have someone on the inside, so we can keep track of what he knows. And with our guy on *their* inside, we can know when they get onto something. Like this. I'm just saying be careful and maybe try to wrap it up before too long. Otherwise, y'know, I don't know you."

Trent knew damn well he'd get no support from Nikki or anyone else if the Bureau stepped in.

"Jesus Christ, Nikki."

"Don't worry about it. This is just a courtesy call. Let me know what you find when you find it."

Nikki hung up. Trent felt sweat on his upper lip.

He had only made it as far as Gallup when the sun started dipping below the mountains, and his one-eyed driving style wasn't going to lend itself to night vision.

Besides all that, he needed a damn drink.

On the outskirts of town Trent pulled into a liquor store.

He caught a reflection of himself in the rounded wide-angle mirror over the door. He was walking roadkill coming in for a six-pack.

Trent grabbed a cold six from the cooler and set it on the counter. He scanned the choice of tequilas behind the counter. A man, fifty if he was a day, struggled to turn his head up over his hunchback. He wore a flannel shirt, to fend off the air-conditioning running at full blast, and a week-old beard born out of neglect for personal grooming.

"You got any Negra Suprema?" Trent peeked around the counter hoping for a secret stash.

"What the hell is that?"

"Tequila."

"Never heard of it."

Didn't have the connections to Cuba. Dumbass.

"Give me a Patrón."

With much difficulty the man waddled down the row of multicolored bottles to the tequila.

Trent turned to evaluate his damaged face again in the wide-angle mirror, and he saw the guy before he even made it inside. Just the way he walked Trent knew meant trouble with a capital T.

The kicking of the door drowned out the electronic *ding-dong* of the touch-pad welcome mat. The double glass doors swung wildly on their hinges as the young man—XXL T-shirt, baggy-to-the-point-of-stupid jeans and a meth user's excess energy—barreled into the store.

"Hands up, motherfucker. Hands the fuck *up!*"

His across-the-border accent was almost as obvious as the chrome-plated .357 he waved in front of him as if he were swatting flies.

Trent lifted his hands. The hunchback behind the counter did too but could barely make it over his stooped shoulders. His hands made it as far as his arthritic joints would allow.

"Gimme the money, man. The register, man. Give it up!" His tone came out like a whiny child who didn't understand why no one could get his cookies fast enough and without being asked. The hunchback obeyed in an all-too-practiced manner.

The tweaker turned to Trent. "Cash, Holmes. All of it. Right now, Jack!"

Trent spoke calmly. "You better make up your mind, man."

"What?"

For the first time the .357 stopped swishing through the air and came to rest leveled at Trent's nose. The man behind it wheezed, permanently out of breath with crystal adrenaline.

"I said you better make up your mind. You calling me Holmes or Jack? Both are wrong."

The meth-head couldn't process the words, let alone read the sarcasm in them. "Man, shut the fuck up. I'll call you whatever I motherfucking want, Jack. Empty your pockets."

"Listen, take what's in the register. I couldn't give a shit. Leave me out of it, man. I've had a really bad day." Trent gestured to his damaged face.

The .357 took two steps closer. Nose to nose. His voice lowered to a register used to intimidate.

"We all had bad days, Jack. Yours is about to get much, much worse. Now. Empty. Them. Pockets."

The hunchback finished filling a brown paper sack normally reserved for a bottle of Boone's Farm.

"All right, all right. Keep your shirt on," Trent said.

The gunman's feet skipped, he sucked in and out through his mouth, eyes darting, lip sweating. Lars would have had to admit that Trent was in the one scenario in which keeping your gun tucked in your belt behind you was an advantage.

Trent reached for his wallet but came back with his 9mm and blasted a hole in the tweaker's chest. The .357 went off four times in rapid succession, but they weren't aimed shots, only muscle spasms of the trigger finger in a dying man's hand. Bottles exploded and rained liquor.

Trent put two more in his chest simply for the therapeutic feeling of firing a gun. The .357 clattered to the floor, and the man holding it followed. As he fell, his pants finally gave up the futile task of staying around his waist. They dropped and left him bleeding into the white of his boxer shorts.

The hunchback peered out from behind the counter. He saw the robber down and Trent standing over him, the 9mm still smoking.

"You got him," said the hunchback, like Trent had bagged a pheasant.

"Looks that way."

"Hot damn. You got him. Ha-ha! Good for you, son." He reached down to the floor and came back up with the bottle of tequila. "Here you go. Whatever you want on the house. Want some chips? A Slim Jim?"

"No, no. Just the brews and the tequila."

"You're a hero. Yes, you are. Wait till the cops see this. They can't never catch these bastards. Five times in the last year. Cops ain't done shit. Not till a real goddamn hero comes in."

"Aw, come on, Pop."

"You'll get yer picture in the paper I bet. I bet you do."

"Jesus Christ."

Trent fired two shots that caught the hunchback in the forehead. He crumpled to a twisted heap behind the counter, folded like a fist.

Trent took the money, conveniently bagged for him, pinched a thumb and middle finger in the plastic rings of the six-pack and picked up the Patrón with his gun hand.

He stepped over the body by the door, hoping the Mustang would start without a problem.

41

Jules Camponisi twirled a gold pinky ring as he looked out over the Las Vegas Strip, wondering where it all went wrong.

Used to be, in this town, to get anywhere you had to be with the family. You had guys like Sinatra kissing your ring. Now it takes a decent criminal a year to pull down as much cash as Steve Wynn takes in over one weekend of legitimate business.

Jules had inherited Vegas from his dad. He grew up in a first-class apprenticeship and made the most of it. Nine years old, Dean Martin sang happy birthday to him at his party. Even made him a balloon poodle. These days Jules ran a crew of Keystone Cops and post-*Reservoir Dogs* tough guys who wouldn't have been allowed to shine Dad's shoes.

One of the crew, a Dog not a Cop, knocked twice then entered Jules's top-floor office.

"Mr. C, I got some information."

Jules turned away from the candy-store colors of the Strip and faced Tiny, the six-foot-five meathead in the suit. Christ, even their nicknames were stolen.

"What is it, Tiny?"

The large man took his usual place on a rectangular rug in the center of the room. His stage for presenting both good news and bad. If Tiny looked close, he could see two worn patches from the soles of his feet, he'd been there so many times. "Word's out that the East Coast is looking for a hit on a guy. Supposed to be coming into town."

"What's that mean, word is out? I haven't heard about it."

"That's why I'm telling you."

Jules sat behind his steel-and-glass desk. "Who's calling for it? Nikki?"

"Nah, one of the lower guys. Word is that Nikki Junior gives his okay."

"Big fucking deal. His okay stops meaning shit once you get out of New Jersey. He should be asking for my okay."

Tiny offered his open palms as a calming and empathetic gesture. "I know, I know. But here's the thing," Tiny's eyes flashed a glimmer, a magician about to unveil a trick. "Guess who the hit is on?"

"How the fuck should I know?" Jules wasn't one for guessing games.

"That fucker who shot up the poker player last year."

Jules reaction did not disappoint. He sat up straight in his chair like a dog seeing a squirrel. "Lars? That rat fuck who made a mess of my town and didn't even ask permission first?"

"Yep. That's him."

"And now Nikki's asking for someone to take him out? What the fuck is he even doing back here? I made it very clear I didn't want him anywhere near my town."

"I don't know much about it. I came right away when I heard. He's supposed to be heading this way, come to get his money for the job."

Jules tapped his pinky ring against the glass surface of the desk. "You know what," he said, "if Nikki Junior wants to go ahead without my permission—fine. I'll just go ahead without his. Let the boys know. I want that fucker dead as soon as he hits town. I want you to shoot him a minimum of ten times but not in the head. I'm gonna ship that body back east and remind those jerk-offs that we can handle our own problems out here."

"Right." Tiny rubbed his hands together like someone placed a juicy steak in front of him.

Jules steepled his fingers and savored the thought of getting to make a point of the man who caused such a mess. Two dead women, one dead poker champion, two dead security guards and one fucked-up penthouse suite. It didn't look good to have that go down in his city and not get any sort of payback for it. Made Jules and his crew look weak. That sort of thing would never have happened to his dad.

Jules looked up and squinted at Tiny. "What the fuck is that?" He pointed at Tiny's head, noticing the Mohawk for the first time.

Tiny always wore short hair, and the Mohawk walked a fine line, the difference between short hair and very short hair. Looked more like a shadow cast over the center of Tiny's thick skull.

"I dunno," Tiny averted his eyes. "Thought I'd try something new."

Jules rolled his eyes. *In Dad's day...*, his thought began, but he brushed it off.

"You know what? Scratch that. Bring him in alive. I want to see him. Maybe we'll make a little trade with Nikki."

"Sounds good, Jules."

Jules slammed his eyes shut. *Mr. Camponisi,* he swallowed, fucking tired of reminding these disrespectful fucks. Let it go. The brick shithouse with the dumb haircut had done him a favor.

"This is very good news you've brought me," Jules said. Tiny smiled and bounced on the balls of his feet, feeling a bonus coming his way. "I swear to God I'm getting a boner here."

Jules leaned back in his chair to regard the growing front of his pants. He pushed a button on his desk and spoke into a small microphone.

"Bring me a scotch rocks and one of the girls from the club."

A scratchy voice came back over the intercom. "Which one?"

"I dunno. That redhead, whatever the fuck her name is."

"She's gone, Boss. Quit about two weeks ago."

Jules pouted like a kid being told his favorite flavor of ice cream is sold out. "Shit. Where'd she go? Not to the Red Lion, did she? Those fuckers keep stealing the best girls."

The voice came back, matter-of-fact. "No, she went up to Reno to join some political action committee that's trying to legalize pot."

Jules blinked twice, confused. Tiny offered no answers, just a shrug-shouldered look.

"Look," said Jules. "Just bring me the scotch and a girl who can suck cock, okay?"

The scratchy voice signed off with a "Will do."

Jules's erection began to wither.

Tiny stood on his carpeted stage, his eyebrows lifting up and down, pantomiming, "So, huh? What about my bonus?"

"Unless you wanna watch me get blown," said Jules. "You can go now, Tiny."

"Is there, uh, one of those girls for me? Maybe?"

"I dunno. You go ask one of 'em. A hundred bucks and I bet you get yours."

Tiny shuffled his feet on the rug, working up a hell of a shock on the doorknob on his way out. "I just figured, y'know, since I brung you this news..."

Jules sighed. Subordinates just asking flat out for favors. Never would have happened with Dad. "Tiny, you ever heard the expression 'Don't shoot the messenger'?"

"Yeah. I heard it I guess."

"Well, the messenger doesn't get a blowjob either." Jules waved the giant away. "Thanks for the news. Have a good night." Tiny hunched his shoulders and shuffled out. Jules heard a muted "Ouch" when the big man touched the door to exit.

Jules spun his chair to look back out over the Strip, like the deck of a giant pinball machine and just as likely to take your money. He spun his pinky ring again, settling in to wait for his requests. His dad would have already had a drink chilling his palm and a girl working his dick. Things ain't like they used to be.

42

When you arrive in Las Vegas at night, it appears as a mirage on the black desert floor. Out of the darkness rises a glow over the hills, and then once you crest the top and look down on the display, it can only be a dream. Hundreds of miles of near-nothing and then this; like someone placed a magnet under the desert floor and the inevitable draw keeps pulling cars, busses, planes and light itself into its grasp.

The logic center of Lars's brain told him to keep on driving. Take the I-15 and don't stop until Burbank. The city held ghosts for him, ghosts of bodies not yet cold. He'd been told to leave and never come back. He wasn't told what would happen if he did return, but he knew. The dumbest cocktail waitress on the Strip knew what it meant if Jules Camponisi told you to get out of town. As soon as you see the lights over the hill, make sure you've got gas in the tank and take the detour. Don't stop until you can't hear the slots ringing.

But that's the power of Sin City. The magnet attraction of all that green overrides any logic in the human brain. Even when you think you're one up on Vegas, you're wrong.

Lars yawned, exhausted from the drive. He looked at Shaine to watch the thrill of Vegas move over her face. Concentrating on her helped him keep the memories at bay.

He drove down the Strip with Shaine wide-eyed, watching Vegas go by. Virgins are all the same. It must be experienced first from behind glass or else it becomes too intense.

"Can we stay at that one?" she said, pointing to a giant fake volcano.

"No," Lars said, offering no more explanation than that.

They found a good place still close to the action. Lars peeled off hundred-dollar bills at the front desk to pay in advance for their stay. The desk clerk noticed, as she was supposed to. The room was upgraded.

"Would you like to place anything in the hotel safe?" asked the girl behind the counter, a wry grin curling her lips.

"Safe?" asked Lars.

"Yes. Any...valuables?" She, like the best service employees in Vegas, maintained the utmost discretion.

"No. No, thank you." In his head Lars cursed himself. A hotel safe. Much better than a bank. No accountability. No tracking numbers. Why hadn't he moved some of his money there?

On his last trip there wasn't time to move any money. And who knew how long they waited until they used a master key and emptied out the contents. He certainly was back in Las Vegas well before he thought he would be. Before he'd been invited. Waiting for that invitation though, he'd be dead in the ground.

The bellhop threw open the doors to a two-bedroom suite, plus kitchen and a fireplace. Shaine acted like a true sixteen-year-old girl and the bellhop gave Lars a look that said he was impressed by the first-class treatment if the girl was Lars's daughter and even more impressed if she wasn't.

Lars tipped a twenty and put the DO NOT DISTURB sign on the door.

"Aren't we gonna go out? It's barely nine-thirty!"

"You got to sleep in the car, but I've been driving forever. I have to hit the sack. We'll go out tomorrow, go to the bank and then hit the road for Burbank."

"We're not going to stay here and have fun?"

"You're too young to gamble, and if you're not gambling, Vegas isn't that much fun. Trust me."

Shaine looked out the window at the neon temptation outside.

"I see a roller coaster!"

"Order a movie on pay-per-view. Do whatever you want, but don't leave this room. Vegas is not a safe town for a girl on her own." Had he really said that? Lars never felt forty-seven more in his life.

She huffed and slumped to the suede sofa. "Fine." She dramatically exhaled.

Lars stepped into a large bedroom with a king bed. He hadn't lived it up in many years, and he was going to enjoy this even if it was only to close his eyes and go unconscious.

He tossed his small bag with the money, his gun and his very few clothes on an armchair. In the living room he heard the TV go on.

He scrubbed his face, trying to wash New Mexico sand out of his pores and finally felt it working. He did several stretches and a few yoga poses before collapsing on the bed.

He fell asleep in under a minute and dreamed of Mexico and a world of beaches where the sun never set below the water line. A world of pink-and-gold skies and warm trade winds. But each time he became lost in his dream world, a gun would go off, a body would fall, blood would mix with the colors of the dusk—his perfect vision marred by some memory that invaded like an insect. Each time he jerked awake, he knew this would be the same every night for the rest of his life. Sleep was something he sold long ago.

43

Las Vegas in the daytime is a steel-and-glass hangover. The sun bleaches out the dark corners that lure people. The citizens all seem lost. Traffic seems like gridlock, not the nighttime conga line of adventure up and down the Strip. Casinos fight hard to keep the daytime out. Cold air blasts from the ceiling to fend off the heat trying to reclaim ground. Windows are blinded or are nonexistent. On the gaming floor it is perpetual midnight.

Lars and Shaine stepped out into the heat and reflective light. Shaine's eager footsteps slowed, her shoulders slumped, let down by the sight, her memory of last night tarnished. *A good lesson to learn in life*, Lars thought.

"Okay, you're going to stay with me today," Lars said. He carried his canvas bag, emptied now of everything except the gun. "We'll go over to the bank and take care of that, then we can eat some lunch, check out and head to Burbank and Uncle Ted's house."

"Troy."

"Sorry. Uncle Troy." Lars handed the valet his ticket.

"Two things first," said Shaine.

Lars raised an eyebrow to her.

"Breakfast and then we get you some new clothes." She pointed a reluctant finger at his outfit. "Those are starting to stink."

He looked down at his jeans, his black T-shirt (better to hide stains) and the jean jacket tucked into the crook of his elbow. She had a point.

"And I get to pick."

"Fine. I guess it's early anyway."

Eight-oh-five flashed on a clock across the street. Two couples, the men in tuxedos with ties undone and the women in cocktail dresses and carrying expensive shoes, stumbled toward the entrance. It wasn't morning, merely the end of last night.

After another filling breakfast, Shaine led Lars around a small outlet mall and made him buy new jeans for a hundred and fifty dollars on sale. He liked the way they fit but wondered why he was paying for jeans that came with holes already in them. He said no to several T-shirts with skulls, bat wings and other slightly Gothic-looking designs and some that looked like they'd been lifted from a tattoo artist's doodle pad.

She picked a shirt with a small Japanese robot that he quite liked. He couldn't say why, and he certainly couldn't read the Japanese written on it. It could have said, "Idiot White Man paid fifty bucks for this shirt," and he wouldn't have known.

When they got back in the Honda, the clock read ten-ten. He drove to the bank. The low building sat well off the Strip. Billions of dollars exchange hands every day in Vegas, and banks, or storefronts that call themselves banks, are as common as Starbucks. Again Lars chose a small bank with a no-questions-asked policy.

He parked the car and felt the hairs on the back of his neck tingle when a navy-blue Lincoln rolled past them a little too slowly. He brushed it off.

Shaine came inside with him this time.

"Wait here," he instructed, and she stepped to the side to read brochures about home loans and savings accounts.

All right, if all goes well, Lars thought, *in about five minutes I'll be walking out of here with two hundred twenty thousand dollars. Even though this is Vegas, I'm not placing any bets though.*

"May I help you sir?" said a bored teller. She could not

have been less interested. *Help me what?* Lars thought. *Go fuck myself?*

"Yeah, I need to check my safe deposit box please."

Lars followed the pantsuit into the back. He began to remember the place, even though it had been a while since he placed the bundles of cash in the long steel box. The safe deposit room measured no bigger than a walk-in closet. Stuffy too. Lars looked up at the vent, clogged with enough dirt to choke a buffalo.

He went through the motions. Pulled the right ID. Waited for her to turn the key, slide out the box. Tried not to look like a dog waiting through the excruciating time it takes a can opener to go around in a full circle. The teller exited with a weak "Press the buzzer when you're done."

The box sounded empty when she set it down. Some kind of rattle, but cash doesn't make that noise. Lars prepped himself for bad news, promised he wouldn't swear at the top of his lungs.

He popped the top. No green. Not even enough for a blade of grass. No little numbers, no pictures of dead presidents.

A cell phone. A shitty one at that. And a Post-it note: "CALL ME."

Oh well, what the fuck?

He dialed. Three rings. Like Lars knew he would, the kid answered.

44

"Yeah?" Trent answered, annoyed.

"Hey, don't get all pissy with me. You said to call."

Trent straightened his back. The traffic passing by at highway speed made it hard to hear, but he knew that bastard's voice. Lars. He dropped the tire iron and sat in the passenger seat of the Mustang, ignoring the flat tire for the moment.

"Well, well. I see we've made it to Sin City."

"You got a cold or something? Maybe you've been crying missing me."

Trent touched a finger to his swollen nose, the inside of his left nostril clogged with clotted blood. He ignored Lars's jibe.

"So you got my phone, you missing something else?"

"Yes, yes. Very nicely played. So I'm broke. Two decades of work down the shitter. You happy now?"

"Hey, you put them in the toilet. All I did was flush. You don't think you still deserve to get paid for not doing the job, do you?"

"Forget the money. Are you done trying to fuck with me or do I have more treats in store?"

Trent checked his nose in the rearview, touching it lightly. "Oh this is just the beginning, motherfucker."

Lars wanted to hang up on him. Changed his mind. Figured he could get a little information first.

"What do you want?" Lars asked.

"You know what I want."

"No, if I knew, I wouldn't have asked, fuck-face. Quit being cute. It doesn't suit you."

"Fine. You want me to spell it out for you. I want you dead. Or more to the point, Nikki Junior wants you dead. That's a hell of a lot more dangerous."

"A puppy with a squeak toy is more dangerous than you, kid. What about the girl?"

"Dead as you."

Lars heated up, felt like he'd drained all the oxygen from the tiny room. Old habits die hard, and the only thing he could think at the moment was how much he'd love to rip off an entire clip of bullets into Trent. No silencer either. He wanted the full impact. The sound, the jump of the gun, the dull thud of bullets hitting flesh. But Trent was somewhere far away. On the road from the sound of it.

"Listen up, kid. You come after me and it's fair game. You'll lose, but at least we're both playing. You go after the girl and that's against the rules. You take a shot at her, I kill you. You prank call her, I kill you. You eat in the same restaurant as her and I kill you. She's got nothing to do with this. Your beef is with me. Me alone."

"Hey, I'm not the one who kidnapped her. You dragged her into this. It's not my fucking fault Mitch decided to have a kid."

Lars ignored the young punk, continued his warning. "I hear you're after her and you're dead. You and everyone you know. I got seventeen years of making up to do and I'll do it on your entire family tree. You got me?"

"Hey, Lars, one question, who's the one standing over an empty safe deposit box? Oh yeah, you. So shut the fuck up and start counting your days. If it's not me, it'll be someone else, but god fucking dammit I hope it's me. Oh, and did I mention the feds are on your ass now? Yeah, that little tidbit came down the pike. Bet they'd love to get their hands on you. No chance they'd be looking for you in Vegas, would they? You wouldn't have any priors there, would you?"

Lars could hear him smiling through the words. "Nice

chat. Give my best to Nikki. You tell him what I said."

Lars punched the END button and let the phone drop back into the thin metal box. He slammed the lid. A cold sweat crept over him. He couldn't get out to Shaine fast enough.

45

Trent laughed when Lars hung up. He had the old boy on the run. Couldn't wait to tell him the new kill total. Up to eight now. And killing Shaine right in front of the old man would be nine. Lars would make ten. If that wasn't the start of an illustrious career, he didn't know what was.

Smiling to himself, he pictured it, leaned back in the seat. A semi-truck passed in the right lane closest to him, and the car shimmied in the draft. The jack buckled, and the Mustang flopped to the gravel like a giant's boot squashing a bug.

Trent bounced to the floorboards and, disoriented, exited the car to see if the rim had been bent and if he could jack it back up again.

It took three urgent blasts of the buzzer to get the lazy girl off her ass to let him out of the safe deposit closet.

Lars blasted past her, ignoring the niceties, unzipping the canvas bag as he went, for easy access to the gun.

When he reached the bank lobby, all appeared quiet. Shaine leaned on the counter browsing a pamphlet on retirement accounts. Lars eyeballed the clientele. One woman, mid-fifties, no threat. One man, baseball cap announcing his intention to GET MONEY GET PAID. No threat.

The two other bank employees seemed as bored as the no-name tag girl. Lars scooped a hand under Shaine's armpit as he made for the door.

Back in the Honda. AC cranked. Shaine noticed the deflated-playground-ball look of the canvas bag.

She watched Lars's eyes, saw a hawk on the hunt. Searching, scanning, taking inventory. The smallest rat couldn't escape his scrutiny.

"So, that went well?" she asked sarcastically.

Lars relaxed. There was no imminent danger. He cursed himself for letting that little shit Trent get to him.

"Not so great."

"Are we out of money?"

"No, no. We're okay. We should have more, but that's my problem to deal with. But we're done with Vegas."

"I didn't even get to pull a slot machine."

Lars started the engine. "We'll stop at the border. Looser slots there anyway. They want to grab the people crossing over from California. Skim a little off the top before they go the extra thirty miles to the Strip."

As Lars clipped in his seat belt, he saw it again. Navy-blue Lincoln. Parked and idle. Shit. Trent's goon squad or the feds now? This was not like the buffet at the Palms—more choices did not make it better.

Lars breathed in through the nose, out through the mouth.

"We need to make another stop."

46

I wish I could get through to Nikki Senior, Lars told himself. *Tell him what his shitbag son was up to. Would it do any good? I doubt it.*

Lars knew the son was well on his way to sending the old man to an early grave. He knew, really, that Nikki Senior should have been six feet under ten years ago. Bad lungs, oversized gut, high cholesterol, plus he operated in a business that didn't lend itself to longevity.

What really bothered Lars was that Nikki Junior wanted to sit in the big boy chair before the seat even got cold.

Trent didn't pose the same threat, just an annoyance. He was harmless without Nikki Junior backing him up. Trent was the finger at the end of the arm poking Lars in the ribs. But now they'd reached too far.

Lars felt sure his threat to Trent didn't make it up the chain. The guy in the Lincoln was on the job well before that phone call anyway.

He meant what he said, though. They come for the girl, he would show no mercy.

Lars felt young again, knowing exactly who to kill. He'd found what he'd been missing all those years. Motivation. Like with Barney's sister. He didn't need to get paid for it to know he wanted to do it. He had skin in the game again.

Back in the saddle once more. A little different this time. Kill them, protect her. He had to admit it felt kind of nice to be looking out for more than his own ass for a change.

Lars made lazy loops around block after block, driving like

a mouse lost in a maze. Everywhere he turned the Lincoln followed. A safe distance; if Lars hadn't known to look for him, he wouldn't have been seen. The guy was good.

"I need to drop you off for a little while."

Shaine was puzzled, but not entirely surprised. The frayed-nerve way Lars had been acting reminded her of her father. "What for?"

"I need to take care of something."

"Something about the money?"

"Related to that, yeah."

Shaine was no fool. She could see his eyes glued to the rearview mirror. She might not have known which car followed them, but she knew Lars well enough now to know what meant trouble.

Lars veered the Honda quickly into the driveway of the Palazzo casino. The front overhang swallowed them as a trio of red-jacketed valets rushed to open doors and greet the new big spenders.

"Stay near the front, always in view of the registration desk. That's where I'll find you, okay? Don't hang out right in front of it or you'll draw attention, but don't go far. If I need to get you in a hurry, I don't want to be looking all over the casino floor. Stick where the crowds are. Understand?"

Shaine nodded. A young valet tried the door but found it locked. He tried again.

"How long will you be?" she asked.

"I'm not sure. Not long." He checked the rearview again. The Lincoln hadn't followed them in. "Right up front, by registration, right?" She nodded. "I'll find you. Please stay out of trouble. Promise?"

"I promise."

Lars popped the electric locks and the valets sprung the doors open.

"Just dropping off," he said to them.

Shaine brought her bag with her, all she had in life. She felt scared and suddenly naked without Lars. He pulled away fast. A sinking feeling she'd been dumped crept over her.

"Can I help you find your party?" asked the young valet, his eyes hinting for a tip.

Shaine ignored him and powered up her cell phone.

Lars rejoined the Strip traffic. The midday heat kept people indoors, so he maneuvered through quickly until he spotted the blue Lincoln ahead of him making a right turn to circle the block. He fell in behind it. Damn. Big navy-blue American sedan. Could be just like the FBI to drive an antique like that.

Off the Strip, traffic got lighter. Another right turn. They traveled along the road behind the casinos. A peek behind the curtain. Service entrances, employee parking, construction. Always construction.

On the back road it became harder to remain unseen by the Lincoln. Lars wasn't trying very hard either.

The Lincoln slowed. Red brake lights said, "I see you." Lars slowed with him, saying, "I know and I don't care."

The Lincoln stopped. Both cars frozen and staring like the sheriff and the outlaw in the Nevada of a hundred fifty years ago.

The brake lights winked, and the Lincoln lurched forward, cutting a hard right into a small lot under construction, daring the Honda to follow. Lars did.

Into the same lot Lars passed a sign advertising the new Palazzo Greco Roman Day Spa. Grecian baths, olive oil body treatments, the slogan promised "Treatment like the gods for the price of mere mortals." It jutted out of the casino like an afterthought, all of four stories high, incredibly modest by Vegas standards.

Four concrete slabs, no walls, and next to it another four-story concrete-and-rebar structure—a soon-to-be parking garage. For the masseurs and olive oil girls no doubt, not for patrons.

No workers. No hammers, saws, cranes or jackhammers.

Times were tough. Guests at the Palazzo would have to wait for a Grecian massage.

The Lincoln kicked dirt across the lot as it aimed for the parking structure. It hit the ramp and spiraled dangerously up the loop of unwalled floors to the roof. His way of inviting Lars into the open, onto even ground. Yeah, this guy knew his stuff. He wasn't about to give Lars an advantage.

The way he was barreling around in that car, he wanted to be the first to put it in park.

Lars followed, the Honda's tiny engine barely keeping up. The tight spirals of the ramp playing hell with his inner ear.

By the time he crested the roofline, he could see the driver of the Lincoln opening the trunk and reaching in.

Lars stopped the Honda at the top of the ramp, thirty feet away from the Lincoln, and got out, not before reaching over and digging out his gun from the bag in the backseat.

47

Shaine pocketed her phone and tried to take in the cacophony of the casino floor. Slot machines rang their electronic siren call, crowds of Midwestern tourists urged one another into spending more money at the roulette wheel. The employees outnumbered the guests, between dealers, pit bosses, cocktail waitresses, busboys, valets and bellhops, all swirling around her in a race to land the one-dollar tip cupped in every guest's hand.

The carpet practically buzzed with a dark diamond-and-swirl pattern that made her dizzy, the smell of shrimp cocktail and disinfectant mingling in the air. A fake stream ran through the lobby, choked with the coins of a thousand people making good luck wishes. Shaine saw a fish floating belly-up above the penny-strewn bottom.

Shaine sought refuge against a low wall crawling with fake ivy. She searched the wall for a clock to keep track of how long she was waiting for Lars but found none.

"Hey, girlie, you lose someone?"

She turned to see two men, mid-thirties and tight on mixed drinks before noon, on the other side of the wall, in a lounge called the Bella Notte. Half-empty tumblers sloshed, one in each of their hands. The men used the drinks to gesture around the casino floor.

"You lookin' for a friend?" asked the one in the green tie. Lapel pins named him Brian and his partner Duane. The badge indicated they both came to town for the Consumer Electronics Show and were a long way from home. Tiny breaks in the golf course tans on each left hand indicated they had left their wedding rings back at the room.

"No one should be alone in Vegas," Brian said.

"Friendliest town in America," Duane added.

Shaine knew they must be desperate if they looked twice at her. Maybe the booze limited their vision or maybe there was only one day left on the convention and it was time to throw a Hail Mary. Whatever the reason, she blushed, somewhat flattered that older guys would flirt with her, and she saw comfort in numbers. If she stayed wrapped up talking to them, she might blend in better and avoid whatever had Lars so spooked.

"I'm waiting for someone," she said, friendly.

Brian smiled. "Well, don't wait alone. Come, come. Sit." He gestured with the glass, guiding her around the low wall and into the lounge. Duane grinned like a salesman.

"Yes, join us...um...?"

"Shaine."

"Shaine. Come. Don't make us watch you suffer out there all alone."

Shaine rounded the vine-covered wall and entered the Bella Notte. Up close now, Duane's radar went off.

"How old are you anyway?"

"Eighteen," she lied.

Brian lit up. "Eighteen. Is there a more beautiful number?"

Duane nodded in agreement.

48

Okay, so now what? Lars thought.

The two men stood on the roof of the unfinished parking structure, out in the open. Good for both Lars and the man sent to kill him. Open air protects against ambush.

No one shouted "FBI." No one flashed a badge. Lars ruled out that option, found it hard to get excited at the alternative.

The man stayed beside the open trunk, and Lars wondered what he had in there. The man straightened, lifting an object out. *Oh, great. A shotgun. Fantastic.*

Lars calculated the distance between them, concluded that the assassin would scatter-shoot and Lars might end up with a few welts, but the man would have to cover a lot of ground before the shotgun could be truly deadly. By then Lars knew he could pop three in his heart and one in his head.

The man didn't shut the trunk, and Lars assumed he hid more of an arsenal inside. The sun reflected off the man's bald head, a beacon in the desert. Lars hoped the man used sunscreen, but then reminded himself it didn't matter because he'd be dead in a short time.

"Lars!"

He knows my name, Lars thought. *No big shocker. I wonder if he had a chat with Trent since our talk in the bank.*

"Lars, it's Joey."

Who? Holy fuck! When did he lose all his hair? Jesus, it's been almost twenty years. Joey. Damn. They sent one of my old disciples to kill me.

Joey held the shotgun over his head, a peace flag. Lars kept his silenced Beretta by his side.

Joey began to walk, a hitching limp in his right leg. Desert sand mixed with concrete dust on the flat roof of the unfinished building and crunched underfoot as he slowly stepped across the divide.

Joey knew who he was dealing with. Lars trained him. Twenty-two years ago, when Joey was eighteen, Nikki Senior put the young gun under Lars's belt. At first Lars didn't think he had anything to share. The job had never been anything he had to think about. He had no special technique, but he came with a set of brass balls and a willingness to get one in him before he got one in you. That seemed to be the biggest single job skill.

Lars brought Joey on four jobs then let him loose in the wild. Joey's first solo hit came with problems, the cause of his limp, but since then he'd become a trusted gun for hire. Along the way his hair had gone missing, but it happened to the best of them.

Joey stopped about fifteen feet away. Lars hadn't moved.

"How are you, Lars? Been a long time out here in the desert."

"You doing errands for a kid now, Joey?"

"You mean Trent? He doesn't give the orders. I get my gigs from Nikki Junior."

"That's the kid I meant."

Joey looked sheepishly at the ground. They both used to make fun of Nikki when he was a boy. His braces, the weak attempt at a mustache, the entitled attitude. Now Lars knew Joey called him sir.

"This is fucked up, Lars. Real bad."

"You here for me or for both of us."

"They're saying some shit, man. Bad shit. About you and the girl."

"Fuck 'em."

Sweat beaded on Joey's pale dome. Planes overhead could see his SOS call.

179

"You're not...You didn't...I mean, with the girl."

"You know better than that." Lars wasn't interested in defending himself on such an outrageous claim.

"I do, I do. Just..."

"Just what?"

"It's been a long time, man. A lot can change."

"Tell that to your hairline."

Joey wiped a hand across his head, squeegeeing off the slickness.

Still the student, Lars thought. "So what do we do now?"

"You fucked up, man. You didn't fill the contract."

"Mitch is dead."

"Yeah but the kid had to do it. Then you shot the kid. You don't shoot family members. You taught me that for fuck's sake."

Lars shifted his weight from one hip to the other, dying for a good stretch. He knew he should just kill him and be done with it. Get off the roof and out of the sun. He could tell by the puddle on Joey's head and the swamp under his arms that Lars had gotten acclimated to the desert heat over the years. Joey still seemed on East Coast settings.

Shooting Trent Lars could do. Joey? That would feel like a violation. Like he said, a member of the family.

Lars wondered if he could talk his old student down. Lars could tell Joey didn't want to be there any more than Lars had wanted to be pointing a gun at Mitch.

"You didn't answer my question," Lars said. He paid attention to body language. The fumbling for an answer. The reluctance. *Answer the fucking question, Joey.*

"She's seen too much." Joey immediately studied the roof. Still making mistakes, Lars could see. Never take your eyes off the target, even if you're filled with shame.

"What's that mean?" Lars wanted to hear it. Clear and simple.

"I got...I got orders."

"So both of us then?" *C'mon, say it Joey. Nut up and pull the trigger.*

"Yeah. Both."

Fuck him. He dies.

Lars whipped the gun up next to his hip like an old-time gunfighter and squeezed off one round. It jumped off the stock of the shotgun and caromed down into Joey's forearm. The shotgun fell, the trigger leaning hard against his finger as it went.

Before the blast hit, Lars had already turned. The shot went wild, unplanned, but the spray of the shell spread wide, and the sound of a shotgun blast will make any man put a hurry in his step. Cold killer or not.

Four tiny steel balls of buckshot pierced the back of Lars's new robot T-shirt as he fled.

49

"You sure this is iced tea?" Shaine asked.

"Yeah, totally sure," said Brian. "Hey, you ever been to Long Island?"

Shaine wasn't entirely sure what he and Duane thought was so damn funny.

"Well, it tastes like crap. Don't they have any Snapple?"

"You don't like that one, we'll get you something else. No problem. Be right back."

Brian jumped up and speed-walked to the bar. Duane stayed and grinned like a little brother left alone with his sister's hot best friend. Only this best friend was quite ordinary.

"So, you in college?"

"Um, no. I'm taking a year off in between high school. Y'know, see the world."

Duane leaned forward as if that was a fascinating plan.

"Yeah, yeah. I always wanted to do that. Totally regret that I didn't. I thought it would be awesome to backpack across Europe."

"Yeah. Fun. Listen, where's the restroom?"

"Oh, uh, right back there. Behind the Grecian urn."

"Cool. Be right back."

Shaine took her bag with her as she left, a sudden head rush catching her off guard when she stood. She righted herself and threw a small wave over her shoulder.

She thought about ditching them and exploring the rest of the casino, but the two dweebs offered a certain sanctuary from the mysterious threat frightening Lars. And if something scared Lars...

No, Brian and Duane would do for protection. She found the men mildly creepy, but harmless. It felt good to be the focus of attention. She was sure they thought she was lame. Seemed to buy the eighteen thing though. Must be drunk, she thought.

Brian returned with a bright blue drink, three sticks, one each with a pineapple, a cherry and a lime wedge.

"Where'd she go?"

"Bathroom. Hey, dude, you think this is even worth it? We can do better."

"It's been six days and we haven't done shit. Besides, ugly girls are more grateful. When else is she gonna get an offer for two cocks at once? Trust me, she'll do it for no other reason than the story to tell her other fugly friends."

They slapped fives.

50

Lars huddled behind the Honda. It offered only temporary shelter. After a few cathartic curses he heard Joey's limping gait crunch across the rooftop.

"You broke the rules, Lars. Stand up and take it like a man!"

Lars spun out from behind the sedan, making for a stack of empty pallets a few feet away. He reached out and grabbed the loose end of a tarp half-attached to the stack and flung it up in the air behind him, a smoke screen.

The shotgun exploded again. Tiny ball bearings ripped into the tarp, but none reached Lars. Pausing for a second, breathing in through the nose, out through the mouth, he set his sights on the open stairwell in the corner of the structure. Open on all sides, it offered refuge in the spiral downward.

Joey struggled with the pump action in his left hand. Without the power of his right to brace the stock, he found it difficult to chamber the next round.

Lars took off, a jackrabbit across the desert floor.

Behind him he heard a shell seat into the chamber. Lars kept low, wove back and forth, becoming more sidewinder than jackrabbit.

A shot erupted. Lars hit the top step. His feet slid on the dusty surface like a million tiny marbles had been thrown under his shoes. He leaned back and put a hand down behind him to keep from landing on his ass. Gravel dug into his palm.

Joey got the hang of pumping the gun one-handed. The

ratchet sound echoed across the vacant lot.

With his sore hand, Lars reached out to grab a stick of rebar and used it to pivot his body down the loop of the staircase. His palm screamed back at him as it grasped the steel bar, and he let go prematurely, almost flinging off through the open side of the stairwell.

As his feet landed on the top step, a volley of small arms fire greeted him. It took three steps to slow his progress down the stairs, his feet scrambling like a cartoon coyote's.

He began reversing up the steps, wondering why he hadn't seen Joey's backup, then remembered Joey and the shotgun that awaited him on the roof. Damned if he did, damned if he didn't.

A larger-caliber shot sailed through the air. Lars poked his head above the rim of the stairwell to see Joey scanning the adjacent rooftops, looking for an unseen shooter.

Another shot rang out, and Joey's shoulder jerked forward, spitting blood. His gimpy leg gave out and he fell to the roof deck. Under Lars, another pistol shot hit only a few steps below.

Lars scrambled to the roof as a glint of sun reflected off the scope of a rifle on top of the building across the street.

Why would Joey's men shoot him? Surely they didn't think Lars had lost that much hair.

They wouldn't hit him, dumbass, Lars thought. *These aren't Joey's guys.* He'd been so focused on the Lincoln, any number of other cars could have been tailing them.

Joey crawled with the undignified flailing a man only ever uses when he's under fire. He backed into the Honda and braced himself against the passenger door, sheltered from the sniper.

Lars took refuge behind the stack of pallets, grateful to them for saving his ass twice. He could hear footsteps below as the shooters made their way up the looping staircase.

Joey forgot about Lars, went into self-preservation mode.

He yanked open the door to the Honda and climbed in. Lars heard the engine turn, saw Joey's shiny dome peek over the dashboard trying to stay low.

Another rifle shot and the brightly lit target of Joey's scalp took a dead bull's-eye. The inside of the Honda became instantly reupholstered in red. The car drifted slowly forward, Joey's slumped corpse leaning gently on the gas.

The footsteps below grew louder. At least two men, maybe more. If he stayed at the pallets, Lars would be exposed when the shooters reached the roof. He could take out the first one for sure, but depending on how many came spewing out, most likely he'd be a sitting duck.

Lars made a quick decision and dashed forward, sliding in beside the Honda on its slow trajectory forward. Using the car as shelter from the sniper he crouch-walked backward, gun aimed at the lip of the stairwell, waiting to pick off anyone who gophered their head up over the edge.

With each step he took, Lars realized his plan would run out of real estate in a few yards. He had no plan B.

The Honda jerked to a halt as it smashed the back end of the Lincoln. Lars froze, pinned in place behind his shelter and waiting for the trigger-happy team below to arrive. Joey's body must have shifted with the impact, because the Honda's engine gained a little life, a heavier weight on the gas pedal. The Civic's wheels spun and spit gravel as the smaller car warred against the much larger sedan's parking brake.

The first gopher poked out of his hole. Lars had the instant thought *I wonder if he saw his shadow? No wait, that's woodchucks. No, beavers. Fuck! Groundhogs!*

He fired. The shot skipped off the concrete and the rodent slipped back down his hole.

Slowly the front wheels of the Lincoln slid toward the edge, the carpet of gravel and cement dust offering no grip to its worn tires. Lars swiveled his neck to try to see if the sniper had a clean shot, while at the same time he kept an eye on the stairs. The unfastened trunk of the Lincoln swayed as the car began to lean forward. Lars glanced inside. A case with the foam outline of Joey's shotgun sat open, a neat row of brass cartridges shone in the sun like ten tiny tributes to Joey's obliterated skull. Lars could try to reach in and snag the shotgun from Joey's lap, but the buckshot would be no match for a sniper rifle and a scope.

He checked the trunk again for anything to help his cause. He prayed for Joey to be carrying some hand grenades. Seated next to the gun case, a black attaché made Lars think of the flight recorder boxes from a downed airplane. A backpack leaked small flaps of paper. Green paper. Green rectangles of paper. With numbers. Pictures. Presidents.

The front tires of the Lincoln slipped off the edge of the roof. The Honda continued to kick gravel from the wheels driving the car forward.

Lars focused on the backpack. Money. Most of it still neatly wrapped in strips of bank paper identifying thousand dollar clumps of cash. His cash. The bag held no more than fifty thousand.

Lars did some calculations. If Joey was their man in Vegas, then he would have put the cell phone inside the safe deposit box. To do that, he would have had to clean out the box first. He filled the bag and then did what with the rest?

But the bag wasn't filled. The bag was the overflow. The attaché...

Gravity took hold and the Lincoln lost the fight. The big blue sedan pitched over the edge and the Honda followed close behind.

Lars peered over the brink to see the Lincoln land roof side down on a pile of dry concrete sacks. The Honda followed and punched its nose into the underside of the big American car and rolled off. As it tumbled, Joey's body flopped out the broken window and landed in the dusty mess, his bald head no longer an issue, being mostly gone and all.

Lars stood exposed. Naked on the edge of the four-story rooftop. He could feel the heat of the sniper's aim on his back. He watched as three gophers scurried out of their hole.

"Drop it, Lars! Now!" said the lead rodent.

Lars did what the varmint said.

The three shooters, in suit jackets over T-shirts, with beefy pistols extended out in front of them, marched in a V formation and, to Lars's pure shock, did not kill him. They turned him around, two men hooked meaty paws up under his armpits, the leader made a waving signal across the street to the sniper, and the trio walked him downstairs.

"That's twice you made a mess in our town. I think you got some explaining to do," said the leader, a huge man with a tight Mohawk carved across the granite ridge of his head.

"So that's who you are," Lars said to the large man.

Yep. Should have taken the detour and kept on driving.

51

"Like this?" Shaine asked.

"Yep. You can just press the button, but you haven't been to Vegas until you've pulled the old one-armed bandit."

Brian had gone MIA about ten minutes ago, leaving Duane to babysit. When Shaine started saying she'd never played a slot machine, he obliged her, even supplied the quarters.

She pulled the lever, came up three across with a plum, some cherries and a bell. The machine ate her three quarters and begged for more. Duane slipped them into the slot. He checked over his shoulder, looking for Brian.

Shaine had seen Duane's wingman chase down a blonde and attempt to buy her a drink. She knew the score. Shaine would end up as disposable as the quarters she pumped into the machine if the stacked blonde fell for their sweet talk.

Might as well have a little fun until she got thrown over for a real woman.

Where the hell was Lars anyway? The feeling she'd been ditched became more of a reality with each pull of the lever.

The next set of coins hit. Loud *ding-ding-ding*s sounded over the clanging of fifty quarters being vomited back out at her. An aging woman with deep nicotine wrinkles in her skin shot a stink eye to the young girl for taking her good luck.

"Hey, look at that." Shaine smiled, the electronic bells ricocheting around her skull. Her first alcohol buzz felt good.

The noise of the win brought Duane back to attention. "Way to go."

"Now what, should we quit while we're ahead?"

"Quit? Is that any way to have fun?"

Shaine smiled. Duane smiled. His own six cocktails gave Shaine an alcohol makeover. Her tits seemed bigger, her thighs seemed smaller, and her mouth seemed just right.

From down the row of slots, Brian approached, defeated. He signaled silently to Duane with a waving motion across his neck and mouthed the words, "No go." Shaine spotted it in her periphery but pretended not to.

Duane refocused his full attention on the teenage girl presenting their last best hope.

"Hey, who wants another drink?" he asked.

Lars seemed to have left her behind. *Why the hell not?* she thought through a growing fog. Inside, her liver waved a surrender flag.

52

Tiny hauled his capture from the roof into Jules Camponisi's office. He thrust Lars out ahead of him, parading the prize for Jules to see. If this didn't earn him a blowjob, nothing would.

Lars let himself be manhandled. The air had gone out of him. It hadn't taken long, maybe a half hour, for his whole world to go to shit. He'd been caught, brought to bear for his crimes. Deep down he knew he'd have done the same for someone who betrayed the family the way he had. The time for explanations had passed. Lars stood on the brink of giving up, taking what was coming to him.

Jules placed his palms down on the large, clear desk. His pinky ring and its newly added twin on the other hand clanked against the sheet of glass. Lars noticed the unusual desk. Most boss types liked the imposing slab of wood. Better to hide a pistol or a buzzer to call for help. Jules's open-air approach let others know he felt no fear. In his office, the man behind the desk had nothing to hide.

Lars stepped onto a rug, swore he felt indentations of feet like Bigfoot had been the last appointment.

Tiny beamed. "Here he is. Signed, sealed, delivered."

Lars stared ahead, a blank slate.

"So I see," Jules said, looking Lars up and down like he was a racehorse. "So you're the one who's been shooting up my town every chance you get." Jules started punching numbers into a phone.

"Look," Lars said. "I never meant to—"

"Shut him up," Jules said to Tiny, who threw a fist into Lars's gut.

When Lars recovered, he straightened up, coughed out the words to Jules "I thought you wanted to talk to me."

"No. You, you're a piece of shit. I don't talk to a piece of shit." He punched a final button on the phone and engaged the speaker. The other line rang four times, then picked up.

"Who the fuck is this?" said the voice on the line.

"Nikki. Jules. How are you, you limp-dick motherfucker?"

A pause as Nikki Junior scanned his internal Rolodex for a Jules. "Jules? What the hell do you want? I'm busy over here."

"You have any idea how little I give a shit? I got your boy." Jules's eyes glinted as he winked at Lars. Lars looked beyond Jules to the wide view of the sun-bleached Strip outside the window, and the reflection of the men behind him: Tiny, his good-report-card smile glued to his mouth, and the two bodyguards, who lounged on leather couches.

"What boy? Jules, this had better be good."

"Oh, it's good. You wanted him caught and I caught him. Now you can see how professional I am. How capable I am of doing a simple job. The question is...why didn't you call me in the first place?"

"Lars? You got Lars?"

Jules raised his chin. "Hey, piece of shit, your name Lars?"

Lars nodded.

Jules smiled. "Yep. That's the piece of shit I got."

An image flashed. A face down on the Strip. A girl. Shaine. Alone.

The giving up option vanished. Once again she offered him a reason. He wouldn't get out of this quicksand for himself, but he'd damn well try for her.

His killer instinct returned, charged through his veins like a shot of adrenaline. All he needed was a plan.

There was no scenario Lars could think of where this

ended well. Nothing to do but improvise and go on instinct. Let the big boys jaw all they wanted and decide his fate. Just two more chumps in this fixed town thinking they're one up on the house. Lars knew he had odds stacked against him, but so did every sad sucker down there in the neon candy dish of the Strip. Most were losing. But a few numbers came up. A few cards turned out to be aces. He only needed one.

He scanned his mental jukebox, searching for just the right tune to focus his thoughts. He had it. Motorhead. "The Ace of Spades." Fast, aggressive, perfect. He dropped the needle and Lemmy urged him on with that gargling razor-blades voice.

Lars rotated his body, stretching his spine. Tiny watched him, inquisitive. Lars spun his torso in the other direction. Just a guy, stiff with age, working out the kinks. Nothing to see here.

"What the fuck do you want from me, Jules?" Nikki Junior said.

"First off, an apology."

"How about this, I'm sorry you're such a cocksucker. How's that?"

"What I'm sensing here is a lack of respect. Maybe I need to ask your dad to pull down your shorts and spank your ass like he used to do."

Lars bent backward. The trio of thugs watched him with animal curiosity.

Lars kept bending back until his hands reached the carpet behind him, his body making a bridge, his back arched high into the air. Jules snapped his fingers at Tiny, gesturing a "What the fuck?" hand motion.

Lars exhaled a slow, deep breath. No one knew what to do about the strange contortionist moves their prisoner suddenly displayed.

They didn't have time to wonder.

Lars brought his legs the rest of the way over, kicking Tiny in the jaw as he flew past, the toe of his cowboy boot connecting more solidly than Lars expected. He continued his motion, bringing the boots down, one on each, to the chests of the two seated bodyguards. Both men gasped to refill their lungs.

Lars moved faster than forty-seven years should allow. He reached under the jacket of the nearest seated thug and came out with a Sig Sauer 9mm. Two shots, each to the heart, and the men could stop worrying about catching that breath.

"What the fuck was that?" Nikki Junior said. Jules slid back his desk chair, stunned into inaction.

Tiny worked through the pain and charged Lars, who shot a hand out and grabbed the big man's wrist. Using Tiny's immense bulk against him, Lars spun the man around and flung him at Jules. Tiny crashed through the desk, cleaving the six-foot slab of tinted glass in two.

Lars advanced, the Sig out in front. Jules began screaming. Lars looked down to see a three-foot section of glass had severed Jules's left foot. A steady flow of crimson pumped out over the glass shelf that cut through his ankle.

Tiny writhed in a dazed fog of pain. Lars fired once, put him out of his misery. Dying with thoughts of an unfulfilled blowjob on his mind.

Lars stepped through the wreckage of the desk, grabbed Jules by the tie and pulled him close.

"I never meant to cause you any trouble. If people would just leave me the fuck alone, maybe we could all be a little better off. You think?"

Jules couldn't concentrate through the pain. Lars shoved him away, banging the desk chair against the window. Jules kicked his leg up and sent a spurt of blood from his shortened leg. The blood ran down the incline of the broken desktop like a slow-flowing serenity fountain, a must for any feng shui office decor. Lars fired once more and bits of Jules's brain hit the window, adding a wet reflective pattern to the colors of the Strip below.

Lars sifted through the shattered glass, found the phone, could still hear Nikki Junior shouting.

"Jules? What the fuck, man!"

"You leave me the fuck alone. Me and her. If I see anyone I think even knows your name, I'll kill 'im on sight. You hear me?"

A pause. "Lars?"

Lars picked up on the fear coming three thousand miles through the phone line. He hung up.

The cold killer was back. Lars hoped he could send him back to retirement soon, but not until the girl was out of danger.

He checked a wall clock. He'd been gone way too long. His only consolation was that Shaine couldn't have gotten into as much trouble as he had.

53

She pressed down the tape on the gauze, covering her tattoo again.

"Can I say this?" began Brian. "That is freaking awesome. I always wanted a tattoo."

"Oh, man, me too," said Duane. "Something cool. Like one of those old-time, like, hula dancers on your biceps or something."

"Dude, can you imagine if you had the balls to do the full-on battleship? Across your chest, dude. Balls out. No joke."

They cracked up. Shaine smiled, her head fuzzy. She felt like she needed a nap, but she wasn't tired. She felt fresh-from-the-dentist numb. She felt wanted.

"You guys crack me up."

Brian and Duane shared a look. Brian leaned in close.

"You know what, we could take this party upstairs. You should see the suite they hooked us up with." He emphasized the syllables, "In-sane!"

Duane chimed in. "Yeah, you should come up. We can order room service. Much quieter up there. And the view."

Brian caught his breath, like he'd suddenly remembered. "Oh, the view! You totally have to come see the view." He snapped his fingers in the air for the check.

"I don't know, guys," said Shaine. "I'm kinda waiting..."

"Is it a twin sister?" asked Duane before spitting out a laugh.

"You know what?" Brian said. "Let's get another one of these to go. Take it with us."

He pointed to the candy-flavored drink sitting next to its empty twin on the table in front of Shaine.

Her hazy-edged thoughts came slow, no match for the hustle these two put on getting up and out of the lounge.

These guys like me, she thought. She'd been reluctant to believe it at first, but now she knew. *What the hell?* said the devil on her shoulder. *Maybe I will go up with them. Maybe I'll totally make out with them. Brian at least. I bet they would have such a story to tell when they get back home.*

The protestations of her better judgment were buried under her brain's sudden initiation to alcohol.

Duane stood, a semi-erection pushing at his business slacks. "Waitress!"

If he hadn't shouted, Lars might not have seen them.

Sweating from his walk, Lars approached the low, fake vine-covered wall of the lounge. "Shaine. Let's go."

Shaine turned and looked at him without recognition.

Brian and Duane froze and each looked to the other for a cue.

"Sorry, pal. Just leaving," said Brian. He threw down a fifty in the absence of a check and hoped that bitch of a waitress appreciated the tip.

"Not with her you're not."

Shaine had a surge of recall and felt a sudden wash of shame. She searched for her bag and began gathering her things like a scolded child.

"Look, pal—"

Lars reached out and grabbed Duane's hand across the low wall, promising himself control but finding it difficult. His body remained in kill mode, a hard habit to break.

Lars spun Duane's wrist and turned the hand backward, crippling him in an instant. Using Duane's body weight as ballast, Lars vaulted over the plaster wall and landed on his feet next to Shaine. He scanned the table.

"Are you feeding her drinks?"

Brian stammered.

"You know she's sixteen, right?"

Both men reacted, stricken. Duane fell to a knee. Lars released him.

"Buddy," Brian said. "She told us she was eighteen. Hand to God."

From the floor Duane spoke, "What the fuck, man?"

Of the two, Duane was the angry drunk. The boner in his pants wasn't putting him in a good mood either since it was not going to complete the mission.

Lars stood over him and looked down. "The *fuck* is that you and your pal here tried to rape a minor. A minor in my custody. That makes me mad."

Lars swung his boot into Duane's face. It connected with his nose, making a satisfying crunch.

"Hey, hey now!" protested Brian. "There's no call for that."

Shaine sulked low in her seat, her head pulsing from fat and blurry to thin and sharp.

Late to the party, a waitress arrived with the check. She saw Duane on the ground, looked up at Lars.

"Hey, buddy. Take it outside."

Lars drew his stolen Sig Sauer. The barrel almost reached her nose. The tray she carried crashed to the carpet. Out on the casino floor someone hit three cherries on a slot. Bells rang, people screamed.

"Money's on the table. Take it and go," Lars said to the waitress. She bent down slowly, retrieved the fifty and backed away. "Shaine, get your stuff. We're leaving."

Brian showed concern for his new friend. "Wait, how do we know she's even with you, dude?"

Lars swung the gun around to his face. "Because I said so." Brian put his hands up like he was being mugged.

Shaine stood and slunk around the wall back out to the lobby.

Lars lowered the gun. "Sorry," he said. "It's been a bad day."

Brian softened. Grinned a little. "No shit."

Lars cracked him across the nose with the Sig. Brian collapsed, both hands to his face.

Lars stowed the gun, leaned in and rifled through Brian's inside coat pockets as he writhed, came up with a valet ticket. He hopped the wall, checked around him for curious eyes and hustled Shaine out the door.

54

Lars hoped for two things: that the waitress was too freaked out to run to her boss right away and that those dipshits drove a decent rental car.

He handed over the ticket. The kid lingered on the sight of a wobbly teenager being propped up by a late-forties dude in a robot shirt. He let it go and dashed for the car. One of the perks of Las Vegas is that you're never the biggest freak in town.

Lars looked at Shaine. Drunk. Feeling her first alcohol regret too. We all get it. Things are going along great and then it hits you. Now you're that person. The drunk girl at the party. He felt no need to shame her further about it.

Mid-afternoon in Vegas is what 5 a.m. is to any other town. Slow and sleepy. The valet arrived with the car mercifully fast.

A grin crept across Lars's face. Praise the lord for the company travel budget. A fucking Mustang. No '66, but it'd do the trick.

Lars slapped a twenty in the kid's hand, who took it as a sign to keep his trap shut. Poured Shaine into the front. Buckled her in.

Burbank here we come. Well, two little stops.

First, he returned to his rented room, snatched his bag of clothes and the cash he'd gotten so far. He tossed the room key to a cute girl at the front desk.

"Checking out," he said.

"I hope you had a lucky stay," she said with a smile.

"That's one word for it."

He didn't wait around to sign anything.

Shaine hadn't opened her eyes and kept them closed as he got back in the car. He palmed a fifty into the valet's hand as a thank-you for watching the car. The young Latino didn't complain but noted to himself that normally a fifty-buck tip came from a guy in a much nicer ride.

Lars looped around to the backside of the Strip again.

He parked the Mustang on the gravel lot next to a pile of concrete sacks and two flattened cars. On the back road and at midday, the shooting and the wrecked cars had gone unnoticed. Only in Vegas.

Lars cut a wide path around the already ripe body of his old student. He reached the Lincoln, struggled to push open the trunk. With a little effort he liberated two hundred twenty thousand dollars of his money from the wreckage.

He hit the remote and the trunk on the Mustang gaped open. The money went in and Lars took off jogging. He took the steps two at a time, winding his way to the roof.

Shaine leaned against the door, eyes closed in a futile attempt to keep the sunshine out. When Lars's footsteps faded from earshot she tentatively opened her eyes.

Blasted by the light shining off the bone-yellow color of the concrete sand, Shaine held a palm over her eyes for shade. It allowed her irises to open enough to make out the shape of a body. She squinted, not sure what she was looking at. It seemed like a person, but somehow not all of one. She sat up straighter in the seat and recognized the landmarks of a human body. The legs, torso, arms splayed out, shoulders, neck and... nothing. Just a pulpy remnant where a head should be.

Shaine barely got the door open in time before she vomited.

* * *

Lars reached the roof and saw his baby. He jogged lightly across the crunching gravel of the roof deck and picked up his Beretta, the long silencer still in place. The metal singed his hand, hot from the direct sun. He stuffed the gun, barrel first, into his front pocket. He lifted the Sig Sauer from his belt and tossed it over the back wall of the parking structure.

When he got back in the Mustang, Shaine moaned and covered her eyes with her hand.

He revved the engine, finding it lacking. Not the same throaty growl as its grandfather.

As long as it got them to California.

"Ready?" he asked.

"Unnngh."

He dropped it in gear.

The Mustang roared west, several hundred more miles of Joshua trees and dirt and then—L.A.

Lars kept his eyes focused on the road ahead, willing the West Coast closer. He didn't notice the broken down '66 Mustang on the side of the road leading in to the Strip. He didn't see Trent kick the back panel of the Ford and take out his iPhone. Couldn't see him touch his swollen nose as he talked.

The rental Mustang would be a mile away by the time Trent got the news that Lars wasn't dead—but a whole lot of other people were.

55

Nikki Senior shuffled down the main hall of the estate, his oxygen tank wheeling behind him like a well-trained dog. In order to wrestle back any goddamn control over his empire, he had to get his ass out of bed.

He pushed open the double doors of his office and found his son behind the desk. A violation almost as bad as finding your only son in bed with your wife. Not his mom, your *new* wife. The better one.

"Dad. What are you doing here?"

"It's still my office, is it not?"

"I guess so. Things are a little bit busy right now, Dad. Trying to sort some stuff out from the Vegas branch. Why don't you go lie down? You look tired. I worry about you."

Little prick wanted his dad dead and Nikki Senior knew it.

"You're in my chair." His voice gravel.

"In more ways than one, Dad. If not for me, who else is gonna fix these problems?"

"I'm here now. I've come to sit in my chair and make a few phone calls. Try to clean up some of your mess."

"Dammit, Dad," Junior said, leaning back in his dad's chair. "This mess is your mess, not mine." He tossed down a gold Mont Blanc pen.

"You show me some respect!"

"Look, I'm trying to get rid of your golden boy who's gone fucking nutso out there. I can't get a goddamn straight answer from any of our guys in the field, and I sure as hell don't need to hear it from you, too."

"What do you mean, get rid of him?"

"What do you think I mean, Dad?" Junior said. "We sweep the place twice a week for bugs, right? No one's listening. I'll say it. I'm trying to have him killed. Okay? I just don't happen to have anyone who can fucking shoot straight. You go west of the Poconos and it's all fucking amateurs."

"You don't kill one of the family."

Junior sat forward again, back to work. "You should have told him that."

Two men appeared at the door behind Nikki Senior. Bodyguards. Linebacker-sized hooligans who were still shitting in diapers when Nikki built his business to the top.

"Gentlemen, my father needs his rest. See that he finds a quiet place to lie down."

Nikki Senior stared daggers through his son. He sucked up the oxygen with a force that made the tubes whistle.

"You make me think things no father should ever think about his son."

"Love you too, Dad." Junior put his head down and went back to work.

56

Earl Walker Ford entered Agent Barry's office late. Special Agent Whitney, Mitch the Snitch's handler, sat on the couch, the beginnings of a tan on his forehead.

Ford slipped in without knocking. He knew better than to interrupt Agent Barry during a tirade.

"Well, why the hell *wasn't* it in the file?"

Whitney swallowed hard. Vacation time was over. "Well, sir, during the transfer some of the information was misplaced—"

"Misplaced?"

"The previous handler, Agent Heath, left rather suddenly, so..."

Agent Barry waited. "So? So what? So mistakes happen? La-de-da and life goes on? Bullshit." Without missing a beat, he noticed Ford. "Siddown, Ford." Then back to Whitney, "This is the FBI dammit. We don't let things slip through the cracks. We do that, people die. Case in point, Mitchell Kenney."

"I'm sorry, sir."

"Well, I will pass on your apologies to this mystery daughter if we ever find her. Alive."

Agent Barry sat hard into his chair. Whitney cowered on the couch.

"What've you got, Ford?" Agent Barry said, not expecting anything.

"Nothing that can be confirmed as related." Agent Barry sighed. "A pile of bodies in Las Vegas." Agent Barry perked up. Ford continued. "And a hit on the cell phone of Trent, our possible out of the Jersey office. Seems like he's headed west."

"And he did the Vegas thing?"

"No word yet. All I know is that he was there, and now several men are dead."

"Son of a—" Agent Barry picked at the frayed edge of his desk blotter. "What now?"

"We can keep tracking the hits we get on the cell phone. Alert the nearest field office. There's not much else we can do. She's underage, so she's not using credit cards. No driver's license, so a traffic stop does us no good. She could be any-where."

"Well, we did hide her after all," Agent Barry said, thick with sarcasm. He turned to Whitney. "Anything else you neglected to tell us before you went fishing?"

"No, sir, not that I know of."

"Well *that* should cover it." He shook his head at the floor, turned his focus to Ford. "Keep me updated."

"Yes, sir," said Earl Walker Ford as he left to get on the phone.

57

There's something about California that lends itself to yoga.

Lars reached and stretched, feeling the atrophy even a few days could do to his ability on several poses. Jeans aren't the most effective yoga pants either, but removing them at a rest stop was not exactly proper etiquette.

The sun rolled downhill toward the ocean, casting long shadows of his origami shape against the scrub brush and sand. Lars waited to stop until they made it out of Nevada, despite Shaine's repeated warning that she was going to hurl. Something about crossing the border into the Golden State lifted a weight off Lars's shoulders.

Shaine returned from the women's room, still a little wobbly.

Lars parked at the far end of the single row of spaces, keeping a good distance between them and the other tourists and disappointed weekend gamblers.

"Did you puke?" he asked her while she still stumbled toward him.

"No. I really kinda want to though."

"You didn't drink near enough for that. I told you so. What you're experiencing is what people strive for when they drink."

"Why on earth would you do this to yourself?"

"When you do it on purpose it feels different."

"I guess so." Shaine deposited herself in the passenger seat of the Mustang and shut her eyes. Lars finished his last few poses. He opened a bottle of water he got from a vending machine and leaned against the front quarter panel of the car.

"You want to talk about it?"

"Not really," she groaned.

"Okay. You listen then. Do I need to tell you how stupid that was?"

"I thought you said I didn't need to talk."

"Sorry. I'll take that as a no. You know you messed up. I'm not going to beat you up about it. I guess I really should have come clean about the danger we're in. I thought it was best to keep you out of it, but I can't keep telling you to keep an eye out if you don't know what you're looking for."

Shaine grunted an agreement.

"The men who killed your dad want to kill you and me. They have resources. They have people. They had people in Vegas and they'll have people in L.A. Also," he dropped his eyes down, not wanting to see her reaction to more bad news, "we might have the FBI after us too. After me, anyway. None of them can find you without me, so as soon as I drop you off, I'm heading the opposite direction and they can follow me all they want. It's not far to go, but we're not safe yet. I don't need you making it any harder, okay?"

"Yeah."

"Okay. I'll get you to your uncle Troy and we'll be done with this."

Lars downed the rest of his water and circled around the back bumper, got in and fired up the brand-new engine.

"They'll still come for you though," said Shaine behind closed eyes.

Lars paused. "Yeah. They will."

Shaine opened her eyes and turned to him. "For how long?"

"As long as it takes."

Seventeen years maybe. Shaine understood.

"Thanks, Lars. You could have killed me. Woulda been easier on you."

"I could have killed a lot of people, kid. My life would have been a lot easier."

He threw the car in gear.

58

The '66 limped into the short-term parking lot at the Las Vegas airport wheezing like a coal miner at his retirement party.

Trent parked it, got out, gave it a swift kick in the bumper and walked inside the airport to buy a ticket for Los Angeles.

Another call from Jake had confirmed a recent pop-up of Shaine's cell phone along the I-15 corridor headed from Vegas to L.A. It was a calculated guess for Trent, but there was a whole lot of nothing along the I-15, so thinking L.A. wasn't much of a stretch. If Lars drove all this way only to stop in Barstow, then he deserved what he got there. Boredom. Chain restaurants. Drought.

Getting on a plane meant ditching his gun, his knives and the bag of coke he kept for emergencies, but it meant beating Lars to the coast. Before buying his ticket for the hourly shuttle to LAX, Trent worked his iPhone, setting up contacts in Los Angeles. In ten minutes he had three men, a pair of guns and a change of clothes waiting for him when he landed. Nikki Junior was anxious to get this wrapped up.

When news came down that Lars had escaped the Vegas trap and killed his old protégé, along with four of the Vegas crew's top men, Junior started to get worried that he had traded one slow-ass fuck-up for another. And Lars was no Mitch the Bitch. Lars knew the game, knew he was being hunted, knew how to fight back.

Trent reassured Junior that his own desire to see Lars and the girl dead far exceeded Junior's.

Once he landed and met up with his new crew, it would become a question of sitting back and waiting for that cell phone to show up on the grid and then swooping in with maximum force.

Trent surged with anticipation, the same feeling he got at a strip club before he went back to the champagne room. He could not wait to get his rocks off, or kill Lars as the case may be. Either way the release of pent-up energy would feel like a shot of heroin directly to his brain.

As he handed his boarding pass to the woman at the X-ray machine, she glanced at his ID, disinterested, and waved him through.

Beeps, buzzers, bells. She woke up. Suddenly his bruised face and distorted nose seemed suspicious. Time for the wand.

Five tries, his belt, two earrings, buckles on his boots and change in his pocket later he reached the gate, but his flight had left. Forty-five minutes until the next one.

Trent visited the bar. There's always a bar.

"Got any Negra Suprema?"

59

Duane's nose whistled as he sat in the tiny room. He started to wonder if it would do that for the rest of his life. Crusted blood and swollen flesh clogged his nostrils.

In the tight confines of the security office no one could ignore the high wheezing sounds coming out of him. Brian tried to tune him out and concentrate on the images being rewound in hopes of identifying the man who'd assaulted them.

"That's it." Brian called, announcing that the videotaped evidence of their beating had been found.

Briggs, an ex-military crew cut in a suit and also the security officer in charge, signaled to the tech manning the console to play it in real time.

There was no audio, but the overhead wide angle caught the whole event happening in the far right corner of a shot focused mostly on a row of slots. Among the two dozen other nine-inch monitors stacked in a grid on the wall was one other shot you could see the beat down happen in, but only in the far background.

"That's the guy," said Duane although it came out muffled enough that Brian felt the need to repeat it.

"That's the guy. That's him."

The tech paused the image. It was a clean shot. High-definition. You could practically pull a set of prints from an image like that.

Briggs moved closer to the screen.

"Yes, well, no doubt this is the guy who assaulted you. You say you'd never met him before? Not even maybe on the convention floor sometime this week? Lot of people out there. Easy to forget a face."

Brian spoke up. "No, we never laid eyes on the guy. He was with the girl, at least that's what he said. Look at the way he kicks Duane. Totally unprovoked!"

The tech hit play and Duane's nose was crushed again in high-def. Duane had to look away.

"Wait a second..." Briggs studied the screen. "Pause it." He leaned over and hit an intercom button. "Hey, Mike, come in here a sec."

Focused on the screen even when Mike, the second in command, entered the room, Briggs spoke like a character on *CSI*.

"Does he look familiar to you?"

Mike examined the image. "Holy shit."

"It is, right?"

"Could be."

"Could it?"

Brian leaned in closer to the monitor, curious. "Who is it? You know him?"

Briggs clicked his teeth, unable to commit. "I'm not sure."

Mike seemed like he wanted it to be true. "Sure as hell looks like it."

Muffled and slurred came Duane. "Who the fuck is it?"

Mike and Briggs exchanged a look. Briggs sighed and explained. "A while back a few of us on the security team here were with another casino. A man entered without our knowledge and..."

Brian leaned forward.

"...and he killed five people, including two of our security officers."

"And this is the same guy?" asked Brian.

"Could be."

"So he could have killed us?"

"If it's the same guy."

"So call the cops. Do an APB or whatever. Catch him and lock him up."

"It's not that easy. We don't know where he went."

"Well, he stole our rental car to get wherever he was going."

"Which you already reported, right?"

"Yeah."

Briggs and Mike studied the screen, becoming more certain.

"You still got that guy's number?" Briggs asked.

"Yeah," Mike said, pulling out his wallet. He dug deep into the leather and pulled out a stack of small cards: insurance, Triple A, a business card for a masseuse and one in simple bone-white with raised black letters detailing a name, a phone number and the initials FBI.

"I'll call it in." Mike stepped away to use the phone.

Briggs turned to Brian and Duane. "Look, guys, you want my professional opinion?" Brian and Duane both nodded. "Leave it alone. This guy is a pro. What he did last time...let's just say you don't want to get on this guy's shit list."

"So we let him beat the crap out of us and steal our rental car and he gets away with it?"

Mike chimed in. "If you know what's good for you."

"Look," Briggs continued. "You're not hurt too badly." Duane shook his head in disagreement. "The insurance will pay for the rental car. Let it go. The way this guy worked at the last place, he meant business. If you almost get bit by a snake, you don't go back and try to whack it with a stick. You keep on walking." Brian and Duane saw the logic but felt like idiots for not seeking retribution.

Briggs looked them square in the eyes. "Boys, keep on walking."

60

Earl Walker Ford knocked sharply on Agent Barry's door.

A muffled "Come in!"

Ford clutched the file in his hand and stepped through the door.

"Two things."

"Yeah?" Agent Barry said, looking up from the three files open on his desk.

"I got relayed onto a call from Las Vegas. Apparently our poker player shooter turned up again on a surveillance tape beating the holy hell out of two conventioneers."

Agent Barry closed the other files. They could wait. "Is that right? The one you think might be in on the Mitch Kenney thing."

"Yeah. So that's an interesting turn. The young gun," Ford checked his file. "Trent. His cell phone gave up a hit in Vegas too. It's gone dark since then, but I don't figure that to be a coincidence."

"No such thing." The phrase had been beaten into Agent Barry at the Academy.

"Here's the other thing—we found the wife."

"What wife?"

"Mitch Kenney's ex-wife, sir."

"Really?"

"Yes, sir. And there's something else."

Agent Barry raised an eyebrow. "Curiouser and curiouser."

"Yes, sir."

61

Dusk settled over an ARCO station on the I-15 outside of Victorville.

Lars pumped gas while Shaine sat on the hood and watched the truckers and locals move in and out, paying for gas, buying lottery tickets, six-packs of Bud.

Lars would have been putting premium into his '66. For the rental, the cheap stuff.

"So, could you kill that guy?" Shaine wondered aloud.

Lars did a double take. "What?"

"That guy." She pointed to a trucker climbing back into the cab of his truck holding a Taco Bell bag and a soda too large for human consumption. "You could kill him easy, right?"

Lars was stumped. "I guess I could. But why would I want to?"

"Like if I hired you to do it."

"You couldn't afford me." The pump's auto shutoff engaged and Lars removed the nozzle.

"What about him?" Shaine watched a young Hispanic man jog from his white pickup to the mini-mart. Whatever he needed, he needed in a hurry.

"What is this little game?"

"I don't know. I wonder how you do it, I guess. You could have killed those two guys back in Vegas, but you didn't. Why some people and not others?"

"No one was paying me for those jerk-offs. And trying to get laid in Vegas is not a crime or the prisons would be overflowing. You remember you told them you were eighteen, right?"

"Fine, not those guys. But, like, a lot of people, huh?"

It was her way of asking how many. Lars opened the driver's door. "Enough. That's all that matters. Get in."

She slid off the hood and took her place in the passenger seat. "Is it easy?"

"Jesus Christ, Shaine!"

"Last question. Is it easy?"

"No. Not even a little bit. If it was easy, everyone would do it." He cranked the engine to life.

"Not everyone."

"A lot more people than you think." Lars scanned the exits, looking for the way back to the I-15 south.

"Can I drive?"

"What?"

"I started taking lessons in driver's ed. I only had, like two weeks to go. I'm a good driver. My dad never let me practice though."

"Of course you can't drive. Relax, we're almost there."

She huffed a teenager's disgust and sank into her seat.

From behind them came flashing lights. Red and blue.

Lars took in the reality of it in the rearview mirror. Cops. He thought about gunning the engine and running, but he wasn't a getaway man and he didn't trust his driving skills. He needed to rely on his wits.

"Stay put," he commanded and got out to meet them half-way so they couldn't get a good look at Shaine.

Gawkers stared as the cop, alone in his patrol car and wiping his mouth with a napkin, signaled for Lars to stay where he was. Lars could feel their stares. Bored fucking cop running license plates in a parking lot while he sucked down his Big Mac the way some folks play solitaire. The worst kind of cop is a bored cop. Of course the plates came up stolen. One more bump in the road.

Fuck yeah I could kill them. All of them. Easy.

"Sir, please stay by your vehicle," the cop said. "Hands where I can see 'em." A veteran, not likely to be fooled easily. Potbelly and thick mustache gave away his years of riding highway patrol. He moved stiffly under the bulletproof vest and heavy utility belt.

Lars stopped. Acting wasn't his specialty, but he had to try.

"What's the problem, Officer?"

"Sir, I have reports that this vehicle was stolen." Lars noticed the cop's hand on the butt of his gun. Lars also noticed he had left his own in the car.

"Stolen? Are you serious? I told those people...goddammit. Excuse my language."

"Told who, sir?"

"The rental people. I get to the place and they send me out to space seventeen. I get out there and there's no car. I say there's a car in space eighteen, but not seventeen. They said, take it anyway. I told them I would wait until they figured it out, but these people, no sense of customer service anymore, am I right? They all want to hustle you out the door. And now this? I swear...I know it's not your fault. I'm so getting a refund from these people."

That hand stayed firmly on the gun, the officer's eyes suspicious. A static charge crackled the air between them, threatening to spark the gasoline fumes to fire.

"Sir, can I see some ID?"

"Sure, yeah, sure. Sorry. This kind of thing really burns my bacon, y'know?" Lars opened his wallet and took out his Arizona license, handed it over. "You go on vacation and you don't expect this kind of thing to happen, am I right? I mean, I only get one week a year and they go and get me arrested? Come on."

The cop read the fake info off the license. "Do you have your rental agreement, Mr. Kellen?"

"The rental agreement?"

"Yes, sir."

"I guess so. Probably. What do you need that for?"

"I need to match the names, sir. To back up your story." The snap came undone on the gun belt. "Why don't you wait over here for me, sir. I'll see if we can get this sorted out." The officer reached down and undid the snap on his cuffs, ready to hold Lars while he searched the car.

On the opposite side of the pump the man filling his pick-up stopped short of a full tank and cradled the nozzle, slipping behind his wheel and driving off, leaving his gas cap open.

Behind Lars, a body pressed into him. Shaine. Lars startled at first. She hugged close in to him, her body half-hidden by his, and faked wiping sleep from her eyes.

"Daddy, do you have some money? I need to buy more tampons." She looked up, pretending to notice the officer for the first time. "What's going on?"

Behind his back, using Lars to block the officer's view, Shaine pressed the Beretta into Lars's belt. Lars felt a smile creep across his lips involuntarily.

Goddamn I could kiss this girl right now. I couldn't be any prouder if she was my own daughter.

Lars turned and looked at Shaine, his smile beaming like a proud papa's. The gun settled into a comfortable spot in the small of his back, the metal of the long silencer cold on his skin, but he kept himself from flinching.

Lars played his part. "There's some sort of mix-up with the rental car, sweetie. It's nothing to worry about."

Her ploy worked. The officer was flustered. Say "tampon" in front of any man and you buy yourself a little bit of diversion time.

"Ma'am, can you return to the vehicle please?"

"But, I need to go buy tampons. It's…kind of an emergency."

The cop's jaw opened to say something, but no words came out. It was enough hesitation for Lars.

The Beretta came out and three shots went quickly into the

cop's legs. One in his right kneecap, one in the thigh and one in the shoe on his left foot.

The shots came out silenced, but the cop screamed loud. He dropped the cuffs and fell after them. His belt clattered a mag light, radio and spare set of cuffs onto the concrete. The small crowd gasped but didn't know exactly what happened.

"Go! Now!" Lars shouted. He and Shaine spun and lunged for the car. When the crowd saw the officer sink to the ground and the two fugitives dash in a sudden movement, there were screams. Nothing panics like a crowd. Even a crowd of four.

Lars slid behind the wheel, skipped the seat belt and cranked the gearshift into drive. Shaine landed hard in her seat.

"Did I do good?"

"You did great, kid."

The Mustang's tires squealed on the oil-slick gas station pavement. It was no '66 but the old pony had some pep.

Lars knew a shot to the kneecap meant it would be quite a while before the cop could even call for backup. He kept the engine hot as he wove through streets like a Prohibition boot-legger. He stabbed the car forward up residential streets and back out on more major drags, all the while scanning for a replacement car.

Shaine was hanging on, white-knuckled, for the ride.

Lars passed a low-rise industrial park. He saw something that caught his eye, and he spun the wheel suddenly. Shaine let out an involuntary shriek.

The Mustang hit two wheels on the curb and bounced as he swung the car into a large parking lot with only one car in it. This was his mark.

He stopped the Mustang next to his new car and got out, reaching over the seat to get his bags of money.

"We're taking this one?" asked Shaine.

"Only one in the lot after five. He's not coming back until

tomorrow. Or maybe even on a business trip and will be gone longer. All we need is a few hours anyway. Get in."

Lars smashed the back window on the four-door Toyota and popped the locks. He placed the duffel bag and briefcase in the backseat and then ducked under the front panel to see if he remembered how to hot-wire a car.

"Did you kill that cop?"

Lars was trying to concentrate on the tangle of wires he had ripped free from the steering column.

"What? No. Of course not."

"How do you know?"

"I wasn't trying to."

Sparks lit the well beneath the steering wheel, and Lars cursed when one landed on his lip and burned.

"But, you could have," Shaine added.

The engine turned over and started. Lars slid up into the driver's seat, checked the gas gauge—three-quarters full—and put the car in drive.

"Sure, I could have. I could have killed you back in Albuquerque too. Best not to keep reminding me of that."

He steered the Toyota out of the lot and picked his way through the streets to I-15.

62

"Okay, time to find this Uncle Troy."

Downtown L.A. loomed over the moonroof of the stolen Toyota. Shaine stared up at the sky. A police helicopter, the California state bird, swept a spotlight down into the street canyons.

"Right. I'm pretty sure my dad has his number in here. He copied over his entire sim card onto my phone so if I ever needed him I would have any number he could possibly be at. He was a little paranoid like that. Of course it would have been helpful if he ever went anywhere instead of sitting around the house with the doors locked."

Shaine pressed the power button on her phone. Nothing happened. "Shit."

"What?"

"My battery is dead."

"Don't you have a charger?"

"No. It's at home. I kind of left in a hurry." She shot Lars a look.

"Well, we can get one."

"Yeah, there's a port right here." She pointed to a small black cap by her knee that popped open, revealing a socket.

"Really? They have those right in the car?"

"Seriously?"

Lars got defensive. "I've been driving a car that's more than forty years old. Give me a break."

"Well, this thing has it all, I gotta say. Dad never sprung for the XM radio. I always wanted that."

"This thing has satellite?"

Shaine pressed a button on the dash and a screen illuminated. Lars stared, unsure where to begin. "Is there a channel listing?"

Shaine pulled one from the glove box.

"Shit," Lars said. "Find something good."

Shaine ran down the list of channel descriptions.

"Country?"

"No."

"New country?"

"No."

"Bluegrass?"

"No country. Next."

Fifteen *Nos* later and she hit it. "Hard rock classics. Sixties, seventies and eighties."

"Bingo. Dial it up."

Shaine rolled her eyes and punched in the numbers. They caught the very start of Rush's "Limelight." Lars's pulse quickened. He turned up the volume to near concert levels.

"Now *this* is how to roll into town."

Geddy Lee's strange falsetto serenaded them off the 5 north into a shopping plaza and an electronics store. Lars made Shaine wait in the car until the song ended, then sent her in to buy a charger. She made it ten minutes before the store closed.

The music left Lars in a good mood. He'd gotten her this far in one piece. Very soon he would hand her over to someone else and could set about getting lost in the world.

As soon as she returned, they would find an address and Uncle Troy would have a new problem for a while, not him.

It could have been the Doors song that came on next, but Lars's good mood turned dark. Never was much of a Doors fan. Get a fucking bass player, then we'll talk.

He found himself already missing her a little bit. It would be a hell of a lot easier to lose Trent without her, though.

Head to Denver, see if any of his money was still there. He had enough. A little more never hurt anyone.

He turned in his seat, stretching his back muscles, rolling his neck side to side. After sitting still for so damn long, it felt good to work out the kinks.

Oh damn, the Kinks. I wish they would play "You Really Got Me."

Shaine returned with a charger. She plugged it into the car jack and found the number for Troy in the address book. Smart phones indeed.

"Now I need to go get a map," Lars said.

Shaine sighed and punched the address into the GPS system on the Toyota.

"Wow." Lars marveled like a man seeing his first motion picture.

63

As soon as Trent received permission by the flight attendants to power up his iPhone, he saw three messages. He dialed in.

"Dude, it's Jake. We got another pop-up in L.A. Are you there yet?"

Next message: "Dude, this time the signal is steady. No more on and off. Call me when you land."

Last one, five minutes ago: "Dude, this rocks if I do say so. I have the signal routed into a GPS software with live tracker, and I am literally sitting here in my underpants five hundred miles away following a little blip on a map of L.A. Burbank, actually. But I got 'em. Real time baby. This is some cool shit. You gotta call me back, bro, you gotta see this!"

Trent dialed. Jake answered. "Where you been, man?"

"Flying. You got 'em?"

"Yeah, it's awesome. Like a fucking video game. I am so geeked about this."

Geek is the word, Trent thought. "Tell me where."

"You can track them, man. I can send this signal to your phone. All you need to do is download the app."

"How the fuck do I do that?" A woman who had been eyeing Trent the whole flight turned a suspicious stare at him again. She sped up her walk, her carry-on bag crossing the floor tiles in a *click-click* rhythm.

"Hold on, I'll send it to you."

"Who am I looking for, by the way? The guys I'm meeting up with."

"I don't know. I never seen them."

"Never mind. I got 'em."

At the bottom of the escalator stood three of the scariest men Trent had ever seen. Kill-you-and-piss-on-your-corpse types. Skull-crushing hands on the end of bench-press arms. Deadly stares from seen-too-much eyes. Break some fingers before breakfast, drag a guy behind a car after lunch, two to the brain and one to the heart before dinner and one more to the balls for dessert.

This was Trent's help. He felt like king of the badass brigade, and for the moment, he was.

64

"So what happens to us?" Shaine asked.

"What do you mean?"

"I mean, you're leaving me here, right? I'll never see you again?"

"That's the plan. Isn't that a good thing?"

"It's just that..." She shifted in the front seat, turning an eye to the two-story suburban home they sat parked in front of. "I owe you that money. I'll need some way to get it back to you."

"Oh, come on. You don't owe me anything. I'm still a little pissed about the tattoo," he smiled, "but you don't owe me a dime. Forget it."

Shaine looked doubtfully at her new home.

"Shall we do this?" asked Lars.

"I guess so."

The two walked to the front door, smoothing clothes, trying to look presentable and not so on-the-lam.

Lars waited until she nodded the okay to him, then he rang the bell.

Lars didn't like the guy right off the bat. From the moment Troy answered the door, it took way too long for him to recognize her. Granted she said it had been a few years, but...it gave Lars a sour taste.

"Shaine! Oh my...oh my God. What are you doing here?"

Lars read more than recognition. He heard panic. No, he didn't like Uncle Troy one bit so far.

"And who are you?" Troy asked the middle-aged stranger on his doorstep.

"Why don't you invite us in and we'll all get to know each other. We can tell you a heck of a story while we're at it."

Troy stood his ground, blocking the doorway. "I don't understand. Where is your dad, sweetie?"

Lars tensed when he called her that.

"Umm..." Shaine hadn't had to spill the news to anyone yet. She couldn't find the words. Lars stepped in to save her, like she had for him at the gas station.

"He's dead. Can we not talk about this out on the porch? You got bugs out here. I'm getting bit."

Troy balked, in the middle of an internal argument. His feet shuffled back and forth in an indecision mambo, finally clearing a path for Shaine and Lars to enter.

The two fugitives examined the well-appointed home. Art on the walls, hardwood floors, big TV. No kids. That much you could tell at a glance. Lots of glass and ceramic down low on coffee tables and shelves.

Troy spoke quietly. "How did he...what happened?"

Lars rested a hand on Shaine's shoulder. "Why don't you use the restroom? It's been a long drive." Shaine got the hint and excused herself.

"Uh, down the hall on the right," said Troy, unsure why he was letting these people into his home, his bathroom.

"Look, Troy, before we get to that, my name is Lars. I brought Shaine here because she has nowhere else to go. I need to know, can you take care of her?"

"What?" With her gone, Troy was emboldened. "Who the hell are you and what the fuck is going on?"

"Her dad is dead. She's got no one. I can't take care of her because the men who killed her father are after me now, and if they find her with me, she's dead too. That's about as much as you need to know. Now, will you take her in?"

Troy had tuned Lars out mid-sentence. He held a hand over his mouth. "Was it Nikki?"

Lars cocked an eyebrow.

"Did they find him?" Troy knew. "They found him, didn't they? After all this time." He gave a shake of his head as if he was impressed.

"What do you know about it?"

"Probably more than you."

Lars doubted that. He raised an eyebrow at Troy, trying to figure out what the jerk-off wasn't telling him. He couldn't be a family friend. Nikki would have mentioned him. In all the years, Lars had been the only man in the know. Besides, if Troy worked for the family and he knew Mitch, he could have killed him anytime.

Maybe Mitch told him. In all that time Lars figured he had to crack and tell at least one person. Lars bet Troy didn't even believe it until right at that moment. Probably left town thinking his friend was a nutcase.

Just because you're paranoid…

"Look," Lars said. "If you know about it then you know she's in danger. So will you take her?"

"It's complicated."

"No shit, pal. This damn thing wrote the book on complicated. Any way you cut it though, her being in your life is less complicated than her being in my life."

"Troy?" a voice, a woman's, called from upstairs. "Who are you talking to?"

"No one!" he answered quickly. Then to Lars, "You've got to go."

"What? No."

"Call me tomorrow. Seriously…you've got to go now."

The woman descended the stairs. Lars stood firm.

"Oh, hi. I didn't…sorry. I'm Ella."

"Lars." He took her extended hand, waiting for Troy to explain who he was.

"Are you from the office?"

"Not exactly."

"Lars was just heading out, honey." Troy put a hand on

Lars's back but found a stone statue not willing to budge. "You head back upstairs and I'll be right up."

Down the hall the toilet flushed. Ella cocked her head at Troy.

"Lars brought...they're both going now. I'll be up—"

"Mom?"

Shaine stood in the shadow of the hallway, staring at her mother. Ella stared back waiting for someone to shout "April fool" or "You're on *Candid Camera*" or "Wake up!" No one said a thing.

65

Agent Barry checked his watch again as Earl Walker Ford entered his office. "I *really* should be home with my wife by now."

"I'm sorry, sir. We've tracked down an address and confirmed the identity of Troy Heath. He is the same man."

"One of ours."

"Used to be."

"And now he's shacked up with the wife of a man he was supposed to be hiding."

"Yes, sir."

"Who screens these agents? This kind of shit wouldn't have happened under J. Edgar Hoover."

Ford swallowed hard, bracing himself for delivering more bad news. "Trouble is, the man we need approval from to take action is out of town. Diplomatic mission."

Agent Barry stood, slamming his hand down on his desk blotter. "Why the hell do I need to seek approval to go arrest one of my own men, goddammit?"

Ford spoke calmly, "He's no longer our man, sir. NSA needs prior approval to move in a case like this."

Agent Whitney entered the room without knocking. "We got a hit on the young gun. Los Angeles. And get this, video surveillance puts our man Lars as the shooter in that Vegas thing with Camponisi. Got him leaving the building two minutes after shots fired."

Agent Barry rubbed his hands together like a starving man eyeing a steak. "So let's go get 'em. They've gotta all be connected."

"This Lars is a ghost though. No records. No fingerprints. No ID. If we hadn't put him in the database after the other Vegas thing, the poker player, he wouldn't have even registered."

"Well, then get the other two. Get somebody for this fucking thing!"

Ford again played spoiler. "If we move on Troy Heath, we need approval."

Agent Barry paced behind his desk. "All this interagency bullshit is driving me to an early retirement. The FBI never used to have to jump through hoops. Get permission from Homeland Security to wipe our asses. Where is this guy?"

"Cayman Islands, sir," answered Ford, reading the e-mail printout in his hand.

"Diplomatic mission my ass. What's the time difference there?"

"Same as ours, sir."

"Call him. Due diligence. If we can't raise him in thirty minutes, I'm sending in men myself. Fuck 'em. Let them fire me. I need the rest."

66

The quartet sat in the living room, Shaine sulking like a TV stereotype of a teenage girl. Shooting daggers at her mother. Ella slumping low into the couch to avoid the laser beam of guilt and disapproval being fired her way.

After a long silence Lars spoke first. "Y'know, I'll be honest with you, when we showed up, I thought we had the most screwed up story to relate. I was wrong. Leaving your husband for his FBI handler. That, lady, takes the cake."

"You don't know what it was like to live with him. He was broken. He lived in fear."

"He kept living in fear even after you left," said Lars, an accusing tone rising in his voice. "But you left him with your daughter. Everything you hated about living with him you sentenced your only child to live with, only worse because now he was damaged twice as bad by you."

Ella sat forward, forcing her words at Lars. "He was so damaged because *you* were hunting him for all those years. You couldn't leave him alone. Each time we had to leave a town in the middle of the night he got quieter, more sullen. He aged. The desert air is supposed to be good for you but it was killing him. But then I guess that was your job, wasn't it?"

Lars met her stare, silently.

Ella turned to Shaine, got an equally cold stare. "I'm sorry." Shaine said nothing.

"So the question now becomes," continued Lars, "not will you take her in, but will she stay with you?"

All eyes turned to Shaine.

Troy did his best impression of a father. "She's too young to make a decision like that."

"No, I'm not."

Troy didn't protest.

Lars looked at her, spoke calmly. "Whatever you want to do. I don't know how we'll make it work if you don't stay here, but it's whatever you want."

"Well, she can't stay with you!" Ella said.

Lars spun and gave her his best cold killer stare. "You don't get to decide. You made your choice a long time ago."

Ella fell quiet.

A fountain outside dripped white noise. A dog next door barked at nothing. Everyone waited for Shaine's answer.

Music played. High, tinny. A Black Eyed Peas song. A cell phone ringtone. Shaine's.

She answered it. "Hello?" Waited. Held it out to Lars. "It's him."

Lars took the phone. Troy and Ella shared a look of confusion. It had become their normal expression.

"Hello?"

67

This fucking little punk. Stubborn as a donkey. Clamps down like a pit bull and won't let go. Wouldn't ever tell him that, it'd go to his head.

Lars spoke into Shaine's phone. "What do you want, Trent?"

"Just calling to say hi."

"How'd you get this number?"

"This number? You should be asking how I got this address." Lars stiffened. "Mitch did me a huge favor the way he was so damn afraid. Had a GPS put into her phone. He could track her, keep tabs on her. So afraid. Afraid of you, so I guess I have you to thank for leading me right here."

"How did you find us?"

"What did I just say?" Trent said, his temper shortened by the air travel and the painful infection in his nose. "I tracked you using her cell phone. What are you in the fucking Dark Ages, man? You still use Western Union?"

Didn't take much to remind Lars why he hated the prick.

"Since I'm a nice guy, I'll give you one chance to come on out and take your medicine so we don't have to disturb the lucky couple who you decided to crash in on. One chance. Then we're coming in. I don't need to tell you what happens then." With a fake chipper song in his voice Trent signed off, "Call me."

Lars turned to Shaine. "I thought you said the battery was dead on this. Isn't that why you bought a charger?"

"I've been keeping it off, mostly."

"Mostly? He's been tracking us with the signal. How often did you turn it on?"

"I don't know. Every now and then."

Even Lars found the fatherly exasperation in his voice surprising. "For what? Who were you calling?"

Shaine's expression changed. A hurt puppy, her eyes hovered close to tears. "My dad, okay?"

The words slapped Lars across the face, clawing a little with sharp fingernails. Ella let out a tiny gasp.

"I called home to hear the voice mail message. His voice."

Lars felt a tug of emotion he hadn't experienced in years.

Shaine hung her head. "I'm sorry."

He wanted to hug her, to comfort her, to be a father to her. He sat still.

The first bullet came through the bay window and smashed a red-and-blue glass vase on the dining table. The shattering made an epic sound, like a glass factory in an earth-quake.

Troy still maintained some of his Bureau training and leapt up from the couch, moving across the room to shield Ella, whom he tugged by her wrist. Lars spun and stood in a crouch, his Beretta in hand so quickly Shaine thought it magically appeared there.

"Get upstairs. Both of you. Now!"

Shaine ducked and ran across the living room to her mother. Troy shielded them as they made it to the stairs, which ran halfway up, hit a landing and then jogged off to the left. Ella tried to take Shaine's hand, but Shaine shook her off.

The two women disappeared around the bend of the stairs as another round smashed through the window and sank into a couch cushion with a muted *thump.*

Troy made it to the hall closet and pushed aside a tangle of coats to reach the back wall. Lars crouch-walked over to him. Troy worked the spinner of a wall safe tunneled into the back of the closet.

The front door rocked. Powerful boot-clad feet kicked at it. The frame started to splinter. Windows rattled.

Troy swung open the safe door. He reached into the blackness and came back with a Bureau-issued 9mm in each hand. Lars couldn't help being impressed.

Another thundering kick at the door and then a final crash and tearing of wood. A figure came through at full speed, like a boulder had rolled down out of the hills above. Troy raised both guns, John Woo-style, and started firing.

Lars dove for the back of the couch as Troy ripped off a half dozen shots with each hand. After the volley of fire, he veered off to his left, into the dining room, to seek shelter from the inevitable return fire.

The human boulder who was Trent's muscle man stood up straight and brushed plaster dust off his black sweatshirt. Not a scratch on him.

You've got to be fucking kidding me, Lars thought. *He must have let loose a dozen rounds and not one landed? Shit, no wonder the feds are always one step behind criminals like me. They don't train them like they should. All that paper target practice. I bet I've gotten more honest to goodness head shots on real heads then he has on a firing range.*

No time to give lessons but Lars did hope Troy watched.

Crack.

That's how it's done. One shot. Dead. Another lesson though: you never leave it at one.

Lars blasted another round through the top of the boulder's head as he lay face down already in the entryway.

He wasn't surprised the first one through the door wasn't Trent. Mr. Hardass on the phone still sent someone else to do his dirty work.

Lars dashed across the open space to join Troy in the dining room. Three shots came late, chasing the fast-moving shape of Lars passing by the destroyed door.

"Did I miss?" asked Troy.

"Sure did."

"Been a while."

"Yeah."

"So who are these guys?"

"The one that killed Mitch. He brought a few friends it would seem. Not sure how many." Troy nodded, sucking wind. Out of shape or nervous, Lars didn't know. "Look, if they were just here for me, I'd cut out the back door and lead them away, but they also want the girl. That's not going to happen."

"I need to reach the phone. I can still make a call and get backup."

"Tell them to bring body bags. By the time they get here, this is gonna be all over."

68

Trent paced in the street. The two towers of muscle looked to him for a decision. They seemed willing enough to storm the castle, but Trent stalled, uncomfortable with making the call. Mostly because he knew he would have to join the rush.

"Fuck!"

"Well? What is it? Do we go in?" asked the one with a flame tattoo up his arm, disappearing under his short black sleeve.

Trent knew the more time he gave Lars the worse it would be for them. He thought about the fat bonus coming when he delivered the corpses of Lars and the girl. He gave a quick glance to the garage. This looked like a guy who might have a workshop. Someplace Trent could dig up some tin snips or some kind of big scissors.

Fingers. Proof positive.

Lars drew a deep breath in through his nose and let it out through his mouth.

"We should split up."

Troy nodded, eyes popping around rodent-like. Lars felt less than confident. "Try not to shoot at me, okay? Stick to the bad guys."

A relative term. Lars—the good guy, contract killer of over forty men—moved back into the kitchen.

Upstairs, Ella checked the lock on the bedroom door again. Still tight. She chewed a nail and marveled at Shaine's calm, sitting on the bed like it was an average school night. A loud movie playing below, not real gunshots.

"Shaine, I want to say—"

"Don't. Please don't."

"But I—"

"I don't even know you, okay?"

Ella felt hurt. This hard shell of a girl was her creation. She could have taken her along. Could have given her a new life. But she would have been a constant reminder of Mitch. She had to get as far away from that life as possible. Troy gave her the way out, but at a cost.

She'd already picked up her life and left behind everything she knew once before. Doing it again turned out to be far easier than she'd expected. She barely thought of Shaine at all.

Ella could see that Shaine did far too much thinking for a girl her age.

With military precision the two hired musclemen slipped quietly past the ruined door.

From under the dining table Troy saw both pairs of black pants step sideways into his house. His body involuntarily jerked and his head hit the underside of the table. The vase on the table above tipped, spilling orchids and the decorative glass beads that surrounded the vase. Tiny clear balls ran off the edge, making hail around Troy's hiding place.

Panic set in.

More two-fisted gunfire erupted from the dining room. The muscle dove for cover, one of Troy's wild rounds catching a leg. He wasn't sure which one.

From the kitchen, Lars recognized the wild frenzy of Troy's shooting technique. He waited for the madness to end. It did with the telltale clicks of two empty guns.

A flame-tattooed arm swung around the half wall of the entryway and a coal-black .40-caliber pumped three shots into the dining room.

Lars heard Troy's cry of pain.

The kitchen island Lars hid behind reminded him of the marble slab that became his refuge at the bank in Albuquerque. Lars sat on the floor, back to the island and to the kitchen entry. Above him and off to the side, a double oven with tinted black glass acted as a mirror, reflecting two TV screens of action. In the reflection he could see a grizzly bear of a man, with close-cropped hair carved into a V shape down the back of his neck, step around the corner into the kitchen. He moved slowly, with the trained and deliberate moves of a martial artist.

Lars watched the grizzly's image grow bigger in the reflection on the oven door, hoping the man wouldn't look into the glass and see Lars's hiding place behind the island. When the bear's torso filled the black rectangle, Lars brought his Beretta around the edge of the island and fired a single bullet that pierced the man's heart from below. The silenced gun made no more sound than if the man had stubbed his toe going to the fridge for a beer. The bullet traveled up and lodged itself in his neck, the bear grasping at his jugular, which bled from the inside.

A little maze game for the coroner's office to play during the autopsy. Entry below the navel, no exit wound. Holes in the stomach, liver, pancreas and left lung. Slug lodged next to the esophagus. The nerds always acted so proud when they determined the path of a bullet.

The man fell and cracked his V-shaped skull on the kitchen tiles.

Lars moved to the door of the dining room. He saw under the table. Troy's chest still rose and fell, but the impact of the three bullets was easy to trace. One to the jaw, one in his chest and one through his hand, open in front of him in a futile attempt to stop a bullet. It's human instinct to protect your heart, even if you know it'll do no good. Anyone would have done it.

69

"Okay, that does it." Ella opened the closet and reached to the top shelf, where the sweaters sat folded, waiting for the weather to turn cold enough during the few weeks it is appropriate to wear a sweater in Burbank.

Shaine watched her mother paw blindly among the cashmere and wool until her arm stopped and Ella's face brightened with recognition.

Ella brought back a small wooden box, opened it and removed the gun. A modest .38 revolver, unloaded. The way Ella lifted it from the box Shaine could tell the gun was a new sensation for her. She tried to hold it firmly enough to load and yet not have it in her possession at all.

"Here, let me." Shaine stood and took the gun from her mother, who was too stunned to protest. The last thing Ella could remember Shaine holding was a Barbie doll.

Lars sat watching Troy's slow chest movements, waiting for the moment they would cease. Another life ruined by Lars butting in. No sense dwelling on it. You could fill Yankee Stadium with all the lives Lars had upended.

His focus under the table, Lars didn't see the tattooed arm reaching out. A canon blast boomed across the bow of the dinner table. Shrapnel from the door frame exploded onto Lars, and he moved quickly back into the kitchen. Not the best hiding place. A door on each end. Very little shelter. Right when he thought he was getting his touch back, he made another mistake.

Impromptu firefights were not Lars's forte, though. Planned executions were more his game. He wasn't about to feel bad for not knowing an unknowable.

"You get him?" came Trent's shout from the front porch. Brave as always.

Cowering on the floor of the kitchen, Lars had to give Trent his due; maybe the kid was smart enough to know when to leave it to the experts. *Well*, Lars thought, *I don't have any experts. Only me and my balls.*

"Not yet fucker!" Lars said.

When in doubt, antagonize the little bitch.

Another blast from the canon and Lars wanted to say out loud, *Jesus Christ those .40-cals are loud as fuck.*

A quick scramble to the back of the island, hoping for a break in the bullets. He couldn't tell if Trent had come inside. Lars listened closely for the sounds of two men.

He cursed himself for his hiding place. *Why the fuck did I hole up in the kitchen? Bad idea, dumbass. Can't really hide behind a toaster.*

More shots from the .40-caliber. The granite counter sprayed shrapnel. The sugar, the spice rack both took fatal hits. It suddenly smelled like an Indian restaurant. Off the counter tumbled a knife block, an egg timer, and a bottle of red wine. The bottle didn't break. Lars knew what he'd be popping open to celebrate if they made it through this.

A momentary distraction.

A boot came down on the hand holding his Beretta, pinning Lars to the ground.

"This him?" said the voice at the end of the tattoo.

Trent called from the entryway. "He look like Father Time?"

"He's old."

"That's him."

Lars saw blood leaking from a wound in the man's leg. He acted like the bullet that hit him had been no more than a mosquito at a picnic. Lars knew about guys like him. A little blood fuels the engine. The kind of guys to be afraid of.

Mr. Tattoo Arm had apparently been told to save the prize kill for Trent, like a bullfighter who pushes a sword through the bull's heart only after a cadre of smaller men have stabbed it repeatedly with spears and swords. The wrong man walks out of the ring holding the severed ears.

Trent smiled as he turned the corner into the kitchen, his nose big and purple like an infected Rudolph's. Gun drawn, chain wallet jangling, he loved seeing Lars on the ground, helpless.

"We meet again."

Lars took momentary pleasure in the bruising Trent's face had taken since he last saw him. "This isn't Superman and Lex Luthor, you little shit."

"True. This is real life and I'm lovin' it right now. Tell you what. You got another minute. Sixty seconds, give or take. I need your girlfriend to see this. Or maybe you should see her get clipped first. Oh, decisions, decisions."

Trent laughed as he turned and started for the stairs.

70

Nikki Senior went through the list of everyone he'd ever known and respected, thinking, *What would they do?* He stopped short of Jesus. Long-haired hippie freak hadn't done shit for Nikki in seventy-two years. Be fruitful and multiply, he said. And what did it get Nikki? A backstabbing ingrate for a son. Letting the kid die on a cross sounded pretty damn good. The big man upstairs did it, why not Nikki? If only he had some wood.

Nikki Senior dug up many different answers from his mental catalog of influential people. None of it fit. He couldn't rely on what someone else would do, because none of them had ever been in his situation. A son. His only son. Betrayer.

It wasn't until he thought *What would I do? The younger me. The powerful me. What would he do with a bastard son trying to overthrow the family?* That he knew the answer to.

He needed help. He was not without influence in that regard. Nikki Junior hadn't made it a priority of his new rule to make friends.

When Nikki Senior knocked on the door to his former office, he brought two young men with him. Add the two together and they were still young enough to be his grandson.

Junior called, "Come in."

There was absolutely no way to be intimidated by a man wheeling an oxygen tank, no matter how many goons he had flanking him.

"Dad. You're up late."

"I had a nap. Did some thinking."

"Oh yeah?" Junior put his head down again, reading the spreadsheets in front of him. Calculating ways to shave a percent off overhead here, a percent off payroll there.

"Yeah. I decided…" He waited for Junior to look at him. It took a full thirty seconds.

"Decided what?"

"You're not my son."

"Okay. Except, you fucked Mom, right?"

Nikki Senior bristled. "No son of mine would do this disrespect. A true son would have more of me in him."

"Look, Dad, I'm busy—"

Nikki Senior lifted a weary hand. The two youngsters both drew guns. Junior stopped.

"No son of mine." Nikki Senior waved a tiny gesture, like the pope from the Vatican balcony.

The guns fired in stereo. Wounding shots.

Nikki Senior strode over to his old desk, a matador proud and regal. He ignored his shocked son sucking for air and leaking blood. Nikki Senior pulled open the center drawer of his desk and reached back to retrieve the gun.

He cradled the pistol that had been his companion during his rise to power. Held it gently, same as he'd held Nikki when he was a baby.

"Dad…Dad…Da…" Breathing became harder. Lungs collapsing. Blood left his heart and made the trip halfway but detoured out onto the floor before returning.

Nikki Senior lifted the old gun to his son's head. *What would the young me do?* he thought.

"This."

He fired.

71

The man with the flame job tattoo may have had one up on Lars for karate training, but no one had it over Lars for flexibility. Even with his lack of time in the past few days to really get a decent session in, Lars could still twist his body like a gymnast. Just ask a room full of corpses in Las Vegas.

Guys like the big brute holding a gun on him, and mashing Lars' own gun hand into the tile floor, cared only about the muscles. Lifting, squatting, pumping. For what? A thick neck that can't turn to check out a great ass anymore. And why did evolution put a swivel on the neck if not for that?

Lars heard Trent's deliberate footsteps hit the landing on the stairs and make the turn to the left and continue up. Time to act.

And act he did. A little drama to conceal his true motives.

The smile on the end of the tattooed arm curled vicious in the corners. "Gonna like this, fucker. Heard what you did. Shot one of the family. Not cool, bro. Maybe before we put a bullet in this girl of yours, I should give her a little—"

The man grabbed his crotch with his free hand and did several hip thrusts, pinching his tongue between his teeth like a teenage virgin's idea of a sex face.

"I wouldn't bother. She's not that cute," said Lars. Truth hurts. His hand hurt more as the boot twisted and ground down.

"Shut up!"

Exactly what Lars needed. He twisted his body in mock agony, some of it real, and used the fake agony to contort his torso around so he could reach back in a modified version of the twist bound lunge pose and reach the fallen knife block and the scattered weapons around it.

Seeing Lars in pain only made Tattoo Arm grind harder with his boot.

Lars wrapped a hand around an eight-inch chef's knife and spun his body back around, using the torque built up in his abdominal muscles to fling himself quicker than Tattoo Arm could react.

The knife flashed, arced across the space between them and came down more like a cleaver. The blade hit the wrist above the hand that held the gun, below where the flames died out on the tattoo, and Lars tugged down on the hilt, pulling the thick steel across the open wrist.

It became quickly apparent why that was a prime spot for suicides. Blood burst out of the gaping slash like kids through the doors on the last day of school. The boot came off Lars's hand and he rolled away, but not before a warm bath of blood splashed down on him.

The .40-caliber dropped to the floor, and Lars passed it on his way to standing. With his non-flame arm the hired muscle grabbed at his wrist, but the cut was too deep. Trying to staunch the flow now was like putting a wine cork in Old Faithful.

Lars went for the stairs, took them two at a time, made the left turn and sprinted for the only closed door in the hallway. His mind ran white with hate and a protective instinct for the girl that still felt strange. *I'll kill him if he hurts her. I'll fucking kill him.*

Well, he thought, *I'm gonna kill him anyway, but still.*

Foot to the door, broken knob, gun at the ready. Lars stopped. Blood spattered, deep breathing, gun wielding, wild-eyed.

Well, goddamn. Did not expect that.

72

Shaine stood, feet spread, arms out straight in front of her, the .38 aimed steady at Trent's face.

Trent wavered, mute and uneasy on his feet. Hands up like at a stickup in the Old West. His nose leaking pus.

Ella sat on the bed, breathless, a hand over her heart. The shattered door swung slowly to a stop.

"Shaine," Lars said. "You got him dead to rights. Now let me take over. You don't want to go and do something you'll regret."

"He killed my dad."

Trent swallowed hard.

"He did do that, true. He's a killer. But not you. Let me take care of this and we can be on our way."

"You'll take me with you?"

"If that's what you want."

Shaine stared daggers at Trent. She sucked in a deep breath through her nose then turned the gun on Ella.

Lars immediately brought his gun up to cover Trent, making a little cough so Trent knew he was there.

Ella, because it seemed like the only thing to do, put her hands up as well.

"Shaine, what are you—"

"Shut up. You don't follow me. Don't ask about me. Don't tell anyone what you saw here. I was never here. I'll never be back. Don't try to find me. I don't exist to you. You already don't exist to me."

Ella's heart genuinely hurt, but she wasn't in a position to argue. She nodded, her eyes swollen with tears. Not exactly the way any mother plans for her little girl to leave home.

Shaine lowered the gun, stuck it in her waistband.

"You two go downstairs," said Lars. Then, to Ella, "Mrs...?"

"Ella."

"You won't like what you see. Stay out of the dining room. Curiosity killed the cat you know."

Shaine passed through the door first, not looking back at Trent. Ella followed, her sobs finally cresting and bursting out as she went.

Lars stood over Trent's back shoulder, only the crescent-moon shape of his face visible. Enough to see real panic.

"Aren't you gonna try to make a deal?" he asked Trent.

"Would it do any good?"

"Nope."

Trent stayed silent. A slight nausea came and went, Lars's body still adjusting to the thought of killing again. He seemed to be settling into a rhythm, knowing when the right time and the right person could make it okay. His decision to pull a trigger had always been based on some numbers and a dollar sign. Now he based it on right and wrong. Deserving or not.

The old way was easier.

"Can I borrow your phone?" asked Lars.

"What?"

"That fancy phone you always play with. I need it. To make a call."

Trent reached into his pocket and drew out his iPhone. He held it out for Lars. Lars took it and regarded the lack of buttons. "You got the manual for this in there, too?"

Trent shook his head, let out a condescending laugh. "I can't believe this old bastard got me," he seemed to say with the laugh.

"You really think I'm that old, huh?" Trent said nothing. "Yeah," Lars said. "Old to you I guess. Older than you'll ever get."

He fired a single shot into the back of Trent's skull. Clean, efficient, experienced.

73

Lars and Shaine left Ella behind in the war zone of a house. They got out as sirens wailed a mile away on their approach.

Lars waited until they were both in the car and moving before he handed Shaine the iPhone and told her to figure it out.

He called Nikki Junior, got Nikki Senior. Was going to tell Junior to leave him the fuck alone. Found out the news.

Talked with Nikki Senior for a long time. Like old war buddies. Been in the trenches. Nikki sounded better than he had in years.

Lars turned down an offer to come back east, sit on the right hand of the new organization. He'd always been a man Nikki could trust. They shared the same sense of honor, duty, commitment to the job.

Lars declined as politely as possible. He had new responsibilities now. Was going to be a stepfather, of sorts.

Nikki understood. "Kids," he said. "You give them everything they ever wanted and they turn on you. You treat them like dogs and they stay loyal for life. Why is that?"

Lars had no answer.

Lars sprang for a suite at a hotel that catered to celebrities, not hit men.

After a hot shower, a good stretch and room service, Lars and Shaine sat on the couch looking out over Beverly Hills, which, from their window, seemed very flat.

"So, I'm staying with you?" Shaine asked, less than confident.

"I suppose so. I can't dump you at the bus station, can I?"

"You could. A lot of people would."

"Yeah, I know things a lot of people *would* do." Shaine smiled a half smile. "Look," he said. "There's no way to phrase it that sounds good. I've thought about it, believe me. You're my mess to clean up, my responsibility now, my burden to bear. It is what it is. Yeah, I'm responsible. Yeah, I'll take care of you, but you really don't seem to need a whole lot of that. We'll keep going as long as you like. I'm not going anywhere. I've been around this long, and as far as I can tell, the devil doesn't want me, so I'll be here a little while longer. For as long as that is, you're stuck with me."

Shaine couldn't hide a smile. Lars grinned too. "This is where you're supposed to say you're not stuck with me. You want to stay with me." She smiled openly, let it fade, picked at her fingers.

"Are you gonna keep working?"

"No. I'm retired. I've been retired for seventeen years. I just didn't know it."

"We'll be okay?"

"You mean money? Yeah. Fine. Nikki said he left a little bonus. For time served, y'know? They do it for all the guys they send to prison on a false rap. The guys who didn't do squat and end up renting seven to ten years of their life. I'm glad I had a skill. Kept me out of that employment pool."

"Oh, pool sounds good. Want to go for a swim? They have one on the roof."

"Yeah, sure. I guess I'm cleaned up enough I won't scare people."

"No one will be as scared of you as they should be."

"That bad, huh?"

"Not anymore."

Lars smiled. It felt good.

74

A week later Earl Walker Ford brought his final report to Agent Barry.

"Run it down for me."

"Okay," Ford started, referencing the file in his hand but mostly speaking from memory. The case had been so intriguing it took up most of his waking hours in the past week. "The shooter in the Mitchell Kenney case was found dead at the scene."

"We're sure it's him?"

"Relatively. His blood matched the second blood type at the Kenney murder scene, so we know for sure he was there."

"But not that he pulled the trigger."

"Technically, no."

"The other three?"

"Hired help. Above average records of assault and attempted but otherwise undistinguished."

"And the girl?"

"Still missing."

"Presumed dead?"

"Depends on who you ask."

Agent Barry scratched his chin. "The wife?"

"Not talking."

"Great."

"It's got loose ends, but there hasn't been any activity related to it in a week, so we think this last incident—"

"The shootout at the OK Corral?"

"—was the culmination of whatever contract was being fulfilled."

Agent Barry held out a hand for the report. Ford passed it over.

"Well," said Agent Barry as he uncapped his pen to sign. "It sure beats me. We got a possible shooter who we're calling the shooter to anyone who asks. We got a missing girl who is easy enough to bury since no one knew about her to begin with. We got an agent who ran off with the wife of a man he was protecting, but there's no prosecution there since he's dead." He finished his signature with a flourish.

"Not exactly tied up in a bow, is it?"

"No, sir."

"Well then, Special Agent Ford. On to the next one. Let's hope it's an easier knot to untie." He dropped the file folder in his out-box, both men silently thinking it would never be read once it reached Washington.

"Yes, sir." Earl Walker Ford didn't feel special, but then again he never did.

75

Lars left the bank, an empty canvas bag in his hand for a change. He'd made a deposit into the account number Nikki had given him. The one already started with an even million dollars.

"For loyal service," Nikki had said the night before. Lars struggled to contain his glee when he saw the actual number on the balance sheet. Add to that the cash he'd been toting around and his retirement was starting to look better than planned.

He climbed into the driver's seat of the '67 Mustang he'd bought that morning. It was the wrong color and one year off, but it would have to do on short notice.

Shaine waited to hear the plan. "So? Where now?"

Lars smiled. "You still want to see that beach?"

"Hell yeah. Let's go."

"No, we should do it right. We don't need a beach to stand and stare at. We need to be surrounded by beach on all sides."

"Mexico?"

"No. An island. Hawaii. Now, *that's* a beach."

"Really?"

"Absolutely."

Shaine and Lars both drew breaths in and exhaled.

The seat-belt sign dinged off, and the pilot announced that the plane would land in Maui on time and, to no one's surprise, the weather would be great.

Lars watched Shaine as she pressed her nose against the tiny window to watch the wide expanse of ocean through bright white clouds below them. He couldn't help being amused that she sat in the same spot, to his right, as she had during their very strange road trip. The big difference being the sustained smile on her face.

This is crazy. I never even owned a hamster and now this. Scary responsibility, but something tells me it can't get any worse or weirder than our first two weeks together.

The tattoo didn't even look too bad to him anymore. All healed up, sitting like it belonged up there on her arm, exposed in the tank top she wore.

They'd had fun packing for the trip by buying everything they needed, including suitcases. Lars particularly enjoyed asking for seats in first class.

He knew he'd made it beyond creepy old guy status and onto Shaine's real friend list when she gave him Trent's iPhone.

"I wouldn't use it as a phone," she said. "Never know who's listening. So I canceled the plan. Told them he was deceased. Still works as an iPod though. Camera too."

Darn it if the kid wasn't learning already. Protecting them both.

Lars turned the black rectangle over in his hand. "I wouldn't know how to use it as a phone anyway."

He'd watched her working the tiny screen all day, not knowing she'd been buying and filling it with downloads of songs, all bought with Trent's account—a nice touch.

Zeppelin, Van Halen (the good stuff, none of that Van Hagar crap, the kid was well on her way); she even put Iron Maiden "Live After Death" on. She got a little overzealous and put on some Steely Dan. He'd have to teach her that just because it's of a certain vintage doesn't make it good.

Lars settled in, put his brand-new headphones on, and reclined in the comfiest airplane seat he'd ever been in. He ran a finger along the screen, scrolling through the entire AC/DC catalog. He found one he liked.

Dirty deeds? Hell yes. Done dirt cheap? Hardly.

Eric Beetner has been called "Noir's James Brown—the hardest working man in crime fiction." (Crime Fiction Lover) and "The 21st Century's answer to Jim Thompson." (LitReactor). He is the author of nearly two dozen novels and novellas including *Rumrunners, Leadfoot, The Devil Doesn't Want Me, The Year I Died Seven Times, Dig Two Graves* and *Criminal Economics* as well as over a hundred short stories. In all his free time he manages to co-host the podcast Writer Types (with author SW Lauden) and host the Noir at the Bar reading series in Los Angeles where he is a TV editor by trade, contributing to the erosion of reading in America.

Eric has designed over one hundred book covers for crime and mystery novels including the one in your hand.

EricBeetner.com | Twitter @ericbeetner

On the following pages are a few
more great titles from the
Down & Out Books publishing family.

For a complete list of books and to
sign up for our newsletter,
go to DownAndOutBooks.com.

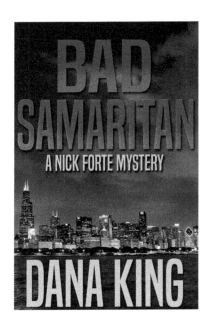

Bad Samaritan
A Nick Forte Mystery
Dana King

Down & Out Books
January 2018
978-1-946502-38-4

Nick Forte has a hard time leaving well enough alone. He seriously injures a man for slapping a woman Forte has never seen before, so when Becky Tuttle comes to him with disconcerting letters sent to her author alter ago Desiree d'Arnaud, he does more than a cursory investigation. Following the thread of Becky's problem leads through a local cop who takes the situation too lightly for Forte's taste and into the disturbing world of men's rights activists, for whom he has no use at all.

A Scholar of Pain
Grant Jerkins

ABC Group Documentation
an imprint of Down & Out Books
February 2018
978-1-946502-15-5

In his debut short fiction collection, Grant Jerkins remains—as the *Washington Post* put it—"Determined to peer into the darkness and tell us exactly what he sees." Here, the depth of that darkness is on evident, oftentimes poetic, display. Read all sixteen of these deviant diversions. Peer into the darkness.

Route 12
Marietta Miles

All Due Respect, an imprint of
Down & Out Books
November 2017
978-1-946502-77-3

Two haunting novellas set in Appalachia in the seventies and eighties. These are stories of people down on their luck—a girl crippled by a bad dose of polio vaccine, a young pregnant woman with no one to turn to, a mother desperate for cash who makes a terrible mistake.

In this debut book from Marietta Miles, God's country is as corrupt as any place on earth and trusting anyone is a dangerous proposition.

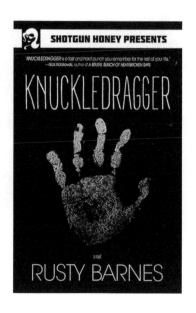

Knuckledragger
Rusty Barnes

Shotgun Honey, an imprint of
Down & Out Books
October 2017
978-1-946502-07-0

Hooligan and low-level criminal enforcer Jason "Candy" Stahl has made a good life collecting money for his boss Otis. One collection trip, though, at the Diovisalvo Liquor Store, unravels events that turn Candy's life into a horror-show.

In quick succession he moves up a notch in the organization, overseeing a chop shop, while he falls in lust with Otis's girl-friend Nina, gets beaten for insubordination, and is forced to run when Otis finds out about Candy and Nina's affair.

CPSIA information can be obtained
at www.ICGtesting.com
Printed in the USA
LVHW03s1607160618
580973LV00002B/482/P

9 781946 502414